1

Triple Threat

The Perfect Triple Threat

THREE DAKOTA STEVENS MYSTERIES

CHRIS ORCUTT

The Perfect Triple Threat

Three Dakota Stevens Mysteries

by

Chris Orcutt

First Print Edition: 2016

ISBN-13: 978-1539823605 (Have Pen, Will Travel)

Book cover image "Wedding Decoration" by Pandorabox, used under license from Shutterstock.com. The original design for the Dakota Stevens Mystery Series covers is by Elisabeth Pinio. The cover artist and book formatter for this book is EBook Converting|High Quality Ebook Conversion: www.ebookconverting.com.

Also by Chris Orcutt:

A Real Piece of Work (Dakota Stevens Mystery #1)
The Rich Are Different (Dakota Stevens Mystery #2)
A Truth Stranger Than Fiction (Dakota Stevens Mystery #3)
The Man, The Myth, The Legend (Short Stories)
One Hundred Miles from Manhattan (A Novel)

www.orcutt.net
www.dakotastevens.com

For Alexas:

My Véra, My Hadley, My Muse

'I'll love you, dear, I'll love you
    Till China and Africa meet,
And the river jumps over the mountain
    And the salmon sing in the street,
. . . .

— W.H. Auden

TABLE OF CONTENTS

THE ADVENTURE OF
THE BABYSITTING DETECTIVES

After the paradoxically grueling Auchincloss case—a yacht burglary in Newport, Rhode Island—Svetlana and I were recuperating over Columbus Day weekend in an unusual way. We were babysitting my college buddy's 12- and 11-year-old boys, Jack and James, at the family's vacation house in Vermont.

It was Saturday morning of the three-day weekend and the activity began at dawn, when the boys and I watched a rafter of wild turkeys feeding under an apple tree. We went fly-fishing, caught and released a few trout, launched and recovered a model rocket, then made breakfast together—French toast and bacon and buckets of Vermont maple syrup. By nine o'clock, the boys were practicing their archery skills in the yard while I watched them from a rocking chair on Ryan and Nina's deck.

Jack and James were about equally matched with a bow and arrow, but James was determined to show up his older brother. He set up the zombie target on the very edge of the woods and positioned himself far across the meadow, by the barn—a good 50 yards away. His first eleven arrows flew deep into the birches and poplars behind the target, but on his final shot James drew the bowstring back, took careful aim and let it fly. It sailed in a high arc. I thought it would be joining its buddies in the woods, but it struck the target with a loud thump, landing dead center in the zombie's chest.

"James! Nice shot, buddy!" I said. "But I counted eleven in the woods, dude. There's no way you'll find them in there."

"Yeah we will!" Jack said.

Jack ran into the house and returned a moment later with two metal detectors. Apparently this was a ritual with them. Jack handed his brother one of the detectors and they ran into the trees.

"Come on, Dakota!" James said.

"Nope. You lost 'em, you find 'em!"

I rocked in the rocking chair, sipped my coffee and admired the panoply of reds, oranges, golds and russets on the distant mountainside. Across the yard, at the treeline where the boys had run into the woods, the breeze rustled the birches and poplars, raining down yellow leaves on the lawn. Every now and then the metal detectors beeped and squealed in the woods.

The glass door slid open behind me and Svetlana came out with a steaming mug of coffee. She was dressed in full autumn regalia: brown suede jacket, cream cashmere sweater, scarf, short tweed skirt, knee-high stockings and boots. She looked like a model in the fall fashion issue of *Vogue*. I whistled.

"Wow, *nice* outfit. But I'm a little worried about it."

"Worried? How?" She cupped her hands around the mug and blew.

"I'm worried we're going to walk into some general store today," I said, "where a bunch of old timers are sitting around a cracker barrel, and you're going to give them all heart attacks."

"That would be unfortunate."

With a smirk, she sat in the rocking chair next to mine, pinched her knees together and sipped her coffee.

"What *is* a cracker barrel anyway?" she asked.

"Beats me. A barrel of crackers maybe?"

"Who would eat a barrel of crackers? That cannot be right." She scanned the meadow and the hillside down to the trees. "Where are our young charges?"

"In the woods, finding arrows," I said. "How did your chess lesson with them go last night?"

"Quite well, I think," she said. "Although neither shows much interest in chess. They seem to prefer video games and outdoor sports."

"Yeah, about the chess—I think they're only doing it because they're hot for teacher."

She blinked several times. "Excuse me…'hot for teacher'?"

"The Van Halen song 'Hot For Teacher'? The *1984* album?"

She closed her eyes and shrugged.

"I forget—you didn't grow up here," I said. "You didn't have time for rock bands and songs about guys attracted to their female teachers. You were too busy playing chess and learning how to be a young Commie."

"Well, 'hot for teacher' or not," she said, "they are adorable—bright, curious and good-looking. And you know I loathe most children. Especially the ones their age."

"I know," I said.

A delicious breeze washed over us and floated down the hill, followed by a languorous moment of blissful peace and silence. It was one of those few moments that makes all the trouble of owning a property worthwhile, and I wished Ryan and Nina could be here to enjoy it.

Then, in the next instant, the quiescence was destroyed by a piercing shriek from the trees. Birds scattered from the treetops.

"Oh my God!" James shouted. "Oh my *God*!"

Then Jack shrieked. Svetlana and I looked at each other.

"The joys of parenting," I said.

"Precisely," she said.

We put down our coffees and ran for the woods.

"Jack?! James?!" I shouted. "Where are you?"

"Over here!"

Thankfully there wasn't much underbrush, and Svetlana and I were able to weave quickly through the trees. We found the boys fifty yards in. They were kneeling on the ground and digging through the fallen leaves.

"Guys!" I said. "What are you shrieking about? Are you hurt?"

"No, Dakota, look!"

Jack lifted the base of his zipped-up fleece, forming a basket in which a dozen coins jingled. "Silver dollars!"

James removed his hand from the leaves and held up a gold coin.

"Look, Jack, look! *Gold*! We're *rich*, sonny!"

Jack turned to me. "You hear that, sonny? We're *rich*! Ya-hoo!"

They laughed and rolled around in the leaves. Svetlana stooped over beside them. She held out her hands.

"Let me hold them for you," she said, "until we return to the house."

Using the metal detectors, the boys spent the next half-hour finding more coins—both silver and gold—and eight of their arrows. Then we hiked back up to the house. As the boys ran ahead, yelling about finding buried treasure, Svetlana and I lagged behind. She spoke into my shoulder.

"Did I ever mention that I once dated a numismatist?"

"A *coin collector*?" I said. "Svetlana, my opinion of you just dropped about ten notches."

"Once dated," she said firmly. "It was many years ago, but I learned a few things from him." She patted her jacket pocket, where the coins jingled together. "These are Morgan silver dollars the boys found, and the gold coins are Double Eagles."

"I take it they're valuable."

"You could say that. My estimate is in the range of twenty thousand dollars."

I coughed. "You're kidding."

"No," she said. "And that is a conservative estimate."

When we got back to the house, I hung up our coats and took a moment to admire the place: post-and-beam construction, cathedral ceilings, and floor-to-ceiling windows that faced the colorful foliage on a nearby mountainside. While I loaded the woodstove and poked the coals with a skinny stick of kindling (Ryan and Nina didn't have a fire poker), Svetlana and the boys sat at the dining table and counted out the coins into stacks. When they were finished there were 26 Morgan silver dollars and 3 gold Double Eagles. I looked at Svetlana.

"Do you want to break it to them?"

She nodded. "Boys…these coins are worth a lot of money. A *lot* of money."

"How much, Svetlana?" Jack asked.

"Yeah, Svetlana," James said. "How much?"

"That is not important."

"What's important, guys," I said, "is that before we do anything with the coins, we have to make sure they don't belong to someone else. Silver and gold coins don't grow in the woods."

The boys groaned.

"Aw, come on, Dakota," Jack said. "You're not gonna make us give 'em *back*, are you?"

James clutched Svetlana's arm. "Svetlana, don't let him, *please*."

Svetlana, at the head of the dining table, a faint smile on her lips, held a stack of silver dollars in her fingertips. I'd seen her hold chips this way at blackjack tables in Atlantic City and Las Vegas. She dropped them one at a time into her free hand, picked them up again and repeated. The coins made a satisfying clinking sound. I could understand why the boys were so reluctant to part with them. Svetlana turned to me and pouted.

"*Okay*," I said, "we'll make some quiet inquiries, that's all."

"What's he mean, Svetlana?" Jack said.

"He means," she said, "we will not advertise that we found silver and gold coins in the woods. We will merely ask around the area and see if they are missing from somewhere."

"Exactly," I said. "I know how excited you guys are—this *is* like finding buried treasure—but we need to establish whether the coins belong to someone else. How far down did you find them?"

"They were under the leaves," Jack said.

"This year's leaves?" I asked.

Jack threw up his hands. "What do you mean, 'This year's leaves'? *The leaves.*"

"No," I said, "were the coins under the fresh colorful leaves on top, or last year's—the brown, decomposed ones?"

The boys looked at each other.

"Oh, this year's, definitely," James said.

"Well," I said, "that means whoever lost them, lost them recently."

"Crap," the boys said in unison.

"Tell you what," I said. "Svetlana and I will give you each one hundred dollars against your treasure, and if there's a reward for the coins, you'll get the reward money."

"Sweet," Jack said.

"Yeah, awesome," James said. "Thanks, Svetlana."

Svetlana plucked her magical Gucci purse off the table (magical because it always contained exactly what we needed during investigations, exactly when we needed it). With blinding speed, she counted out two stacks of $20 bills and handed them to the boys. Then she found a canvas grocery bag and, in one smooth motion that hinted at finely honed experience doing this, swept all the coins into the bag. She put the bag aside and turned to the boys.

"Now that you have your money, there is only one thing you have to decide," she said.

"What's that?" Jack asked.

One corner of Svetlana's mouth curled up impishly. Her eyes flashed.

"Why, how you are going to *spend* it, of course."

With their money burning holes in their pockets, the boys wanted to do something with it, so we drove down the mountain to the picturesque village of Newfane. A banner across the road read, "NEWFANE HERITAGE FESTIVAL." There were tents with craftsmen, artists, games, a rummage sale, and a big food tent where the church was serving breakfast.

"What do you say, guys? Shall we check it out?"

I glanced in the rear-view: the boys were playing video games on their phones.

"Yeah, sure," James said.

"Whatevs," Jack said.

Svetlana turned to me and lowered her sunglasses.

"I concur," she said. "Whatevs."

The Festival was on the village green. After we parked, our first stop was the food tent. I had a stack of blueberry pancakes, Svetlana had an egg sandwich, and the boys had a dozen cider donuts in five minutes. Afterwards Svetlana and I trailed behind the boys while they ran over to the games area.

"I wonder," she said, "do they still make leashes for children?"

I squinted at her. "What do you mean 'still'? I don't think they *ever* made leashes for children."

"No, no," she said, wagging a finger, "I was in Bergdorf's once and I distinctly saw a toddler on a leash."

We approached a table for the Lions Club, where a group of male retirees sold raffle tickets. Their heads swiveled in unison as Svetlana went by.

"There might be leashes for toddlers, Svetlana," I said, "but Jack and James are almost teenagers. They're not going to appreciate being walked around on leashes."

"A shame," she said. "It would make watching them so much easier."

When we reached the boys, they were at the dunking booth, hurling baseballs at a wooden target, trying to dunk a stoic man in the dunking chair. After ten dollars' worth of throws, I persuaded them to join me at the high-striker, where I swung the mallet, rang the bell and won Svetlana a small teddy bear. Then I showed the boys how to do it, and gave the carny an extra ten to cover his losses.

In the crafts tent, Svetlana bought a handmade maple and walnut chessboard directly from the craftsman. Once he found out she was a U.S. champion, he asked her to sign one of his other boards. Three booths down I saw a metal worker selling fireplace tools and andirons. I led us down to him. A 30-year-old man with big hands and a beard sat on a stool surrounded by his metalwork.

"Guys," I said to the boys, "check this out." I took a fire poker down from its hook.

"Metal?" Jack said. "What about it?"

"Your parents could use a poker back at the house," I said. "This man does excellent work, and I happen to know two young men who just came into some money."

Jack and James looked at each other.

"A fire poker?" Jack said.

"Do we have to?" James said.

"Come on, it's twenty-five bucks," I said. "The two of you can afford to spend twenty-five bucks on your parents. And trust me, this is the kind of gift you want to get them, because every time they use it, they'll think of you."

"All right," they moaned.

"They'll take this poker," I said to the craftsman. "It's beautiful work."

"Thanks. I do it all from one piece of steel."

Svetlana took down a fireplace shovel. "They will also be buying this excellent shovel."

The boys grumbled, but she silenced them with a glance.

"How much for both?" I asked.

"Forty, even," he said.

Svetlana nudged the boys. "Pay the nice man."

They each handed the craftsman a $20 bill. As he turned around to put the money in a cash box, the boys noticed a big patch on the back of the denim vest he was wearing. It read, "GREEN MOUNTAIN BOYS" and showed a motorcycle on a road that wove up into some mountains.

"What's 'Green Mountain Boys'?" James asked.

"That's my motorcycle club," he said.

"Cool," Jack said.

He put the tools in two long paper bags, handed them to the boys and gave me his business card.

"In case you know anybody else who could use my stuff," he said. "Mike Carver."

"Dakota Stevens." I flicked the card. "Your workshop is on Pheasant Hill in Podunk? My friends—these boys' parents—have a place right down the road from you, on the Podunk line."

"I know their dad." Mike snapped his fingers. "Ryan Connor, right? Bumped into him in the hardware store a couple times."

"Yeah, that's our dad," James said.

"Is he here?" Mike asked.

"No, he and Nina had to go California," I said. "We're friends of theirs, watching the boys for a few days."

"Oh, 'cause I've been meanin' to ask him what he was doing out in the woods Monday and Tuesday night."

"Dad wasn't up here then," Jack said.

"Mike," I said, "are you saying you saw Ryan in the woods this week?"

"No, I didn't exactly *see* anyone," he said. "Let me explain. It was about two in the morning, so it was actually this past Tuesday and Wednesday—I tend bar over at Mount Snow a couple nights a week. I was on my way home and the woods were lit up like a UFO was landing up there."

"Why do you think something was happening on the Connors' property?" Svetlana asked.

"Well, I stopped my motorcycle at that bend in the road—you know, where you have to stay way to one side because you've got that deep ravine with the creek at the bottom—"

"—and no guardrail." Svetlana shot me a look. "Yes, we know the location you speak of."

"Yeah, well, I stopped there and heard a lot of heavy equipment noises. It sounded like it was about a quarter mile in from the road, so I thought it was on the Connors' place."

"Interesting," I said. "A quarter mile from that bend would put it on the east side of their property."

Mike squinted one eye and thought about it. "Yeah, east. That sounds right."

"And about how long was this activity would you say?" I asked.

He shrugged. "Couldn't say. I only stuck around for a couple of minutes."

"Could you identify any of the heavy equipment noises?" Svetlana asked.

"Not specifically," he said. "I mean, I know what diesel engines sound like, and there was a lot of that beeping—you know, when trucks are backing up?"

"I do," I said. "Thanks. Svetlana and I will look into it, but do me a favor—don't mention this to anybody else. I want to ask Ryan about it first. He might have had some workmen up there as a surprise for Nina."

"You got it," he said. "Tell them I said hello."

I shook his hand. "I will."

Svetlana, the boys and I walked away. We bought hot chocolates and browsed the rummage sale.

"So it's a mystery, right, Dakota?" James said.

"Yes, it is. A small one."

"And the coins, they're another mystery," Jack said. "To see if there's a reward."

"Yup," I said.

Jack stopped at a table of used board games. He opened up a Monopoly box with one hand and sipped his hot chocolate with the other.

"We don't have Monopoly back at the house." He looked up at Svetlana. "If I got it, could we play tonight?"

Svetlana's sunglasses were on top of her head, so I saw her eyes widen when Jack mentioned Monopoly. I'd seen her play the game several times before—most recently during "The Adventure of the Heckled Band," when we were snowed in at the lodge in Vale. She became monomaniacal during the game, crushing everyone with her strict adherence to the rules and her Robber Baron ruthlessness. I shook my head.

"I'd rethink that one if I were you, Jack. Svetlana doesn't play nice at that game."

"Ignore him, boys," she said. "Get it. I would love for us to play Monopoly."

"Boys," I said, smiling at Svetlana, "have you ever read Hansel and Gretel?"

"Huh?" James said.

"The fairy tale," I said. "Two kids get lured into a house made of candy, and a witch eats them."

"I don't care, I'm buying it." Jack put the game under his arm and walked to the checkout table.

We left the rummage sale and meandered through the booths of local artists. Jack darted in front and spun around so he was walking backwards facing us.

"Have you ever had to use your gun, Dakota?" he asked.

"Yeah, what about you, Svetlana?" James said, tugging her arm. "Do you have a gun?"

Svetlana looked at me. Suddenly babysitting the boys had taken a turn from the charming—chess, model rockets, video games—to the uncomfortable. Now there was talk of guns and violence. She was treading into unfamiliar territory.

"Svetlana doesn't carry a gun," I said.

She pointed at her temple. "This is *my* weapon."

"Dakota," James said, "is Svetlana smarter than you?"

Svetlana smiled. "Yes, Dakota…am I?"

"Sure, guys, at some things she is. But at other things I'm smarter. On the whole, I'd say we're about equal."

"Yes," Svetlana said, "but I am infinitely better-looking."

James walked alongside her, about six inches away from her hip.

"Yeah you are!" he said.

We passed an artist's booth where all of the paintings were of flowers in vases. Not my bag; if I wanted to look at flowers, I'd just go buy some flowers and put them in a vase.

"As for your original question, Jack," I said, "yes, I've had to use my gun, but it's only been in life or death situations as a last resort."

"We have BB guns," Jack said. "Can we do some shooting when we get back?"

"Sure. But there are other things I need to do first," I said.

"Stuff to do with the mystery?" James asked.

"Yes."

"Can we help?" Jack asked.

James shot his hand in the air. "I'm Svetlana's assistant! I call it!"

"Okay, assistant," she said, peering down at him. "You can start by carrying this for me." She handed him the bag with the chessboard.

"All right, guys," I said, "you're officially on the case with us. But here's the deal. I don't want to worry your folks while they're on their trip. When they call, this is strictly between us for now, okay?"

"Okay," James said.

"Sure," Jack said.

I stopped in front of a Vermont autumn landscape painting. It would look great over the sofa in my Millbrook living room, and it was less than two hundred dollars. I took out my wallet.

"I'm hungry again," Jack said.

"Me too," James said.

"There's no way you guys can be hungry," I said. "You just ate a dozen donuts."

"Can we go to Brattleboro for lunch?" Jack asked.

"Yeah, I want pizza," James said. "And maybe some clam chowder."

I turned to Svetlana. "Thoughts?"

"Whatevs," she said.

When we got back to the house, I parked the car at the foot of the driveway. The four of us got out and examined the gravel.

"What are we looking for, Dakota?" Jack asked.

"Heavy equipment tracks, mostly—like bulldozers or tread marks from big tires. But look for other things, too—little clues that other people have been here."

"Like what?" James asked.

"Litter," Svetlana said. "Gum wrappers and cigarette butts, but also oil stains, shoe prints—"

"Yes," I said, "but large prints, like from men in work boots."

"Got it," the boys said.

We examined the driveway for a good fifteen minutes without finding anything.

"Dakota," Svetlana said, "I believe it rained the day before we arrived."

"Good point. All right, let's check the far end of the property, where Mike saw the lights in the woods. Follow me."

We walked through the apple orchard, past a crumbling woodshed, and along the edge of a broad meadow where it met the woods.

"Same idea," I said. "We're looking for tracks, litter, and any places along the treeline where brush has been trampled. Any signs that men or equipment have been in or out of here."

I walked ahead of Svetlana and the boys, checking for clues and shoe prints before taking a step. I scrutinized the underbrush just inside the trees, looking for broken limbs, and didn't find a thing. Not a single leaf looked out of place. I was gazing into the forest of birches and poplars when I felt bits of sand biting my cheeks. I held out my palm. It wasn't sand; it was very fine sleet.

"Dakota?" Svetlana said.

I glanced over my shoulder. Vaguely I noticed that she and the boys were shivering. In the meantime I was transfixed by the unique weather behind them, where summer, fall and winter were happening at the same time. A sun-splashed green meadow sloped up to a distant ridgeline, crowned with a stand of fiery sugar maples. The sky over the ridgeline was bright blue and cloudless. To the east, a towering gunmetal mist moved over the trees, and across the meadow, sleet was falling. From where I stood, the sleet made a haze like a sandstorm.

"Dakota," Svetlana said, "if you would not object, I would like to take the boys inside."

We went back to the car—the Range Rover that Ryan and Nina had insisted we use in the mountains, instead of my Cadillac—and took our morning's purchases into the house. I put on a scarf, gloves and a hat, and ducked out quietly, taking one of the boys' metal detectors with me.

First I went into the woods where the boys had found the coins and did another sweep with the metal detector. About twenty yards from that spot, beneath some freshly fallen leaves, I found three more Morgan silver dollars. I marked the location and took the coins. Now that I had two points some distance apart where we'd found coins, I wanted to figure out what direction the coins had come from.

I picked up two long sticks from the forest floor, whittled points on the ends with my knife and jammed one into the ground where I'd found the most recent set of coins. Then I walked back to the center of the original find and planted the second stick. Sighting along the top of that stick, I walked in a straight line toward the other stick, and beyond it.

With the sleet pattering the tree canopy overhead, I shuffled through the fallen leaves and swept the metal detector along the ground in front of me. At the base of an old oak, in a patch of mud, I found one large boot print—a men's size 11 or 12 was my guess—its toe pointing toward where I'd found the coins. From the tread marks, it looked like a motorcycle boot. I continued in the direction the boot seemed to have come from.

When the detector beeped again, I was near a rock wall on the edge of the woods, twenty feet from the dirt road. The detector beeped faintly two more times, then went silent. Dead batteries. I shut off the detector, squatted and sifted through the leaves. I came up with a can of Folger's coffee, a box of 12-gauge shotgun shells, a broken pocket flashlight, and a sealed vial of morphine.

"Morphine? What the…?" I said aloud.

The way the items were strewn across the forest floor on this side of the rock wall suggested that the person had tripped on the wall, smashed the flashlight, and dropped some of the things he'd been carrying. With the exception of the vial of morphine, the items pointed to someone camping or poaching (deer season was a month away). I hopped over the wall to the road and looked for shoe prints, but didn't find any, so I turned around and followed the trail back to my sighting sticks and the first find location, and continued from there in a straight line.

Soon I reached a clearing. I couldn't walk into the clearing because it was encircled by brambles and thick underbrush. The only way in and out of the clearing was a 20-foot gap in the underbrush on the far side. From the gap, a wide path sloped gently downhill through a cluster of small evergreens, to the edge of a well-manicured lawn. I followed the bramble around the clearing to the spot where the path reached the lawn.

The sleet had stopped. Down the lawn from the woods was a modern log house with windows that looked out on the surrounding mountains. There was movement in one of the windows. I stepped back into the cover of the trees. I considered watching the house for a while, but it was getting colder and there was one last thing I wanted to check out. I headed back toward the road.

If the coins, coffee, shotgun shells, flashlight and morphine all belonged to the same person, it was possible—although hardly probable—that a neighbor was

CHRIS ORCUTT

bringing the items to the people living in the log house. But if that was the case, why walk through the woods? Why not drive or walk on the road? And what a bizarre assortment. Finding the coffee, shotgun shells and flashlight made sense, but the coins and the morphine? Of course, all of the items could have been lost separately at different times and might have nothing to do with each other. But they all looked new, so this seemed unlikely.

When I reached the road again, I walked down the mountain until I came to the bend above the ravine. This was where Mike Carver had stopped his motorcycle when he saw the lights and heard the engine noises in the woods. I scrabbled up the steep, rocky slope into the trees and climbed about a quarter-mile uphill until I ended up back at the clearing.

There wasn't a single tire tread, machine track, broken branch or trammeled fern. There was *nothing* to suggest there had been heavy equipment in these woods recently. The only signs of any human activity out here whatsoever were the coins and other items, and the boot print—all some distance from here.

I started back to Ryan and Nina's house, noting that while the sky might have cleared up, this little mystery the boys had stumbled upon was murkier than ever.

Back at the house I loaded up the woodstove and warmed myself for a few minutes. Svetlana and the boys were upstairs playing a video game; I could hear automatic gunfire and explosions. I made myself a cup of coffee and went upstairs. The boys sat at either end of a long sofa frenetically clicking on video game joysticks. Svetlana sat between them with her legs crossed, sipping tea.

"What's up?" I said.

"They are in a post-apocalyptic world, killing zombies," she said, nodding at the TV. "At the moment they are looting a grocery store."

"We're not looting, Svetlana," Jack said. "We're *scavenging*. It's not looting if there's no law and order."

"Right on, Jack," James said, staring at the TV. "Hey, Dakota...find any clues?"

"As a matter of fact, yes," I said. "Who's up for more investigating?"

"Sure, but not in the woods again," Jack said. "Is it still snowing or sleeting or whatever?"

"No, it's stopped," I said. "We won't be going back in the woods. At least not today. Svetlana and I need to talk to some of the neighbors."

"Then can we go to dinner?" James asked.

"*Dinner?*" I said. "You just ate lunch."

"Not this second, Dakota," James said. "Like, after your investigating stuff. I'm planning ahead."

Svetlana compressed her lips and gave me a serious nod.

"He's planning ahead."

"Yes, we'll go to dinner afterward," I said. "Maybe in Manchester so Svetlana can do some shopping at the outlets there."

Svetlana sipped her tea.

"Boys," she purred, "I just heard my *favorite* word in the English language."

"What's that? 'Dinner'?" James clicked on his joystick.

"No. *Shopping.*"

The boys giggled. The corners of Svetlana's mouth twitched in a smile. She put her tea on the coffee table, stood and clapped her hands sharply.

"Save your game! Brush your teeth! Put on your coats and boots! We leave in five minutes!"

The boys threw down their controllers and ran out of the room.

"Wow," I said. "Somebody got her second wind fast."

She smoothed out her skirt. "You said there would be shopping."

"And so there shall be. Let's go."

II

The first neighbor I wanted to visit was the log house near the clearing at the edge of the woods. The four of us drove down Pheasant Hill Road and climbed the steep driveway.

"Okay, boys," I said, glancing at them in the rear-view mirror. "These people are your neighbors and they might know your folks, so let me and Svetlana do the talking, okay?"

"I thought we were investigating, too," James said.

"And so you shall," Svetlana said. "Your job is to keep your eyes open and notice anything that seems out of place."

"Like what?" Jack asked.

Svetlana smirked in my direction. "As the master detective Dakota often says to me, you will know it when you see it."

"Are you making fun of my methods again?" I said.

"Yes."

The boys laughed.

At the top of the driveway, a mountain of split firewood sat on the gravel next to the garage. We got out. Down the hill was a huge garden, well past harvest, fenced in with chicken wire. Smoke curled out of the chimney on the house. I was leading us up the walkway when a voice called out from behind the garage.

"Hello there! Can I help you?"

A man walked into the driveway carrying an armload of firewood. He was in his 60s with close-cropped iron gray hair. His eyes swept across me and the boys, then stopped and sprang open at the sight of Svetlana's legs in the short tweed skirt. I was about to speak when Svetlana stepped in front of me. Her suede jacket was open and, as she often did when seeking information, she arched her back to accentuate her curves. She removed her sunglasses.

"My, that is certainly very much *hard wood,*" she said. "I am not seeing this much hard wood since I was little girl in Siberia."

"You're Russian, young lady?"

"*Da.* Well, American now, but one never forgets the cold."

"That's for sure," he said. "You folks lost?"

"Visiting," I interjected. "We're staying at your neighbors', the Connors, just up the hill. Watching their boys"—I nodded to them—"Jack and James, while their parents are away for a few days."

"Sure, I've met Ryan and Nina," he said. "So, how long've you been here?"

"Since yesterday," I said.

"Then you missed the big rainstorm. Not much wind though, so it didn't blow the leaves away."

"Yes," Svetlana said, "the foliage has been quite lovely."

He dumped the firewood and held out his hand to her. "Tom Clark."

"Svetlana Krüsh," she said. "And this is my friend, Dakota Stevens." She winked over her shoulder at me. "We are from Manhattan, so all of this"—she gestured at the house, the yard, the woods—"is novelty for us. We are...how do you say...city mice?"

"Sure," Tom said, "city mice. We used to be a couple of those ourselves." He looked at Jack and James. "Boys, Mrs. Clark has been baking all day. I bet if you went up to the house and asked nicely, she'd give you some cookies."

They raced each other to the door. I picked up some firewood.

"Let me give you a hand, Tom."

"Appreciate it," he said.

The two of us carried armloads of firewood to a stack behind the garage. Svetlana followed empty-handed.

"So what brings you folks down here?" Tom asked. "Couldn't be just to say hello."

"Actually, no," Svetlana said. "We were in Newfane this morning, at the Heritage Festival, and we met the nice young metalworker who lives up the road."

"Oh, you mean Mike Carver, the blacksmith. Yeah, nice fella."

"Right," I said. "Anyway, Mike mentioned that he was driving up this road early Tuesday morning—down by the ravine—and he said there was a lot of light and heavy equipment noises coming from Ryan and Nina's property."

Tom squinted. "Tuesday? Hmm. Oh, I know what it was." He wagged a finger. "But it wasn't coming from their property. It was mine."

"Were you here?" I asked.

"No," he said. "Come on, it's easier if I just show you."

We followed him up to the side of the house, where he disappeared behind some rhododendron bushes. The deafening rattle of a large engine filled the air, and floodlights in trees around the property flashed on. Tom emerged from the bushes with his hands covering his ears. He shouted.

"Generator!" He nodded at the lights. "Those go on whenever the power goes out! We must have had an outage the other night! This is what Mike saw and heard! Hold on!"

He went back into the bushes, and a moment later the lights went out and everything was quiet again. My ears rang. A thick stench of diesel hung in the air.

"I knew there had to be a simple explanation for it," I said. "I was starting to think he'd seen a UFO landing."

Tom chuckled. "Don't kid yourself. Live up here long enough and you see some things."

"How long have you lived in Vermont?" Svetlana asked.

He thought about it.

"We've had the house about ten years," he said. "It's been strictly a weekend and vacation place up to now, but that's about to change. A month ago, I was offered early retirement, so as soon as we sell our place in Manhattan, we're moving up here full-time."

"What did you do?" I asked. "If you don't mind my asking."

He sighed and gazed wistfully to the south, in the direction of New York City.

"Broker," he said. "I'm glad to be out of it, to tell you the truth. The whole thing's a big house of cards, and when it falls, it's not going to be pretty. But anyway you didn't come over here to get a lecture on the market."

We walked back toward the driveway. The front door of the house opened, and the boys skipped out with handfuls of cookies. A trim, petite woman with pewter hair and eyeglasses stood in the doorway and wiped her hands on an apron. She waved. Svetlana and I waved back.

"So," Tom said, "was there something else besides the lights and noise the other night?"

"Yes, one thing," I said. "Did you lose anything in the woods recently?"

"Doubt it. Neither me nor Sandra go in the woods much. You know—ticks. We've both had Lyme a few times. Why, what'd you find out there?"

"Some silver dollars," I said, "a can of coffee, morphine and a few other things."

"Weird," Tom said. "Where the heck was this?"

"Just up there." I pointed. "In the woods between the Connors' place and yours."

"Silver dollars? Morphine? Makes no sense." Tom shook his head. "Want me to ask around?"

"No," I said, "but if you hear that anyone lost something in there, and they're looking for it, get in touch with me or Svetlana, would you? You can reach us at Ryan and Nina's for the next couple of days. You have their number?"

"Sure do."

We shook hands.

"Nice to meet you, Svetlana," he said.

"Likewise," she said.

I watched him steal another glance at her legs as the four of us piled into the Range Rover. We drove down the driveway and headed up the road, past Ryan and Nina's place, towards their next-closest neighbor. Maybe they had seen or heard something.

"Boys," Svetlana said, "what did you observe inside the house—besides cookies?"

"Not much, Svetlana," Jack said. "I asked if I could use the bathroom, and then I snooped around a little bit."

"What do you mean?" I said. "You didn't go in any of the bedrooms or anything, guys, did you?"

"No, nothing like that," Jack said. "She had me use the bathroom downstairs, and I made a wrong turn and ended up in a gun room."

"Gun room?"

"Yeah, there were a couple of glass cases with rifles and shotguns and pistols in them, and deer antlers on the walls, and a stuffed bird, and a bunch of pictures of that man you were talking with hunting and fishing."

Svetlana turned to me and lowered her sunglasses.

"Ticks," she said.

"Interesting," I said.

"What about ticks, Svetlana?" Jack asked.

"Nothing, Jack," she said. "Continue, *mon cheri*."

"What's '*mon cheri*' mean?" James asked.

"'My darling,'" she said. "*Tu es mon cheri aussi*, James. Continue, Jack."

He shrugged. "I don't know. I didn't see anything else. I used the bathroom and went back up to the kitchen."

"And you, James?" Svetlana said.

"What did I see?"

"*Oui.*"

"Nothing. I just sat in the kitchen the whole time and ate cookies."

"Okay," I said, "but did anything jump out at you as unusual?"

James peeked his head around Svetlana's seat. "She was cooking."

"What about it?" she asked.

"You smell good, Svetlana," James said.

"Thank you," she said. "Now, what was she cooking?"

"She had a bunch of stuff on the stove and was putting it in jars. My grandma does it sometimes."

"You mean *canning*," I said.

"Yeah, that's it," Jack said, "and she—"

"Hey, it's my clue! I'm telling it!" James said. "Butt out, Jack!"

"You butt out!"

They punched each other repeatedly on the arm.

"Ow!"

"Ow!"

I smiled at Svetlana as if to say, "Your turn, dear." She took a breath and barked something in rapid Russian or Ukrainian. Instantly the boys stopped fighting and sat bolt upright in their seats. The only reason I didn't jump was because I was used to Svetlana's sudden, violent bursts of temper, and because I knew that they came and passed quickly like summer thundershowers.

"Continue, James," she said.

"It wasn't what she was cooking," he said. "It was how much *stuff* there was. She had like a hundred of those jars all over the kitchen."

"James is right," Jack said. "It was weird, like she was cooking for an army or something."

"They do have a very large garden," Svetlana said. "And canning is hardly a crime."

"True," I said. "Good work, everyone."

A quarter mile up the hill from Ryan and Nina's, a wooden sign hung on a tree over the mailbox. It read, "DUANE HOBART — CHAINSAW ARTIST."

"Chainsaw artist?" Svetlana said. "I do not like the sound of this."

I turned into the driveway and crossed the river on a one-lane steel deck bridge. On the other side we were greeted by an assortment of carved wood sculptures: a grizzly bear, a moose, totem poles and a miniature Stonehenge. The sculptures stood in grassy open spaces between copses of birch and poplar that lined the driveway. We went over a hill and through a densely wooded dell on the other side, until I rounded a corner and the driveway dead-ended.

We were in the middle of a sprawling dirt lot surrounded by towering wooden statues of famous military generals: Caesar, Washington, Napoleon, Grant, Rommel and Patton. They all stood about eight feet tall, and their likenesses were incredible. The boys rolled down their windows.

"Awesome!" Jack said. "I wish we could get one for our driveway."

A chainsaw moaned in the distance.

"The chainsaw artist appears to be at work," Svetlana said.

I turned to her. "I should probably handle this one alone."

"Correct," she said.

I leaned across the center console and whispered in her ear.

"Get behind the wheel and keep the engine running, in case we need to hightail it out of here. I don't like the look of this place."

The boys started to open their doors.

"No, boys," I said, "hang out with Svetlana, okay? If you're sweet to her, maybe she'll teach you some Russian."

I got out and walked in the direction the chainsaw noise was coming from. The dirt lot was festooned with woodchips. As I crossed the lot, the generals glared down at me, and I half-expected them to come to life any second. I passed a pickup truck with three large bumper stickers on its tailgate: Harley-Davidson; the early "DON'T TREAD ON ME" American flag with the rattlesnake; and one I didn't understand, which read, *When the shit hits the fan, I'll be ready. Will you?*

As the chainsaw noise grew louder, I was glad for the reassuring heft of my Sig Sauer .45 ACP under my arm. I glimpsed a cabin atop a knoll about 100 yards away. The cabin was dwarfed by the colorful mountainside behind it.

I rounded the corner of a shed and saw a stocky man, maybe 50 years old, with a thick and grizzled beard. He stood in quarter-profile with his back to me, and he wore shooting earmuffs and safety goggles. His flannel shirt, overalls and work boots were caked with sawdust.

A massive log hung by chains from a tall steel tripod. The man canted his head and evaluated his work, then stepped toward it revving the chainsaw and deftly angling the tip into the wood. The air smelled pungently of exhaust fumes and scorched wood pulp.

I walked in a wide circle around his work area until he noticed me. He killed the chainsaw, put it down, and pulled off the earmuffs so they hung around his neck. Now that I was facing him, I saw how muscular he was. He also had a considerable, hard potbelly. The man was built like a silverback gorilla.

"Can I help you?" he said.

"Your sculptures are terrific," I said. "You do great work."

"Thanks. Which one you interested in?"

"No one in particular," I said. "I live in Manhattan, so I wouldn't have any place to put it."

He took a deep breath and gazed across the work yard, as if looking to his only constant companions, the trees, for moral support.

"Then why are you interrupting my work?" he said. "What do you want?"

"I'm staying at your neighbors' place—the Connors—and Mike Carver, the metal guy up the road—"

"I know Mike."

"Swell," I said. "Mike heard a bunch of heavy equipment on the Connors' property earlier this week. Tuesday and Wednesday mornings—really early."

"I don't know anything about it." He started to put the earmuffs back on.

"Wait," I said, "you haven't heard the best part."

"What?"

"I also found about twenty thousand dollars' worth of rare coins in the woods near their property."

His right eye twitched. "So? What's that got to do with me?"

"Do you have a Harley?" I asked.

"Yeah, so?"

"I found a print from a motorcycle boot near the coins. Do you own a pair of motorcycle boots, Mr. Hobart?"

"What are you, a *cop*?" he said.

"No, not exactly."

"Then get the hell off my property."

"How about a vial of morphine," I said. "Have you lost one recently?"

His face became apoplectic. Snatching up the chainsaw, he started it with one yank of the cord and stepped toward me revving it. He was far enough away—at least ten feet—that I didn't panic; I just pinched open my jacket lapel and revealed my gun. He froze.

"Get the hell out of here!" he shouted. "I want you off my property!"

I backed away, returned to the Range Rover, and got in the passenger seat. I had just shut the door when the boys spoke in unison behind me.

"My lyubim Svetlanu!" they said. *"Ona boginya!"*

"I heard your name in there," I said to Svetlana. "What'd you teach them?"

"That is our secret," she said. "Right, boys?"

"Right!" they said.

The chainsaw noise outside got loud all of a sudden. I glanced out the window. Duane Hobart was running across the lot toward us, brandishing his chainsaw. The boys screamed.

"Go, Svetlana!" I said.

She threw it in drive and floored it, kicking up a dust cloud behind us. Duane got within ten feet of the car before receding rapidly in the rear window. The dust cloud engulfed him.

"So," Svetlana said, "I take it your interview was unsuccessful."

"Yup," I said. "But he's involved somehow." I turned to the boys. "You guys okay?"

"Yeah, fine," they mumbled. Their faces were gray and drawn.

"Sorry about that, guys," I said. "Unfortunately, in the detective business Svetlana and I sometimes have to deal with crazy people."

"Svetlana," James said, "does that happen to you a lot?"

"Men chasing us with a chainsaw?" she said. "No, that was a first. However, I suggest we do not mention Chainsaw Man to your parents."

"Good idea," I said.

"Don't worry," Jack said, "we won't blab."

"Yeah," echoed James, "we won't blab."

When we reached the road, Svetlana stopped the Range Rover and waved a hand.

"Up the hill or down, Holmes?"

"Holmes?" Jack said. "Like 'Sherlock Holmes'?"

"Yes, Jack," Svetlana said. "Dakota likes it when I call him that."

"Down," I said. "I want to talk to the people who live below the Clarks'. Maybe they've seen something that can help us."

Svetlana coasted us down the road, slowing at the hairpin turn over the ravine, and continued on to the next driveway. The name on the mailbox read, "KRAUSSE." She turned in. Just off the road, we were stopped by a closed wooden gate. Beyond the gate, the driveway climbed a long rise to a house. A fenced-in paddock ran along the driveway, and there was an all-wheel drive hatchback parked on the grass next to the porch.

"Now what?" Svetlana said.

"We go up to the house, all of us," I said. "I didn't see any 'No Trespassing' or 'Posted' signs near the gate. The place looks friendly enough, and I think a man, a woman and two boys will be less threatening than just some guy who hasn't shaved in three days hiking up their driveway alone."

"I agree," Svetlana said, opening her door.

Outside, we climbed over the gate. About 100 yards away up the hill, the house was utterly silent. A trio of horses in the paddock stopped grazing and looked at us.

"What if nobody's here?" Jack said.

"Then we—"

"I've got a bad feeling," James said.

"Relax, nothing's going to happen," I said, which is when I spotted two objects darting across the grass up the hill. One ducked under the fence and cut diagonally across the paddock toward us, the other rounded the corner of the fence and bolted down the driveway. Two big German shepherds.

"Holy crap!" Jack said.

"Stay where you are, boys!" I said. "Don't move!"

Running silently, the dogs covered more than 50 yards before they started barking.

"Stay!" I shouted at the dogs. "Down! Sit!"

The dogs kept coming. I put my hand on my gun. When they were almost on top of us, Svetlana stepped in. She snapped her fingers, stabbed a finger at the ground and roared at the dogs with a ferocity I'd never heard in her voice before.

"*Setzen!*"

The dogs instantly halted and sat on their haunches.

"*Bleibe!*" she shouted.

"Wow!" James said, shaking beside me. "What was that?"

Svetlana turned her back on the dogs. They were calmly panting.

"German," she said. "It occurred to me that the surname of 'Krausse' on the mailbox is German, and that many German shepherds are trained to respond only to commands in German."

As I shook my head in awe, the front door of the house opened and a woman walked down the driveway. She was a middle-aged blonde, tall and sturdily built—like she spent her free time chopping wood and running up mountains. In an earth-toned jacket, jodhpurs and tall boots, she looked like she'd just returned from a lion hunt.

As she drew closer, I noticed her face: square jaw, fleshy cheeks, prominent nose. Attractive but slightly mannish, the woman was what you'd call handsome.

"Excuse me," she said with a distinctly German accent, "did you not see gate?"

I was about to respond when Svetlana replied to her in German. The woman visibly relaxed and the two of them chatted briskly for a minute or two. The dogs, meanwhile, lay on the driveway panting, glancing left and right at the two women like they were watching a tennis match.

"My name is Klara Krausse," the woman finally said.

Svetlana shook her hand, introduced herself, and introduced me as Dexter Price.

"I see you meet Ludwig and Wolfgang," Klara said. "Svetlana tells me you wish to know if we see anything in woods recently. Sadly, we see nothing—Bernhard and me."

"Is Bernhard your husband?" I asked.

"Yes."

"If you don't mind my asking," I said, "what kind of work does he do?"

"He is construction engineer. He is at project on Mount Stratton now." She gestured at the property and slapped her arms against her sides. "Is very quiet here as you can see. Now I am sorry to be rushing you, but dogs have doctor's appointment in Bennington in one hour, so I must leave. I see you another time perhaps?"

"Perhaps," Svetlana said. *"Auf Wiedersehen."*

"Auf Wiedersehen."

As we said goodbye, I scanned the trees for security cameras. There was nothing near the gate, along the fence, or in the paddock that I could see. We walked back to the Range Rover.

"Svetlana, you drive," I said.

We got in. Klara and the dogs walked up to the house. As Svetlana was backing us out of the driveway, I tapped her arm.

"I want you to drop me up the road, then go to the house and wait for me."

"Going back for a closer look?" she asked.

"Yes. If old Ludwig and Wolfgang are really going to an appointment, this is the best chance I'm going to get."

"What if the dogs are *not* gone?" Svetlana said, creeping up the road. "What if Klara only said that to get us to leave?"

"Then I'm dog food," I said.

"Can we come?" Jack asked.

"Yeah, Dakota, we want to come," James said.

"No, it's dangerous. Besides, you two need to watch out for Svetlana, okay?"

"Okay."

"Stop here," I said to Svetlana. "I'll meet you back at the house in half an hour or so."

"Be careful, Dakota," Jack said.

"Yes," Svetlana said.

"I'll be fine, guys."

I smiled at Svetlana for a long moment, admiring the rare softness in her eyes, then winked and got out. I jogged down the dirt road as the Range Rover crunched up the mountain and faded into the trees. When I saw the Krausse mailbox ahead, I climbed over a crumbling stone wall on the side of the road, kneeled behind an old maple and peered out at the driveway mouth. The wall gave me good cover in front, but at my back was a big open meadow at a curve in the road. People coming down the mountain would be able to see me.

Hunches are an important part of detective work: listening to your intuition about something you think is going to happen, and then waiting for it to happen. So, for about the billionth time in my detecting career, that's what I was doing—waiting. I waited seventeen minutes before Klara and the dogs got in their hatchback, and the car started toward the road. Unfortunately, that was exactly the moment when, from up the mountain, I heard the unmistakable, obnoxious flatulence of a Harley-Davidson motorcycle. And it was getting louder. I lay down in a prone position with my ribs pressing against the stone wall, and burrowed as deeply as I could into the fallen leaves. If I stayed absolutely still, I doubted the motorcycle would spot me.

Where I lay, there was a hole in the stone wall with a clear view of the foot of the Krausse driveway. Klara reached the gate. I lay motionless while the motorcycle rumbled past me. The driver wore a helmet with no visor. It was Duane, the Chainsaw Artist. He blocked the end of the driveway just as Klara reached the road. Revving the motorcycle, he duck-walked with it over to her window. An interesting observation—as Duane approached the car, the dogs inside didn't bark, as if they were used to him and his motorcycle. Klara and Duane talked, but with the noise from the engines, I couldn't hear what they were saying. It didn't help that I had to focus on lying motionless in a pile of leaves and resisting the urge to sneeze.

Finally, after two minutes that seemed like two hours, they both headed down the mountain and the road was clear again. I sprang up, brushed myself off, and hustled across the road to the Krausse property. I hopped the gate and ran up the driveway.

At the house, I habitually started to climb the porch stairs to pick the front door lock, but I got two steps up and realized I hadn't brought my lock-picking tools. While my TV detective hero, Jim Rockford, is often able to break into places with a story and a credit card, the reality is, it takes a while. Besides, there was a lot outside that I could check out.

I went around the house and tried to peek in the windows, but all of the shades were drawn, so I turned my attention instead to what looked like a large barn. It was metal-sided, and the doors were locked tight. Walking around the perimeter, I passed three pallets stacked high with heavy plywood, and then I found a chink in the barn siding where I could look inside. All I saw were tarpaulins covering big amorphous blobs, and the unmistakable green and yellow of a John Deere tractor. Adjoining the paddock was a small stable with its door open, but all I found inside was a tack room, bins of oats and feed, and three empty stalls.

I walked to the far edge of the property, where the paddock abutted the woods. There were tire tracks on the ground from what looked like a tractor and a large truck. The underbrush along the treeline had been crushed by machinery. It was thick bramble, though, so I just stood at the edge and peered in. The woods sloped down sharply, and I could hear the river below.

The grass along the fence line showed vague traces of tire tracks. I followed them back to the metal barn. From there the tracks led to the other side of the property, continued into the woods, and went up a narrow dirt lane with a grass stripe down the middle. Leaves covered the tracks in some places, but the tracks were still noticeable. The lane pitched uphill beneath a dense canopy of trees, and curved out of sight at the top. I started up the hill.

The tire tracks continued through the woods for close to a quarter mile, until they faded, about 10 feet from the edge of the Clarks' yard. The bed of fallen leaves was thicker here. I squatted and dug through the leaves until I felt tire tracks beneath. Taking a closer look at the leaves, I noticed that a lot of them were from tulip and sassafras trees, two trees I hadn't seen in the woods at all around here. The scarlet, mitten-shaped sassafras leaf was especially curious; I wasn't sure it was even native to this area.

From this vantage point I could see the Clarks' garden, the mountain of firewood and the house, but I didn't see any tracks on the lawn. It was as if a tractor and a truck had driven up from the Krausses', stopped dead at the woods' edge and backed all the way down the narrow lane to the Krausses' again.

The sun was beginning to set behind the mountain, and the light in the woods was fading. I checked my watch. I'd already been longer than half an hour. If I stayed out here much longer, I risked being seen or turning my ankle because I couldn't see where I was walking. Skirting the Clarks' yard, I continued uphill through the woods, towards Ryan and Nina's house.

———◆◆———

The boys and I had promised to take Svetlana shopping, and we did. We drove to Manchester, where the boys and I patiently accompanied Svetlana inside Prada, Kate Spade, and Michael Kors, complimenting her on each pair of boots, each handbag, each skirt. Afterwards I took the boys to Orvis, asked the fishing expert what the trout were biting, and bought the boys a couple flies. And because of their extraordinary patience and good behavior, Svetlana did something shocking: she offered to take them to a pizza-arcade restaurant in Bennington.

Svetlana and I sat on either side of a cheese-yellow Formica booth with our backs against the wall. We had our legs stretched out and were keeping a watchful eye on the boys, who were across the restaurant playing Skee-Ball. I was on the phone with Ryan, who asked me how things were going with the boys. I felt a little guilty saying everything was fine, but he and Nina were three thousand miles away, and I didn't want them to worry or to feel compelled to return. I painted a picture for him of the weekend being nothing but fly-fishing, pumpkin carving, apple picking, leaf-peeping and every other piece of autumnal Americana I could think of.

"God, that's great to hear," Ryan said, sighing over the line. "I was a little concerned, Dakota."

"Why's that?"

"Because you two don't have much experience with this sort of thing," Ryan said. "But…clearly you and Svetlana have things under control."

I assured him that we did, sent our love to Nina, and hung up. The second I put my phone in my pocket, Svetlana narrowed her eyes at me across the table.

"You lie well," she said, sipping her drink and putting the cup down. "What a *fine* pair of guardians we are. Let's see…"—she ticked off items with her fingers—"…allowing them to eat nothing but donuts and pizza. Letting them keep rare coins they found in the woods. Getting them chased by a man with a chainsaw. Nearly getting them mauled by two German shepherds. What else…?"

"Who knows?" I said. "Bigfoot? A meteorite maybe? Heck, the weekend's young. We still have tomorrow and Monday."

"Well," she said, "while you were snooping around the Krausse property, I discovered some interesting items in the local newspaper."

"Uh-oh," I said. "You have that 'you'll never guess what I found' look. Do I want to know?"

The boys ran over clutching fistfuls of Skee-Ball tickets.

"Svetlana, look!" James said. "We won a bunch of tickets. We want to get you something. What should we get you?"

"You never need to ask a woman that," she said. "Jewelry."

"Okay," Jack said hesitantly, "but I don't think there's anything fancy."

"Whatever it is, I will love it. Go! Dakota and I are talking now."

They ran over to the prizes counter and pored over the glass cases.

"So," I said, "what did you find out?"

"There have been several unsolved burglaries in the area in the past year."

I shrugged. "Those happen all the time. A lot of vacation homes up here sit empty half of the year."

"These were commercial establishments," she said with a smile. "Including, unfortunately for Jack and James, two rare coin dealers. Pawn shops, it seems. I did a search for shops that deal in rare coins and discovered one had been burgled, the other one robbed."

"This is big," I said. "Nice work, Svetlana."

She craned her neck to check on the boys, then sat down again.

"Don't worry," I said, "I'm watching them."

"I am merely making sure they stay out of mischief."

"It's okay to admit you care about them, Svetlana. I promise not to tell."

"No comment." She smiled and sipped her drink.

"Continue with your findings," I said.

"There were two other burglaries of commercial establishments. A gun shop and—"

"Let me guess…a medical supply warehouse?"

"No, but close. The hospital in Bennington. A lot of medical supplies were stolen, including a defibrillator kit and controlled substances."

"Like morphine," I added.

"Exactly." She put her drink down again.

"What about the other rare coin dealer?" I asked. "The one that was robbed. Where's it located?"

"Near Brattleboro," she said. "Oh, and there is one thing that all of these crimes have in common. In each case, witnesses reported the sound of loud motorcycles fleeing the scene."

I thought about Duane Hobart and his Harley earlier in the day.

"Okay, let's think about this," I said. "Silver and gold coins, shotgun shells and morphine. Assuming those items all belong to the same person, what kind of person would be stealing those things? For what purpose?"

The boys returned to the table with their hands behind their backs. Seeing their faces reminded me of watching them play video games that morning.

"Guys," I said, "before you give Svetlana her present, I need you to tell me something about that zombie game you were playing today."

"What about it?" James asked.

"When you're scavenging," I said, "what kind of stuff do you look for?"

"Depends," Jack said. "Weapons mostly, but food and medical supplies are really important too."

"If you don't get the medical packs, you die eventually," James said. "Svetlana, here!"

James revealed what he was holding: a faux diamond necklace. It was surprisingly sparkly for something made of plastic and sequins. Svetlana's eyes went from their usually hooded, mysterious look to little-girl wonder.

"Oh, James," she said, "I love it." She gathered up her hair, exposing her neck. "Put it on me."

With trembling hands, James somehow managed to open the tiny clasp and secure the necklace around her neck.

"And here's the matching bracelet," Jack said, putting it on her wrist. "And some earrings."

"*Je les adore.*" She removed the earrings she was wearing and put on the ones Jack gave her. "I love them. Thank you." She kissed them both, leaving conspicuous ruby red lip marks on their cheeks. They blushed. "Now go play and let Dakota and me finish our talk."

They wandered over to a deer hunting video game and put in quarters. I picked up an uneaten slice of mushroom pizza, took a bite and tossed it back. It was no DaVinci's on 18th Avenue in Brooklyn, that's for sure.

"All right," I said, "tomorrow we'll have to visit the dealer that was burgled over near Brattleboro. Maybe he knows something."

"*He?*" Svetlana said with a smirk. "What a sexist you are, Dakota, thinking that a woman cannot be a rare coins dealer."

"Yeah, that's *exactly* what I was thinking." I rolled my eyes. "The combination of items we found in the woods suggests that preppers are behind this, but—"

"Excuse me?" she said. "Preppers?"

"People who are preparing for the end of the world by stockpiling food, ammunition and medical supplies."

"Ah," she said, "*those* people."

"What do you mean 'those people'?" I said. "Need I remind you that I have a decent-sized supply of that stuff in Millbrook myself? Guns, ammo, medical supplies—"

"Food?"

"Yes, I have a pantry *and* a deep freeze," I said. "I also have fish in the ponds—trout and bass—and I have seeds and a lot of acreage, so I could *grow* food. I used to help my great-uncle Holland with the potatoes."

"You, farming," she said. "This I would love to see."

"It's less ridiculous than the idea of *you* farming."

"Perhaps, but I would look incredibly stylish while doing it."

"Yes, you would—in *haute couture* overalls," I said.

She smiled. I smiled back.

"Well, my dear…you're welcome in my compound anytime."

If there ever were a zombie apocalypse, Svetlana was the one person on earth I'd want with me. Even if she did come with a lot of Louis Vuitton baggage.

"So," she said, "what did you learn at the Krausse residence?"

I took a few minutes to describe the layout of the Krausse place, the tire tracks I'd found, the trail through the woods, and the presence of leaves not indigenous to the Green Mountains of Vermont. Svetlana peered across the restaurant. The boys were shooting baskets now.

"The leaves," she said pensively. "Perhaps they were carted over from the other side of the property and dumped there."

"Yes, but that doesn't explain why someone felt the need to use them to cover the tire tracks."

"What if they were not trying to cover the tire tracks?" she said. "They might simply have been dumping leaves and covering the tracks was an accident."

"Maybe," I said, "but none of this explains why there are tire tracks going through the woods in the first place, nor why they just *stop* at the edge of the Clarks' property."

Svetlana closed her eyes and drummed her fingernails on the table.

"*Hmm*," she said.

I sat up. "Your 'hmm's' are usually pretty good. What is it?"

"Is it possible to drive over the ground without leaving tracks?"

"It isn't easy," I said, "but yes, it can be done. However, why would a tractor and a truck be going up to the Clarks' place—through the woods—to begin with? I didn't see any signs of work activity on the property."

She opened her eyes and turned to face me. "Perhaps they were not going to their property. Perhaps they were only going *through* their property."

I nodded. "You might be on to something. Tomorrow, I need to get a better look at the Clarks' property."

"What if I invited them up to Ryan and Nina's for coffee or cocktails?" she said. "And in the meantime, you could do your patented 'poking around.'"

"An excellent idea," I said. "And we'll visit the rare coin dealer tomorrow. *She* might prove useful."

As if they sensed we were done talking, the boys ran over. Jack leaned over my shoulder on my side of the booth, and James did the same to Svetlana on her side.

"Can we go?" Jack said. "We wanna get back and play Monopoly."

"Like I told you this morning, guys," I said, "I'd re-think that if I were you."

"Hush, Dakota," Svetlana said. Then, to the boys, "I would love to play Monopoly with you."

"Said the spider to the fly," I said.

--------◆◆◆--------

At eight the next morning, the boys and I put on wad-ers and went down to the river to do some fly-fishing. The river here was wide, with the woods some distance from the water, making for ideal casting conditions. The leaves on the trees—scarlet, flame-orange, russet and gold—sparkled in the rising sun. The rocky banks were splashed with light. It was a beautiful morning. Yet for some reason, Jack and James waded into the river beside me with their heads hanging.

"Why so glum, guys?" I said. "Missing your folks?"

"A little," Jack said. "But it's not that. It's…"

"Oh," I said, "let me guess. Monopoly with Svetlana last night."

"How'd you know?" Jack said.

"You guys still have that dazed look from the pound-ing she gave you."

"She was scary, Dakota," James said.

"She bankrupted me," Jack said.

"She *is* scary, and she bankrupts everybody," I said. "But you can't say I didn't warn you."

"Yeah," they said.

"Let's forget about Monopoly and do some fishing," I said. "You guys fish this section, and I'll be a hundred yards downstream. See that pool below those steep banks? Little critters sometimes fall in the water in places like that. I have a feeling there might be some big ones in there."

"If you hook one," James said, "can I reel it in?"

"Sure. Work your way downstream to me, both of you."

Once I was clear of them, I pulled some line out of the reel, letting the line float in the water beside me, and worked the rod rhythmically forward and back in controlled bursts with my arm. Careful to keep my wrist firm, feeding out the slack, I made a nice thirty-foot cast in the middle of the river and let the fly drift downstream with some fallen leaves. I didn't get any hits, but I continued to cast well as I made my way downstream through the thigh-deep water to the pool I'd spotted earlier.

The river was narrower here and hemmed-in by undergrowth along the high, steep banks. I was about to do a roll cast because of the tight conditions when the water near the edge of the pool caught my attention. It was rust-orange. As I waded over to it, I noticed a mound of orange dirt beneath the waterline. In fact, the entire hillside leading to the mound in the water was covered in orange dirt. Topsoil is dark brown or black, and there's seldom more than a few inches to a foot of it when you dig; this orange stuff was subsoil, and there were yards and yards of it here, which meant that someone had recently done a lot of digging. And since the hillside was covered with subsoil, it had clearly been dumped from above.

I had a feeling I was below the Krausse property, directly beneath the spot where tire tracks had crushed the bramble along the treeline. But I couldn't be sure without taking a look. I laid my rod and net on a flat-topped rock and started to climb the hillside, using the birch saplings as ropes to pull myself up.

When I reached the top I crept forward to the edge of the trees, squatted and peered out. It was the Krausse place all right; Ludwig and Wolfgang sat sentry at the top of the driveway, their ears pricked and alert. Painstakingly, I backed up, careful not to make noise (no small feat in the cumbersome hip waders), and climbed back down to the river. James handed me my rod and net.

"Where'd you go, Dakota?" he asked.

"Yeah," Jack said. "We were worried about you."

"I'm sorry, guys. I had to check something out."

"Something involving the case?" Jack asked.

"Can we help?" James asked.

"Actually," I said, "you've already been more help than you know."

"But we didn't do anything," Jack said.

"Yes, you did," I said. "That zombie game of yours gave me several ideas. And today, I'd like your help with something else."

"What?" James asked.

"I need you to keep Mr. and Mrs. Clark busy for a while."

"Keep them busy with what?" Jack asked.

"Launch your rocket for them," I said, "show them your bow and arrow skills, anything to keep them occupied at your house."

"What are you going to be doing?" James asked.

"Nothing much," I said. "Just poking around a bit."

"Poking around *where*?" Jack asked.

"Who's hungry?" I said. "I want a stack of blueberry pancakes *this* high." I made a six-inch gap between my middle finger and thumb.

"I'm having a stack *this* high," James said, spreading his arms.

"All right, let's go."

When we got back to the house, Svetlana was stretched out in the hot tub with her hair up, playing chess on her iPad. The jets were on high, causing the water to bubble loudly around her.

"We're going out for breakfast, guys," I said to the boys. "Go change out of your fishing gear, okay?"

"Why can't we go in the hot tub with Svetlana?" James asked.

"Svetlana needs some time to herself," I said. "Go get ready."

They went inside grumbling.

"Good morning, Champ," I said.

"Good morning," she said.

"Speed chess?"

"With the Internet speed up here? *Hardly*," she said. "It is one of my archived games against an old rival."

"When you get dressed, I need you to call the Clarks—their number is on the refrigerator—and invite them up here for brunch at one o'clock."

"Brunch?" She turned to me, raising an eyebrow. "Do you expect me to cook?"

"*Hardly*," I said, mimicking her accent. "I saw a bakery down the mountain. We'll pick up something when we do our errands."

"What errands?"

"Talking to that coin dealer that was robbed, and hopefully a cop."

She floated to the side of the tub and stood up unexpectedly. She was wearing a black bikini. The sight of the water sluicing down her smooth skin made my breath stutter.

"Could you hand me my bathrobe and towel?" she asked. "They are on the deer antlers behind you."

I handed them to her over my shoulder and glanced at the sliding glass door. She was smirking behind me.

———————◆◆◆———————

After picking up a spinach quiche and a box of pastries at an "artisanal" bakery—whatever the hell that meant—we drove south on Route 30 from Newfane and found "Jerry's Gold, Silver, Rare Coins and Pawn" in West Dummerston. The business was housed in an old general store on a barren gravel lot. The best thing going for the place was the view across the highway: a wide section of the West River with the peak foliage on the mountainsides beyond. As I turned into the lot, a Harley-Davidson that had been behind us since Newfane passed us and continued south. The rider didn't appear to be our neighborhood chainsaw artist, Duane.

The boys waited in the car while Svetlana and I went to the front door. There were bars in the windows and a "CLOSED" sign hanging on the door, but we knocked anyway. Nobody answered, and there was no noise inside.

"Shoot," I said. "We really need to talk with this guy."

Svetlana went back down the steps to the lot. She glanced at a pickup truck on the side of the building. The truck bed was overflowing with clear plastic garbage bags filled with beer cans. She pointed at a window on the second floor.

"There is a light on upstairs. I think someone lives here. Keep knocking."

"Okay."

This time, I pounded. I could feel the entire front wall shake under my fist.

"Very good," she said. "There is activity."

She was looking up at the window, shielding her eyes with her hand. I went back down to her. The window banged open and a gray-haired man with an eye patch leaned out. As an added bonus, he was fat and shirtless.

"Christ all-mighty," he shouted, "what the hell is wrong with you people?! It's Sunday! I'm closed! Now go…"

He craned his neck out the window and homed in on Svetlana. She was standing with her hands on her hips and her chest thrust out. The hem of her coat flapped in the breeze.

"Sir," she said, "are you the owner of this establishment?"

"Yeah, I'm Jerry. What are you, a cop?"

"Please…do I *look* like a cop?" she said.

"Not one I ever seen."

"Get down here," she said. "I require your assistance."

"Yes, ma'am."

"And put a shirt on," she added.

"Yes, ma'am." He ducked back inside and slammed the window shut.

Thirty seconds later, Jerry opened the downstairs door. He walked out in white socks and no shoes, trying to tuck in a threadbare Budweiser T-shirt that barely fit over his gut.

"Hey, Jerry," I said, pointing at the plastic bags in the truck bed, "you're a little behind in your can returns. I bet you've got at least fifty bucks in there."

He chuckled. "Ain't that the truth."

"You've got this," I murmured to Svetlana. "I'll be in the car."

I got in the Range Rover with the boys.

"What's Svetlana doing?" James asked.

"Questioning this guy," I said.

"Why's she doing it and not you?" Jack asked.

"Because older, overweight men with eye patches are her bailiwick."

"Huh?" James said.

"Because she can get more information out of him than I can," I said.

"Dakota," Jack said, nudging my arm, "check him out. Doesn't he look like a pirate?"

"Yeah," James said, "he does!"

"Yup," I said. "All he's missing is a wooden leg…and a parrot on his shoulder." I turned around, glanced at the boys, then looked back out the windshield and mimed Jerry's hand gestures as he talked to Svetlana. " 'Arrggh! I be Jerry the Pirate. I got me a heap a' gold and silver in me establishment, lassie. Gold 'n silver bigger than me beer belly. Arrrggh!' "

The boys laughed hysterically. They bounced up and down in their seats and pounded on mine.

"Easy," I said, "it's not *that* funny."

Svetlana nodded to Jerry with her hands in her coat pockets—a maneuver I'd seen her do before so she wouldn't have to shake the other person's hand. She started for the car.

"Look, here she comes," I said. "Simmer down, guys. Svetlana doesn't like it when you're being crazy little monkeys."

They made chimp noises for a second before settling back into their seats.

"What's 'simmer down' mean, Dakota?" Jack asked.

"It's something my grandfather would say to me when I acted up."

Svetlana climbed in. I got back on Route 30 south. The last I saw of Jerry in my rear-view mirror, he was still gazing after Svetlana. She had that effect on men.

"So, what did Jerry the Pirate say?" I asked.

The boys giggled.

"I told him I might know the whereabouts of certain missing coins," Svetlana said, "*if* he could tell me more about the robbery. He said he was off that day, and that one of his employees, Amber Grange, was minding the shop. She quit his employ a week after the robbery. Jerry gave me directions to her place. Head toward Ryan and Nina's. It is near Williamsville on the way back."

I glanced in the rear-view. The Harley-Davidson from earlier was behind us again. If he was following us, he wasn't being very discreet about it.

"Did Amber describe the holdup man or men?" I asked.

Svetlana touched up her lipstick in the visor mirror.

"Apparently she told Jerry it was two people wearing motorcycle helmets with reflective visors, so she couldn't see their faces. The security video corroborated her description. According to her, the one that did the talking was a man, and the other one might have been a woman."

"Of course this is all hearsay," I said. "Jerry might be using Amber as a scapegoat. I'll have to talk to her."

Svetlana creased her lips on a tissue and flipped up the visor.

"One last thing," she said. "Jerry believes Amber was in on the robbery."

"Why is that?"

"Because one of the robbers knew to go upstairs to his apartment to get the gold coins. Jerry keeps them in a box under one of the floorboards, and one day when he was upstairs getting some coins from the box, Amber burst in and saw him."

"Let's go talk to her," I said.

Svetlana gave me directions to her place. It was a pale blue double-wide that sat down in a dell with a broad creek running behind it. A Rottweiler lay beneath a pine tree, next to a weather-beaten doghouse. The moment we parked in front of the trailer, the dog started barking and straining against a heavy chain. Up on the road, the Harley roared by.

"I'll handle this one," I said.

"Good," Svetlana said. "I did not sign on for Rottweilers."

"That dog looks mean," Jack said.

"He probably is, but he wasn't born that way," I said. "Stay in the car, all of you." I leaned over and whispered in Svetlana's ear. "Get behind the wheel. Turn us around and keep the engine running."

She nodded and got out with me, then walked around to the driver's seat. While she turned the car around, I went up to the trailer door and knocked. The dog growled savagely and jerked against its chain.

"Nice doggie," I said.

The door cracked and a pair of eyes peeked out. I heard heavy metal music playing inside the trailer. Then the door swung open wide, revealing a skinny woman in a red satin bathrobe. The bathrobe was untied and gaping. I hoped the boys weren't seeing this. I closed her robe.

"My," she said, "a gentleman."

"I was raised right."

"You a cop?"

"Nope."

The woman was probably only in her early twenties but with thinning blonde hair, glassy eyes and unsightly teeth, she looked 35. My heart winced for her. She wobbled against the doorjamb. Her eyes flicked from the Range Rover, to my face, to my shoes, and back to my face again.

"You wanna party?" she asked.

"Sure."

"Your friends wanna join us?"

"No," I said, "that's my driver and bodyguards."

"Mmm, rich guy out slumming, that it?"

"Pretty much."

"Well, come on in, baby. Heat's getting out."

I stepped inside. She shut the door. Light seeped through partially closed blinds on the windows, illuminating a pig-sty of a living room. A coffee table, sofa and carpet were littered with glass pipes, plastic baggies, junk food wrappers, beer cans, cigarettes and lighters. The air was stifling and smelled of smoke and overflowing garbage. A CD player in the corner blasted heavy metal music. I turned down the volume. An emaciated man with long black hair, his age hard to guess, was slumped over in a recliner.

"Who's he?" I asked.

"Dunno," she said. "He was here when I woke up."

She backed up and leaned against the kitchen counter. A chrome toaster shone behind her.

"You're Amber Grange, right?" I asked.

"That's right." She pushed away from the counter and rubbed my chest with her palms. "Now...did you bring some stuff, or do you have money?"

"Money." I removed her hands and reached in my pocket. "But I don't want to party."

She gave me a questioning look. It was not attractive. "I don't get it...what do you want?"

I pulled out a hundred-dollar bill. Her eyes dilated. "Information," I said.

She glanced over my shoulder and swallowed hard. "Okay."

My eyes flicked to a reflection on the chrome toaster. A dark figure was creeping up behind me wielding a thin pole. The second the figure's arm started to move, I ducked. The pole whooshed over my head, striking Amber in the arm. She screamed and fell against the counter.

"Ah, goddammit, Billy! My arm!"

I spun around. Facing me was the guy I'd seen passed out in the chair. He swung a half broomstick wildly back and forth. His eyes were sunken and crazed-looking, and he staggered on his feet with each swing.

"Billy," I said, "put it down, or you're going to get hurt."

I dodged another two swipes of the broomstick before my back was to the kitchen counter. I had nowhere to go. A memory from when I was a teenager flashed through my mind: punching a guy with rotten teeth, my hand becoming infected, and almost losing the hand. I didn't want that happening again, certainly not with this 100-pound meth-head, so when Billy drew back his arm for another swing, I grabbed him by the arm and hair and slung him across the living room. He went headlong into a heavy brass table lamp and collapsed against the wall. I snatched the broomstick away from him, snapped it over my knee and hurled the two pieces down the trailer hallway.

At this point, Amber was on her feet. She pulled a bag of peas from the freezer and pressed them to her upper arm, where the broomstick had struck her. I yanked the CD player plug out of the wall.

"Tsk, tsk, Amber," I said. "Hoisted by your own petard."

"What? Speak English, jerk. Who are you? What do you want?"

"Dakota Stevens," I said. "I'm a private investigator, and I want information."

I held up the $100 bill. Her eyes flicked to the money.

"The robbery at Jerry's," I said. "He said you quit soon after it happened. Something tells me you know the perpetrators."

"If I say anything, he'll kill me." She winced moving her hurt arm.

"Who, Duane?" I asked. "Duane Hobart?"

She gave me that unattractive confused look again.

"How...how'd you know?"

"Lucky guess. What other robberies has he been involved with?"

"I want my money first," she said.

"Nope."

"Bastard," she said.

"No," I said. "Orphan actually."

"Fine," she huffed, "but you better pay me. Before Jerry's, he and his buddies did a grocery store and a hospital, and I think maybe a gun shop. He didn't tell me he was doing Jerry's though. I didn't know that Duane was behind it until afterward."

"The stuff he steals," I said. "Do you know where he keeps it? Is there a warehouse someplace?"

"I have no idea," she said. "Honest. That's all I know. Can I have the money now?"

I reached in my pocket, replaced the $100 bill with two twenties and gave them to her.

"Hey! You promised me a hundred!"

"I didn't promise you anything," I said. "When was the last time you fed that dog outside?"

She shrugged. "Food's under the sink if you wanna do it."

Over against the wall, Billy stirred. He moaned something and smacked his lips. I found a mixing bowl, filled it with dry food and added water. I went to the door with the bowl.

"Amber, I'll take you to a detox facility if you want. Right now," I said. "You're a young woman, you don't have to live like this."

She stared at me for a second. Her eyes became teary and she appeared on the verge of accepting my offer, and then the moment passed.

"Nah, I'm fine," she said. "Close the door on your way out. Oh, and don't say anything to Duane about what I told you, all right?"

"I won't. Goodbye."

Out in the yard, the dog barked until I showed him the food. He eased up on his chain, and when I dropped the bowl in front of him, he wolfed the food and wagged his stump of a tail. My good deed for the day. I returned to the Range Rover and got in the passenger seat.

"Dakota, what happened in there?" James asked.

I felt a pang of sadness for Amber. Maybe if I'd said something else, something sage and compassionate, she might have come with me. But there was nothing I could do. Svetlana put a hand on my arm.

"Did Amber tell you anything?" she asked.

"Yes, she confirmed a suspicion I had—that Duane—chainsaw man—has committed several robberies and burglaries. But she claims she has no idea what he did with the stolen goods."

"I had a similar suspicion," Svetlana said, "so I called Mike the metalworker, who called his state police friend—the one in the dunking tank at the festival yesterday. They are meeting us for breakfast at Dot's Diner."

"Breakfast? When?"

"One half hour."

"Then let's beat it over there," I said. "We don't want to be late."

Svetlana got us back on the road and laid down on the accelerator. The engine growled.

"Dakota," Jack said, poking his head between the seats, "we're starved."

"Svetlana," James said, "what's worse than starved?"

"Famished," she said. "Or ravenous."

"That's me," James said. "*Ravenous.*"

I turned to face the boys. "I said we were going out for breakfast, and we're going."

"But that was like an hour ago," Jack said.

"You can't be hungry," I said. "I just watched you guys eat two huge cinnamon rolls—each."

"We burned those off already," Jack said.

"We burned 'em off," James said. "We're growing boys."

The boys laughed; Svetlana chuckled with them. She drove us across a deep ravine and through the quaint hamlet of Williamsville until we reached a covered bridge. She stopped at the stop sign before the bridge. The one-lane bridge was empty. As we started across, the deck slats rattled under the tires.

Then the opening on the far end darkened. A black pick-up truck blocked our way. The truck had a raised suspension and a large decal across its windshield: "RED NECK."

"Charming," Svetlana said, pressing the brakes. "Oh, how I long for Manhattan."

"Back up, Svetlana," I said.

She looked behind us. "Someone is blocking that way as well."

It was a pair of Harleys. The two men on the motor-cycles removed their helmets. At the far end of the bridge, the truck doors opened and two men got out. They carried a heavy chain and a tire iron. One of them was Duane.

I had a gun, and if worse came to worst, I could shoot them; but that would create a lot of problems, legal and otherwise, not to mention potentially traumatizing the boys for life, and guaranteeing that Ryan and Nina wouldn't ask me to babysit again. I had to handle this nonviolently. As nonviolently as possible anyway.

"Boys, is that duffel bag with the guns still in the car?" I asked. "Please tell me it is."

"Yeah, Dakota," James said.

"Good. And they're fully loaded?"

"Yup," Jack said.

"Okay," I said. "Make sure they're set to full-auto and give me the bag."

They picked up a duffel bag and handed it forward together.

"Thanks," I said. "Now, guys…I don't *ever* want you doing what I'm about to do. Get down and keep the doors locked. And Svetlana, if things get scary, just throw it in reverse and ram those bikes back there."

"*Avec plaisir*," she said.

"English, Champ."

"With pleasure."

I got out carrying the duffel and leaned against the front fender. Duane and his buddy stood menacingly on their end of the bridge with the bright sun streaming through the latticed bridge beams. Behind us, the guys with the Harleys were closer—only about ten feet from the Range Rover's back bumper.

"Since when is this a toll bridge?!" I shouted to Duane. "It was free an hour ago."

Duane called out from the far end: "Whaddaya talking to Amber for? What'd that bitch say to you?"

"Who?"

I put the duffel on the engine hood and unzipped it. Right on top of the pile of Airsoft guns was a Sig Sauer

556 automatic tactical rifle with a peep sight. *Nice.* Jack and James had awesome toys.

"Nice try, buddy," Duane said. "All weekend you been poking into business that don't concern you and—"

"Doesn't," I said.

"What?"

"*Doesn't* concern me. It's a grammar thing."

"Shut up, prick! What's in the bag?"

"The coins I found."

Duane shouted down the bridge: "Henny! Dwight! Check it out!"

I turned to face the men by the Harleys. The second they were alongside the Range Rover, I pulled out the 556, took aim at their faces and fired. The gun shot its biodegradable BBs incredibly fast. Before they realized what was happening, I had hit both of them dozens of times on the forehead, cheeks, nose, neck and around their eyes. In seconds, red welts began to form.

"Sonova...!"

They covered their faces and ran back down the bridge. Following them with the gun stock wedged snugly into my shoulder, I mercilessly fired at their legs and groins. They threw on their helmets and started the bikes.

"Henny! Dwight! Come back!" I said.

They roared off. With the gun still up, I pivoted about-face and marched straight toward Duane's buddy. He approached from the other end, whipping the chain over his head. When I reached the middle of the bridge, I unloaded on his face. I had to admit: this guy was tough. At first he lowered his head and continued forward swinging the chain, but I adjusted my aim and drilled another hundred

BBs into his groin. He screamed, dropped the chain and ran back to the truck. Now it was just Duane and me. I stopped firing for a moment and lowered the gun.

"Drop the tire iron, Duane," I said.

"First drop the Airsoft."

"Fine." I placed it on the bridge deck and walked toward him. He tossed the tire iron behind him.

"What did Amber tell you?"

"No, that's not how it works," I said. "You lost. You don't get to ask questions. You listen and answer *my* questions. Now…I know that you and your gang have been stealing goods in the area, and that you've got them hidden somewhere—my instinct tells me it's around Pheasant Hill."

"Who the hell are you anyway?" he said.

"I'm a PI from New York. Nobody's paying me to solve this, though, so I'm dropping it. We're leaving later today. However, I will have to tell the Connors about all of this—you *did* chase after their boys with a chain-saw—which means Ryan and Nina will probably get the cops up there. In fact, it wouldn't surprise me if the entire mountain was crawling with them by tomorrow. Maybe even FBI and ATF."

"Is this a *threat*?" He put his hands in his pants pockets.

"No, a friendly warning," I said. "Oh, and if anything happens to Amber, I'm holding you responsible."

He removed his hands from his pockets and clumsily tried to conceal something in his right hand. I knew from experience what was coming next, so I backed up toward the side of the bridge, where the light streamed through the latticed beams.

"Screw you," Duane said.

He flicked open a switchblade and slashed at my face. I dodged it. My shoulder blades were against the bridge beams now. When he slashed at me again, this time backhanded, I ducked. The back of his hand hit one of the iron-hard beams behind me. He screamed, and the knife clattered to the bridge deck. I kicked it through the latticework into the river below. Duane stumbled around cradling his hand and grimacing in pain.

"Darn, it's probably broken," I said. "All those thin bones on the back of your hand? I hear they're really sensitive. Are you in much pain?"

He staggered back to his truck whimpering.

"Have a good one," I said.

I picked up the Airsoft rifle, put in in the duffel and got back in the Range Rover. The pickup truck backed away from the bridge opening, turned around and sped away.

"Dakota," James said, "why didn't you just punch that guy?"

"If an attacker is clearly out of control," I said, "he'll usually end up hurting himself. The best punch is the one you don't need to throw."

"I don't get it," Jack said.

"I'll explain later. Let's get over to the diner."

———◆·◆·◆———

There was a line out the door at Dot's when we arrived, but Mike Carver and his buddy, Vermont State Police Officer Beau Graves, had saved a large table for us. I recognized Graves as the stoic volunteer in the dunking booth at yesterday's Heritage Festival in Newfane. Once the waitress brought coffee and took our orders, I told Officer Graves that Svetlana and I were Manhattan private detectives. I gave him an outline of the case, including the discovery of the coins and other items in the woods, our questioning of the neighbors, the tire tracks around the Clarks' property, and Amber's statement that Duane was behind some of the robberies and burglaries in the area.

"Amber, huh?" Beau said. "Not a very reliable witness. She's a known meth addict, and she's been busted for solicitation more times than I can count. Besides, everyone knows that ever since she and Duane broke up, they've had it out for each other."

"Maybe that's true," I said, "but there's something suspicious going on. There might not be enough evidence to do anything official, but there's enough for a casual inquiry."

Svetlana stirred her coffee. "Dakota and I have already done most of the legwork, Officer Graves."

"Svetlana's right," I said "Look...do a stakeout with me tonight. If I'm wrong, I'll pay you for your time. But if I'm right, you'll be making an arrest that could get you promoted."

The waitress brought our food. Officer Graves, holding his mug in both hands, gazed out the window at the leaf-peepers driving by on Route 100. He nodded.

"You've got a deal. Where and when?"

"The Clarks' place on Pheasant Hill Road," I said. "Tonight at dusk. But we'll have to hike in from someplace else. Duane and the others need to think everyone's left."

"I know where," Mike said, slicing off a piece of ham. "The old Grayson farm. We can park our cars off the road there. It's maybe a two-mile hike over the mountain. No one will see us."

"*Us*, Mike?" Graves said.

"Yeah, *us*. I'm going with you. I'm tired of my club being accused of every crime committed around here. If there's a chance we can catch the real crooks, I want in."

Graves sipped his coffee. "All right."

"Just you, though," I said. "We can't have the whole club along."

"Of course," Mike said.

"A couple of things," I said. "One, if there is criminal activity tonight, Graves—which I think there will be—it'd be great if you could call in the cavalry."

"Sure," Graves said.

"And…if there's any reward for the recovery of the stolen coins—"

"There is," Graves said. "Two thousand dollars if I remember."

"Then those two boys"—I nodded at Jack and James—"get the reward."

Graves smiled. "Agreed." He looked down the table at the boys, who were hunched over eating forkfuls of pancakes. "So, you're the ones who cracked this case, huh?"

"Yes, sir," Jack said.

"Yup," James said, "we cracked that sucka!"

"Hmm," he said. "Guess I can forgive you for trying to dunk me all those times."

———◆———

We arrived back at the house minutes before the Clarks arrived. I helped Svetlana set out the food, and when our guests entered, I said I'd forgotten something at the store. Svetlana, who had taken their coats, lifted their house keys and palmed them to me on my way out the door.

Confident no one would see me, I drove straight down the road to their place, got out and examined the house perimeter for signs of an alarm. It was clear. I used the key and went inside.

Most of the time, a thorough house search takes at least an hour, often two—especially when you're not sure what you're looking for. But today it took only minutes. In the kitchen I found evidence of recent canning, including a countertop full of sealed jars of vegetables. The jars were labeled and decorated with ribbon. Then, behind a closed door adjoining the kitchen I found a large pantry with shelves and shelves of jars, as well as store-bought staples. But this wasn't prepper-level hoarding; these stores weren't much larger than what my grandmother had kept at our country place in Millbrook.

I was looking for evidence that would definitely show that the Clarks were involved in the prepper ring, or evidence that exonerated them. After casually searching the living room and their bedroom, I went downstairs to a TV room and got a lucky break. There were two closed laptops on a coffee table in front of a TV. The laptops were in sleep mode but awoke as soon as I opened them, and they weren't password-protected. I launched their calendar programs. Before, during and after the days that Mike had noticed the commotion in the woods late at night, both Mr. and Mrs. Clark were engaged with a variety of other appointments. Incoming emails corroborated their calendar appointments.

I quit out of the programs, closed the laptops and looked around for another five minutes. I peeked in the gun and trophy room Jack had mentioned, and saw that all of the hunting photos of Tom Clark were from many years ago, so it was quite possible that when he said he and his wife didn't go in the woods much anymore because of ticks, he was telling the truth. My instincts told me the Clarks were oblivious to what was happening on or near their property when they weren't here. Of course, they might have planned it this way—to be conspicuously absent so they couldn't be associated with any illegal goings-on, but I doubted it. Unless I found something damning outside around the house, I would choose to trust them.

Leaving everything as I found it, making sure the door was locked behind me, I went out to the garage. There was no heavy equipment here. In fact, it had been so long since many of the tools were moved that they were connected by thick cobwebs. I left the garage and walked along the upper treeline—the section of woods that abutted Ryan and Nina's property.

As I walked, I searched for signs that the ground had been disturbed. I walked the entire upper perimeter of the property without seeing any disturbances, and then I turned and swept my unfocused gaze along the upper treeline again.

The trees that bordered this property were birches, poplars, maples, and oaks, with the exception of one cluster—the five small spruce trees. I jogged back to that section of the lawn. The ground here among the spruces was covered with leaves. I waded through them. Right away I saw several mitten-shaped sassafras leaves. I brushed them away from the base of one of the spruces and found dirt mounded up around the trunk. These spruce trees had been recently planted.

I waded farther into the leaves, up the path between the brambles and thick underbrush, and when I entered the clearing, my foot hit something. It made a rattling sound under the leaves. I brushed the leaves away. It was a can of orange construction marking paint.

Also beneath the leaves were tire tracks like the ones I'd found yesterday on the leaf-covered lane across the property. From the middle of the clearing, I followed the path out of the clearing and down through the spruce trees, then walked across the lawn, past the house and down the hill. When I reached the leaf-covered lane on the other side of the property, I stopped and turned around.

Tire tracks on this side of the property, and tracks on the other side, but none in between. How was this possible?

Thinking back to something I'd seen on the Krausse property, I broke into a big smile.

The pallets.

Carrying the paint can gingerly by its bottom, I ran back to the Range Rover and put it in a plastic bag. Then I returned to the spruce trees with a rake and covered any signs of my footprints through the leaves. I did the same with the leaves in the clearing, then put the rake in the garage and drove up to Ryan and Nina's house.

Svetlana, the Clarks and the boys were on the deck eating quiche. I went inside, returned Mr. Clark's keys to his coat pocket, and joined everyone on the deck. Svetlana raised an eyebrow to me. I knew she was asking whether the Clarks were involved. I shook my head.

"So," Tom said, "did you get what you needed down at the store?"

"Actually, no," I said, pulling up a chair beside them. "Tom…Mrs. Clark, there's something going on around here, and we need your help to catch the people involved."

"I don't understand," Mrs. Clark said.

"We will explain," Svetlana said.

III

Because it was Columbus Day weekend, all of the moderately priced accommodations in the area were booked, so Svetlana, Mrs. Clark and the boys had to check into a suite at the Manchester Inn for the evening.

Mr. Clark and I had an early dinner with them and then we drove to the abandoned farm where Officer Graves and Mike Carver were waiting for us. After slathering on tick repellent, Tom Clark gave each of us a walking stick. I carried a knapsack that included my standard survival pouch, first-aid kit, water, energy bars and a compass. When everyone was ready, Mike, who hunted these woods during deer season, led the way up the gradually steepening slope and over the ridgeline, and we reached Tom's house just as the light began to fade behind the western mountaintops.

Once inside, I set up chairs in the living room, about ten feet back from the picture window that looked out on the lower treeline, where the leaf-covered tire tracks had been. Tom had a pair of binoculars, and we took turns surveying that section of the woods, where, I explained, a lane through the woods connected Tom's property with the Krausse's.

"I had no idea," Tom said.

"This group is very clever," I said. "I think they've targeted weekenders' properties—places where the owners aren't around enough to notice small changes on their land. For example, Tom—didn't you notice that little grove of spruce trees on the north side of your property, outside the kitchen, about twenty feet beyond the lawn?"

"Nope."

"Those were planted recently," I said, "and the dirt around them was covered with leaves."

"But why would someone do that?"

"I have a theory, and it involves this." I reached into my knapsack, took out the plastic bag and handed it to Graves. "It's a can of construction marking paint. I found it in the clearing just above those new spruce trees. If I'm right, in a few hours there's going to be a lot of activity out there."

Graves put the bag into his knapsack.

"I told my watch commander they might get a call in the middle of the night for backup."

"Good," I said. "Now all we have to do is wait."

Graves had brought a large Thermos of coffee. He poured each of us a cup, and as the light faded and we sat in total darkness, we sipped the coffee and stared toward the picture window.

"Graves," I said, "on the way over here, Mike was telling me about his motorcycle club. I have another theory."

"About what?" Graves said in the darkness.

"Why the Green Mountain Boys have been associated with the burglaries and robberies in the area."

"Who the hell are the 'Green Mountain Boys'?" Tom asked.

"My motorcycle club," Mike said. "I want to hear this."

"Here's what I think," I said. "I think that Duane Hobart is the head of an unsanctioned, underground motorcycle club, a club that doesn't have a patch. They don't have a clubhouse and they probably don't even ride as a group. They're just a gang that gets around on motorcycles."

"Go on, Stevens," Graves said.

"Hobart and his gang know there's an official AMA club in the area—Mike's club, the Green Mountain Boys. They also know that the general public, including most of law enforcement, doesn't discriminate between law-abiding AMA clubs and the 'one-percenter' clubs."

"What's a 'one-percenter' club?" Tom asked.

"The ones that engage in criminal activity," Mike said. "We call them 'one-percenters' because they give the other ninety-nine percent of riders a bad reputation."

"Not a bad theory," Graves said. "But there were a couple cases where witnesses *saw* the Green Mountain Boys' patch."

"The patch was a fake," I said. "If a witness only glimpsed the patch, he wouldn't be able to tell if it was a real woven patch or an iron-on decal. To fake a patch, all Hobart's guys would need is a decent photo of one. In fact, I bet a person could do a web search and find a high-res photo of a GMB patch."

"Well," Graves said, "like you said, Stevens—it's just a theory."

"Maybe," Mike said, "but it's a damn good one."

"Look!" Tom said. "The woods! Lights!"

Down the hill at the treeline, headlights slashed the darkness, silhouetting the trees. The outlines of pickup trucks, with men walking alongside, came into view. The caravan halted at the treeline, and pairs of men walked in front of the lead truck. They were carrying large sheets of plywood. They laid the plywood on the grass in front of the tires, and when they had laid several sheets end to end, the trucks crawled ahead and men laid down more plywood, forming a land bridge across the lawn. I grinned in the darkness.

"I knew it had to be the plywood," I said.

"What do you mean?" Graves said.

"I saw three large pallets of plywood on the Krausse property yesterday."

"I'm calling for backup," Graves said.

"No, not yet," I said. "Let's wait until they cross the lawn first. It'll take backup what—twenty minutes to get here?"

"About that."

"Okay, perfect," I said. "In the meantime, let's have Tom and Mike sneak out to the generator. Tom has an emergency generator that illuminates the entire property. Mike?"

"Yeah?" he said.

"On the nights it looked like a UFO was landing up here," I said, "I believe they were using heavy equipment outside and turned on Tom's emergency generator for additional lights."

"We weren't here," Tom said, "so I thought the power must have gone out. I'll be damned."

"Anyway, Graves," I said, "while Tom and Mike go to the generator, you and I can position ourselves behind the barn. It has a clear view of the spot where they're headed. When our backup is about a minute away, they should call us. We give Tom the signal and he turns on the generator just as they pull in. Then you arrest everybody."

"Sounds good," Graves said. "I'll tell them to block the road up and down the mountain, too—you know, in case anybody makes a run for it."

"Perfect," I said.

"How do we communicate?" Mike said.

"Brought a couple of walkie-talkies," Graves said. "Here, take one, Mike. Make sure the volume's turned down."

"Ready, everybody?" I said. "Let's do this."

By the time we slipped out the front door, the caravan was halfway across the lawn. Pairs of men hustled in front of the lead headlights, dropped a plywood sheet and ran back for another one. Tom and Mike went to the left out the door, through the bushes along the front of the house, and Graves and I went to the right, across the lawn and behind the garage. Peering out, I saw the caravan reach the back of the house. It was approaching the grove of spruce trees.

"Mike," Graves said into the walkie-talkie. "You guys in position?"

"Affirmative."

Five men and what looked like Mrs. Krausse ran ahead of the headlights carrying lanterns. They crossed over the treeline at the spruces and walked up the path through the underbrush to the clearing. There, they laid the lanterns on the ground and along the path back to the lawn.

"Graves," I whispered, "call for backup now."

"Okay."

"Remember…tell them to call when they're a minute away."

Shortly afterwards, the men and Mrs. Krausse returned from the clearing in pairs carrying sealed plastic storage crates, one person on each end. They loaded each crate into a pickup bed, and went back to the clearing for more. Among the men I noticed Duane Hobart and the three tough guys who had accosted me at the covered bridge.

During the next fifteen minutes, the men continued to load the trucks. They must have loaded 100 crates in that time—so many that I worried they might finish before our backup arrived. I heard Graves' phone vibrate in his hand.

"Yeah?" Graves said softly into the phone. "Okay, but no sirens. And when you come up the driveway, go straight up the lawn, above and below the house. Bye." He put the phone away. "Tell them to hit the lights."

I spoke into the walkie-talkie: "Count to ten, then hit the lights. Confirm."

"Got it," Mike said on the other end. "Count to ten and hit the lights. Out."

I handed Graves the walkie-talkie and drew my gun. "Ready?"

He drew his gun. "I'll take point. Got a vest underneath."

"Lead the way."

We left the cover of the garage and ran up the long hill, toward the lanterns. In the next few seconds, everything seemed to happen simultaneously: Graves and I reached the crest of the hill, the generator roared to life, the lights flashed on across the entire property, the state police SUVs sped in and surrounded the caravan, the officers yelled at the perpetrators to get on the ground, and motorcycles swarmed up the driveway.

"What the hell are *they* doing here?" Graves said.

"They're *my* backup," Mike said.

Only two of the crooks made a run for it, but they were soon rounded up, and when it was all over, thirteen men and Mrs. Krausse were handcuffed and sitting on the ground against the pickup trucks.

"Holy crap, Stevens," Graves said to me under his breath. "I'm gonna owe you—big time. Know what's in those crates?"

"I have a pretty good idea."

"We've already found fifty A-R's," Graves said.

"I'm sure that's just the tip of the iceberg," I said. "Follow me."

I led him into the clearing. Directly in the center were two holes, maybe six inches deep, where two hatch doors stood open. There were lights on in the holes. I went to the hatch on the right and climbed down a ladder. Graves followed. He whistled.

"Damn, this is the mother lode," he said.

It was a full-sized shipping container, lit on each end by a halogen lantern. Rows of stainless steel shelving ran the length of the container, and the crates on the top shelves scraped the ceiling. We opened crates at random. Canned coffee. Powdered milk. Rice. MREs. Medical supplies. Cases of ammunition. How-to books. Water filtration kits. Gas masks. Jewelry. And rare coins.

"And this is just one shipping container," I said, "I wonder how much more is in the other one."

A voice called down the hatch: "Graves? You oughta get up here. The woman and her husband are ready to give a statement. I think they want to deal."

"That will be Mr. and Mrs. Krausse," I said. "Their place is down the hill, at the other end of the road through the woods. That's where the trucks came from."

"Gotcha," Graves said.

We climbed out. Graves followed the uniformed officer to a police cruiser, and Mike and Tom joined me in the clearing.

"Shipping containers, huh?" Mike said. "Pretty smart. Glad you caught these guys, Dakota. I was getting tired of having the club accused every time a lawn gnome went missing."

Tom sighed, shook his head. "I don't get it. It's all so bizarre—literally *right* in my backyard."

"It's a very coordinated group," I said. "Duane Hobart's gang burgled and robbed places all over the state to build up their stores for Armageddon. But they didn't want to keep the stolen goods on their own property, so they targeted the properties of weekenders. Like Duane, Mr. Krausse was aware that a number of his neighbors were weekenders, and he possessed the technical expertise and heavy equipment needed to dig holes and bury the containers.

"So, last week, Mike—on the nights you were coming home from your shifts at the bar—they were out here burying the containers and filling them with all of the stolen stuff."

Tom looked around and shook his head in a daze. "All of this for the end of the world?"

"That's right," I said.

"But how did you have any idea this was going on?" Tom asked.

"It started with the coins the boys found in the woods," I said. "I did some searching myself and found morphine, shotgun shells and a broken flashlight. I believe Duane returned to the container to retrieve some loot for himself." I pointed my flashlight into the woods. "But on his way back to his house, he broke his flashlight and the other items and couldn't find everything in the dark.

"That's when I started asking questions—the Krausses, Duane, and you, Tom. And when I found yards and yards of subsoil in the river below the Krausse property, I knew something big had been buried."

"So," Tom said, "did you suspect us?"

"Briefly," I said. "But it quickly became clear that you had no idea what's been happening around here."

"And you first learned of this yesterday?" Tom asked.

"Saturday, yes," I said.

"It only took you two days to solve?"

"Well, me and my associate Svetlana Krüsh, and Jack and James."

"If I ever need a private detective—"

"Same here," Mike said.

Graves walked into the clearing. "The Krausses are spilling everything in exchange for a deal. They claim Hobart coerced them into all this."

"Not surprising, what I know about Duane," Mike said.

"And guess what else?" Graves said.

"There are several sites like this around the area," I said. "Other containers buried on vacant properties."

"Exactly. How'd you know?"

"This one was too well done," I said. "There had to have been earlier ones where they got practice."

"Eight more properties," Graves said. "All within two miles of here."

"Makes sense," I said. "No more than an hour's walk from supplies when, as they like to put it, 'the shit hits the fan.'"

"I just hope they're not right," Mike said.

"About what?" Tom said.

"You know…everything hitting the fan."

We looked at each other in the bluish lantern light and walked back to the house.

———◆———

In Manchester late the next morning, Svetlana, Jack, James and I ate brunch, browsed a used books sale at the library, then headed back to the inn. Svetlana had picked up some vintage chess books for herself and bought the boys a copy of *How to Survive the Zombie Apocalypse*. They flipped through the pages as we strolled up the sidewalk.

"I knew I was right," Jack said. "It says here that an island gives you the best chances of survival."

"Cause zombies can't swim," James said. "Svetlana… will you and Dakota live on our island with us?"

"Absolutely, James."

He grinned. We passed beneath a fiery, brilliant sugar maple. Ahead, up the lawn, sitting on a bench in front of the inn, were Ryan and Nina. They stood, threw their arms out and beamed at the boys.

"Hey, guys!" Nina said.

"Mom! Dad!"

The boys sprinted up the long lawn toward their parents. Svetlana hooked her thumbs in her jeans pockets.

"So, Dakota…are you going to miss them?"

"I am. A lot," I said. "You?"

Svetlana gave me one of her patented silent replies: she closed her eyes, smiled and shrugged minutely.

"I'll take that as a yes," I said. "So, how do you think we did? Babysitting two boys for the weekend?"

She narrowed her predatory eyes at the four of them on the hill. The boys were jumping up and down and talking excitedly to their parents.

"I think we should get up there before they say something incriminating," she said.

"Yeah…good idea."

We strode briskly up the lawn. Leaves drifted down around us.

"You were terrific," I said. "You'd be a great mother, Svetlana."

"Perhaps." She glanced at me. "Someday."

— For the inimitable and legendary
Jack and James Maloney

THE MYSTERY OF
THE VANISHING GREENSKEEPER

I was at the door of my house in Millbrook, about to walk outside with my shooting bag and try out a new gun, when the landline rang. I couldn't imagine who was calling. It was only eight thirty in the morning and very few people knew this number. Svetlana was in St. Louis, at the Chess Club and Scholastic Center, teaching a seminar on the endgame, and no one else knew I was up here. I stood and listened to the vintage answering machine. The man on the other end sounded annoyed.

"Shoot," the man said. "Dakota, it's Brett Vaughn, pro at The Links at Chestnut Ridge. Haven't seen you in a while. Anyway, I'll get straight to the point. A couple of weird things have happened up here at the club recently. I talked to the State Police down at Troop K, and Detective Sutherland suggested I call you. Said you specialized in the weird stuff…"

Hmm, I bet he did.

"Well, guess you're not home," Brett said. "Give me a ring if you get this. I'll try you back later. Bye."

He hung up. I crossed my arms and stared out the window at the woods. Everything was so green and lush. It was the week before Memorial Day weekend, and I'd been looking forward to this time off. I'd planned to do some shooting, horseback riding, swimming, fishing, and play some tennis. At some point I wanted to ask my stylist, redhead Sherilyn Jones, over for dinner and a private trim. Or I might ask Johanna Zeiss, the Austrian tour guide at the Shunpike Winery, to come over and teach me a few things (about wines).

I sighed. *Look into "a couple of weird things" on a golf course?* Honestly, I didn't feel like working, but Brett's call had piqued my curiosity. The club was only a few miles up the road. I could cruise up there, look into these "weird things" and be back in time for lunch—crab salad sandwiches. The thought of them made my mouth water. Suddenly I wanted to get up there, solve this thing and hurry back for lunch. I called him back.

"Brett, it's Dakota."

"Oh, great," he said. "I could really use your help."

"What's going on?" I asked.

"It's kind of hard to explain on the phone. How soon can you be here?"

"If it's urgent, fifteen minutes."

"Make it half an hour," he said. "And bring your clubs."

I hadn't swung a golf club in two years, and I wasn't about to break my fast now, under the scrutinizing gaze of a PGA professional with a U.S. Open title to his credit. I left my clubs where they were—indubitably cobwebbed in the annex storage room—changed into quiet golf attire and went out to the Cadillac.

Spring had come early to Dutchess County this year, and the trees, a pale green the shade of key lime pie, ballooned across the hillsides and crowded the road. I passed the old Middlemiss dairy farm and the farm where Mr.

Schultz had once sold his turkeys, and then I arrived at the Links.

Two magnificent old oaks and a large wooden sign that read, "The Links at Chestnut Ridge," marked the entrance. I followed the drive up a short hill until it circled in front of the clubhouse, and parked in a visitor's spot. Brett was standing in the drive next to a golf cart, wearing the only outfit I'd ever seen him in: golf shoes, high-wasted golf pants, polo shirt with another course's crest (today's was St. Andrew's), and a Links at Chestnut Ridge baseball cap. We shook hands.

"Still got the Caddy, I see," he said.

"Yeah, I do a lot of driving."

He glanced at the trunk.

"You didn't bring your clubs? Thought we'd play a few holes."

"Another time, Brett. Why don't you tell me about your problem?"

He looked relieved.

"Boy, am I glad you said that. What the heck was I thinking? I don't have time to play today. I'm running around here like a chicken with its head cut off. Well, anyway…I'll explain on the way. Hop in."

No sooner had I sat in the passenger seat than Brett floored it, and we raced down the drive. We careened off the cart path, around the clubhouse dining room, past the 18th green, to the starter's booth. A scowling white-haired man stood next to the booth holding a clipboard.

"Simon," Brett said, "anybody needs me, I'll be up at the equipment shed, or the tee on thirteen."

Simon nodded and we drove off.

"Talkative fellow," I said.

Brett lowered his voice. "Simon's not real friendly, but he's a great starter. Really keeps 'em moving. So… here's the deal, Dakota. I've got a charity tournament next week and…sorry, hold on…"

He turned onto a cart path that twisted through a copse of trees and emerged behind the third tee. He stopped the cart. An elderly gentleman teed off, the ball flying in a low line drive and bouncing straight down the center of the fairway, about 150 yards away.

"Nice follow-through there, Mr. Feller. Looks to be about"—he winked—"two seventy-five."

"Flattery'll get you everywhere, Brett," Mr. Feller said.

Brett tipped his cap and drove on.

"Anyway, Dakota, I've got a charity tournament next weekend. Biggest, most important thing I've ever done—a benefit for veterans. It's a veteran-pro tournament, where a vet gets paired with a pro."

He gazed into the distance as steered the cart.

"I've got two dozen sponsors and twenty tour pros coming—including a few big shots like Leo Irons. People are coming from all over the country—*next* weekend—and I need this thing to go off without a hitch, you see?"

"I do," I said. "What are the couple of weird things you're worried about?"

"I'm about to show you the first one."

We crossed a bridge over a stream, skirted the 7th green and drove along the treeline toward the 7th tee.

"Here's my problem." Brett gestured with one hand and steered with the other. "My head greenskeeper—nice Mexican guy, Javier Rodriguez, one of the nicest guys you could ever meet—he took off the other day. Just left when we were talking at the tee on thirteen, and he hasn't been back since. I called his house and his cell at least a dozen times with no answer, and then I went over to his house. Lives on the other side of Tower Hill Road, heading downhill towards Dover. You know where I'm talking about?"

"Sure."

"Well, I went over yesterday and peeked in the windows. Nobody was there."

"When did he take off?" I asked. "How many days ago?"

"Let's see, it was on Tuesday and this is Thursday, so…two days. I asked Brian Sutherland if I could do one of those reports on Javier and his family—"

"A missing persons report?"

"Yeah," Brett said, "but apparently you have to be a relative or not enough time has passed or something."

"Look, Brett," I said, "you might be overreacting. Maybe he had a family emergency and needed to take some time off and didn't tell you."

"No way." Brett drove down a lane and parked in a gravel clearing next to an equipment shed. "Javier's been with me for two years. Hard worker, nice family. I've always paid him well, he's been happy here. He knew he could come to me about anything." Brett sighed. "I need to find him and get him back before the tournament. Frankly, Dakota, I need him. I can't get this place ready without him."

He got out of the cart and pulled a ring of keys from his pocket. We walked toward the shed.

"So let me show you the first weird thing that happened," Brett said. "Jacob Brown—he's my assistant greenskeeper—he was with Javier when Javier saw this. According to Jacob, Javier started hyperventilating when he saw it. Here, see for yourself."

Brett unlocked a padlock and slid the door open. Parked inside were a pair of mowers. Tools hung from the walls. He led me to the back of the shed and snapped on a chain light.

On a workbench in front of us was a painstaking configuration of flat stones in the shape of a two-foot-tall person. Two stacks of small stones formed the legs; a medium stone, the torso. Atop that was a long flat stone forming two outstretched "arms," and crowning the whole thing was a flat stone with rounded edges—the head.

The stones ranged in color from a light bluish gray to charcoal. In Boy Scouts we'd occasionally used stacks of stones to mark the way on trails, and although I'd seen pictures of markers like this one, I couldn't remember where I'd seen them or the name for them, and I'd never seen one in person before. It was impressive in the way an interestingly shaped tree is impressive. I stepped back with my phone and took several photos of it.

"Really something, right?" Brett said.

"Yeah. Give me a second while I do something with these photos."

There was a way I could search the internet for photos similar to the ones I'd just taken, but I didn't know how, and I didn't care to learn. Honestly, the internet and those stupid "apps" exhausted me. Besides, this is what I had Svetlana for. Before she left on her trip, she had teasingly said, *"You may contact me when you need help, Dakota. I say 'when' and not 'if' because we both know you will need it."*

I had half a mind not to contact her, just to spite her, but that would be foolish, not to mention wasteful. Among other things, Svetlana handled the money for us; she paid herself a salary (for all I knew, a considerable salary), so she might as well be earning it. I emailed her the photos with a message: *"Two-foot tall man of stacked stones. Found in a golf course equipment shed. What can you make of it?"* Brett cleared his throat.

"Weird, right, Dakota?"

"A bit," I said.

"Okay, let me take you over to thirteen now."

"One second. Has anything been moved or taken?"

"No, I asked the other grounds guys that same question, and they said everything else was exactly as they found it."

"All right," I said, "let's go to thirteen."

Links courses, like Brett's, are notoriously difficult— tall grasses and bunkers dividing fairways, sharp doglegs, hilly terrain, and very thick rough. We had to drive literally over hill and dale before reaching the tee box at thirteen. Brett allowed a foursome to tee off and get well up the fairway before we went into the tee box.

"This is where I was standing with Javier the morning he took off," he said. "We were looking over there first"—he pointed—"and the next thing I know, Javier turns around to look up the hill, and his face goes *white*. I mean, Javier is Mexican and has reddish-brown skin, so to see his face go pale like that…well, it shocked me, so I turned to see what he was looking at."

From the tee box, the ground rose steadily uphill until it reached the top of a ridge with a post in the center of the fairway. I had played this hole before, and the idea was that you aimed for the post to keep your ball in the fairway when it sailed over the ridge. At the bottom on the other side was a bell that golfers rang to tell the groups following that it was safe to tee off. It was a frustrating hole because a lot of golfers forgot or outright refused to ring the bell, and whenever I caught up with the culprits, I wanted to kick them in the pants. Then I remembered why I was here and got serious again.

"Brett, what did you see up there?" I asked.

He gulped.

"A giant Indian—excuse me, Native American. I mean, this guy was at least seven foot, three hundred pounds. He had long black hair, in those whatchamacallits…"

He motioned with his hands from his ears to his shoulders.

"Braids?" I said.

"Yeah, braids. And he wore one of those round, old-fashioned hats."

"A bowler hat?"

"Exactly," Brett said, "a black one."

"What about his age?" I asked. "Any idea?"

He made a scales motion with his hands. "Tough to say. Mid thirties maybe. Definitely not a young guy, but not real old either. His skin was kind of weathered, know what I mean?"

"I do," I said. "Now, about his height. How do you know he was seven feet tall?"

"Because he was standing right next to the post up there. That post sticks six feet out of the ground, and this guy's head was at least a foot above the top of it."

I was intrigued.

"Let's go up and take a look," I said.

As we drove to the top of the ridge, I checked the sky for the sun. It was well above the trees and dead ahead. He stopped the cart next to the pole. I gestured down the fairway, toward the 13th green.

"That's east, correct?"

"Yup. East *exactly*."

"What time of day did this happen?"

"Just before we opened, so like quarter to seven."

"All right," I said, "so the sun was rising and you were looking east directly into it. Isn't it possible that—"

"Dakota, I know what you're going to say—that we were probably seeing things, that the light was playing tricks on us—but two things. First, yes, it *was* light out, but the sun wasn't over the trees behind the thirteenth green yet. It doesn't get above there until eight o'clock. Second, I *know* what I saw. After Javier took off with the cart, I yelled at the Indian—sorry, Native American—"

"Just say 'Indian' for now, Brett. I promise not to tell the PGA you were using racist or insensitive language."

He grinned. "Okay, so I yelled at the guy and—"

"What did you yell?" I asked.

"I yelled for him to stay put, and I walked up the hill towards him. Boy, was I shaking in my shoes. Thank God he didn't listen to me. He turned and walked in that direction"—Brett pointed in a diagonal toward the distant woods—"and when I got up here, he was gone. I did find something in a bunker on the twelfth fairway, though."

"You say, 'bunker,' Brett, but I say, 'sand trap.' To me, a bunker is where dictators hole up during bombing raids."

He chuckled. "Never thought of it like that before."

"But I'm the duffer, and you're the pro," I said, "so from now on I'll call them bunkers."

"Good man," Brett said.

He raced the cart in a diagonal across the fairway, crossed into the rough beneath some apple trees and stopped at a bunker surrounded by temporary plastic fencing. A typed computer page read, *"KEEP OUT! DO NOT DISTURB! POLICE BUSINESS! If your ball lands in here, please play another, without penalty, outside the bunker."*

Just beyond the bunker was more of that stream we'd crossed earlier. I got out of the cart. There was one ball in the sand, but it hadn't disturbed what Brett had sought to preserve—two giant shoe prints. I walked around the bunker, stooped over the fence and examined the sand. Besides the ball and the shoe prints, there was nothing in the bunker, not even a twig.

"Nice job, Brett," I said.

"Thanks. All the cop shows I've seen, first thing they do is lock down the crime scene, right?"

"Right. The 'police business' is probably a bit much, but better safe than sorry." I handed him my car keys. "I need a bag from my trunk. Big black satchel. It's my CSI kit. And four or five bottles of water, okay?"

"You're *that* thirsty?" he said.

"Well, I am thirsty, but I need a couple bottles to make casts of the prints. Please hurry back. No stopping for chit-chat, okay?"

"Gotcha. *You* keep an eye on the twelfth tee. Don't want you getting hit."

"I won't be here," I said.

"What do you mean?"

"I'm going to try and see where this guy was headed," I said. "If I'm not here when you get back, wait for me. I shouldn't be more than a few minutes."

"Aye-aye, captain." He saluted and drove off.

At first glance the shoe prints each appeared to be over a foot long. Again, huge—at least a men's size 16 shoe. The treads on both shoe prints were odd: they weren't boot or sneaker treads. The soles were segmented with deep grooves between the segments, and instead of traditional treads, the soles had raised, irregularly shaped blocks. The only soles I'd seen like these were soles for swimming shoes—the type a person might wear on a stony beach. I got behind the prints and gazed in the direction they were headed.

From the bunker, I walked toward the stream and found trampled grass on the bank leading down to the water. Looking across the stream, I couldn't see any trampled grass on the other side, so I crept upstream along the bank for fifty yards, until I was in the woods. When I looked across the stream again, I spotted two more shoe prints on the far bank and a clear exit path. I hopped rocks across the water and entered the woods on the other side. Then I lost the trail. Undaunted, I pressed on through the woods in the direction the shoe prints had been heading, until I emerged from the woods onto a dirt road.

I was pretty sure this was Ridge Road, which connected Chestnut Ridge Road in Union Vale with Route 22 in Dover. I paced along the shoulder until, in a turnout, I spotted fresh tire tracks and another one of the shoe prints I'd been following. I took a few photos of both. The tires appeared to have been turned to the extreme left, as if making a U-turn to head towards Dover. I started to walk back when I glanced in the weeds and found a new-looking Links scorecard. I held it by the corner. There were no scores on it, and it had been folded back to show the course map. It was glossy and might have a usable fingerprint.

I carried it all the way back to the bunker pinched in my fingers. When I got there, Brett was waiting with the satchel.

"Whatcha find?" Brett asked. "A clue?"

"Maybe." I put the scorecard in a plastic evidence bag, and slipped the bag in the satchel. "Right now, these shoe prints are the best clue we've got."

"Oh," Brett said, "I put up a sign on the twelfth tee, telling people to skip over to thirteen for now. That way, we won't get beaned while you're working."

"Excellent."

The first thing I wanted to do was take photos. Walking around the bunker, I snapped ten photos of the undisturbed scene from various angles. My next task was to get scale in the photos. I took a tape measure out of the satchel, stepped over the fence and laid it carefully on the sand beside the shoe prints—from the toe of the front one to the heel of the rear one. I climbed out and repeated the photo process again, then climbed back in and took several close-ups of each shoe print.

Now it was time to measure the shoe prints themselves. They were a little over 13 inches long. The ratio of height to foot size is, on average, 6.6 to 1, so I multiplied 13 by 6.6 in my head and came up with 85.8, or about 86 inches. This, divided by 12, came to a little over seven feet. *Maybe the guy really was seven feet tall.* This whole ratio and calculation thing was a rough estimate, of course, so I measured the distance between the shoe prints and the overall stride length as well, and wrote everything in my notebook for later.

I climbed out of the bunker, mixed up a pouch of plaster of Paris to make casts of the shoe prints, then went back in and poured it into each one.

"This takes about five minutes to set," I said. "Well, Brett, I think you were right. Estimating from these shoe prints, I'd put the guy at six feet eleven to seven feet three."

"Boy, I didn't like the look of that guy," he said. "Let me tell you, was I glad he was gone before I got over the hill."

"What was his build like?"

"Huge. Like a linebacker."

"And Javier took off as soon as he saw this guy?"

"Yup."

"Was it out of fright, or did it seem like he recognized the man?"

"Hard to say," Brett said. "When I turned around, he was already running for the cart."

"You told me you saw his face turn white," I said.

"I did. I mean he looked afraid—I noticed his face as he went for the cart—but I didn't see his reaction when he first noticed the Indian up there."

"Okay, I've got a pretty clear picture of what happened. One second."

I retrieved the shoe print casts, slipped each one into an extra-large evidence bag, and put everything in the satchel.

"Let's head back to your office," I said. "I need some additional info from you."

At the clubhouse Brett parked in the shade and we entered through the pro shop. The display shelves and cabinetry were all dark, rich wood. I felt like I'd just stepped into a fine men's store.

"Business is good, I see," I said. "You've upgraded since I was here last."

"Oh yeah," Brett said. "We do a nice business. Members like the convenience."

"Brett, could you make a copy of Javier's W-2 for me?"

"What for?"

"So I have the exact spelling of his name, and his address and Social Security number."

"Sure," he said.

He led me down a hallway to his office. Plaques, trophies and photos of Brett with other golf pros filled the room. The desk was spotless. He went to a filing cabinet behind the desk and opened one of the drawers. He flipped through the file folders, frowned and searched through the second drawer.

"Strange," he said.

"What?" I said.

"Rick," he called down the hall, "could you come in here?"

There were footsteps. A thin man with a gray mustache came into the room.

"Rick," Brett said, "do you know where Javier's personnel file is?"

"Should be in the top drawer. Last time I saw them was after Bud did the taxes. I put them all back in there."

"Okay. I probably misplaced it. Thanks."

Rick hitched up his pants and gestured down the hall.

"Meant to ask you before, Brett," he said. "What's going on with the lost and found?"

"What do you mean?"

"The little storage room down there. Mr. Scott came in a few minutes ago looking for his pitching wedge, and it's a mess in there."

"What?"

Brett and Rick went down the hall. I followed them. Rick opened the door, and the floor was covered with a mound of golf clubs, bags and other equipment.

"Holy crap!" Brett said. "When did this happen?"

"I have no idea," Rick said. "I just noticed it."

"Brett," I said, "don't touch anything. Let me take a look."

I edged past them and stooped over the piles of equipment. Every pouch on every bag and jacket had been unzipped.

"Were there any wallets in these?" I asked.

"No," Brett said. "First thing we do with any bags or jackets left here is look for ID. Any wallets get locked up in my desk."

"All right," I said. "Which golf bag or set of clubs is the most recent addition?"

Brett turned to Rick. "That set of Ben Hogans, right? The blue bag?"

"Think so," Rick said.

I picked it up and felt inside all of the pockets. Empty. Not even a broken tee. Then I shone my Mini Maglite into the club sleeves on top. All of those were empty as well. Except one. A red and white tin box was shoved in near the bottom. There was no way for me to reach it, even with some kind of tool, so I pulled out my pocket knife and cut a hole in the side of the bag, near the bottom. Then I reached in and gingerly removed the box. It was an Altoids tin. I opened it. Inside was a Ziploc bag containing a small scrap of paper and a torn-off section of a course map.

The scrap of paper read, *"It's in the dirt. Max watched for hours."* The section of course map told me even less: just the layouts, pars and yardages of four holes: 1, 2, 17, and 18. Nowhere on the map section was the name of a course, or an address, telephone number or website. I put the Altoids tin in a plastic bag and showed the scrap to Brett.

"Can you make anything out of this?"

"Hmm…'it's in the dirt.'" Brett gazed at the floor. "Reminds me of something Ben Hogan once said. Somebody asked him what the secret to his swing was, and he said, 'It's in the dirt.' But the other thing about this guy Max watching? No clue."

"What about this section of course map?" I said. "The hole layouts, the pars, the yardages—any of it look familiar?"

He shook his head. "Sorry. I wish I knew."

"Could you ask around?"

"Sure, but why?" he asked.

"Because somebody went to a lot of trouble to conceal this little tin," I said, "and somebody else rifled through every golf bag in this room. The two events might just be a coincidence, or it might be that the tin and the slips of paper inside are valuable to someone." I gave Brett the slip of paper and the course map. "Put these in a safe place. Okay, I've seen enough in here."

The three of us went back down to Brett's office.

"What are you going to do next?" Brett asked.

"Check the tin for fingerprints," I said, "and try to track down the Indian."

"Hey, Dakota…all this weird stuff—the stones, the Indian, the files, now this tin—do you think they're connected?"

"That's what I'm going to find out," I said. "While I'm pursuing other leads, could you look into that section of the course map and find out what course has that configuration?"

"You bet," Brett said. "Glad to help. Anything to help bring Javier back."

"Do you guys know Javier's address off the top of your head?" I asked.

"Yeah, I've got it in the other room," Rick said. "I'll go write it down for you."

"And get me a photo of him, please."

Rick left.

"Brett," I said, "have you noticed any signs of a break-in around the clubhouse? Windows broken? Doors jimmied, that sort of thing?"

"No, and I doubt that could happen. The whole place is alarmed after hours."

"But during work hours, if you're out on the course and Rick or whoever's in the pro shop gets busy, could somebody slip down the hall?"

He nodded. "Happens all the time. Some of the members like to use that bathroom outside my office."

"And your employees," I said. "They come and go freely down here?"

"Sure. Oh…I see what you're driving at…maybe Javier took his own W-2 the other day when he left. But why would he do that?"

"If he didn't want someone finding out his address or social security number," I said. "And by *someone*, I'm talking about a certain seven-foot tall Indian."

"But what if the Indian stole it?" Brett said.

I shook my head. "You saw him. Did he look like a guy who could 'slip in' here unnoticed?"

"Good point."

"As for the lost and found room," I said, "it *might* be connected to Javier's disappearance, but what's most important right now is finding Javier."

"Absolutely." Brett sat on the edge of his desk. "Dakota, we didn't discuss your fee."

"Cover my expenses and give me a season pass, and we'll call it even."

"I'll do you better. Since you only come up here a couple times a season, as long as I'm managing this club, you'll be considered a member. You can play whenever you want for free."

"I've never been a member of a club," I said. "Do I have to buy a special tie?"

Brett crossed his arms. "No, but our pro shop features a fine assortment of golf attire with the Links at Chestnut Ridge crest on it."

"Good," I said, "throw in one of those cashmere sweaters while you're at it. I saw a nice sage one in there. Large, of course."

"Of course."

We shook on it.

"Dakota," Brett said, "do you think you can find Javier?"

"I'll do my best," I said.

Rick returned and handed me an envelope. "Javier's address and a photo of him."

I opened it. The photo was of Brett and a shorter man with brown, almost reddish, skin standing in front of the Links sign at the main gate. The man had short, stiff black hair and dark eyes, but no distinguishing characteristics—scars, tattoos, et cetera—that I could see.

"Dakota," Brett said, "when you get to Tower Hill Road, Javier's place is the slate blue Cape with the gravel driveway. Good luck."

"Thanks. If a seven-foot Native American is truly involved in this, I'm going to need it."

II

Early morning sleuthing really works up a guy's appetite. It was only eleven thirty, but I'd earned a break. I went home, took the bowl of crab salad out of the refrigerator and made myself three thick sandwiches on soft rye bread. My paternal grandmother from Vinalhaven, Maine had always used hamburger rolls, but I wanted the bread to be every bit as good as the crab salad, so I went with the fancy, locally baked stuff.

Having just come from a golf course, I poured myself an Arnold Palmer in a tall glass with lots of ice. I put a Sinatra LP on the living room hi-fi and opened the windows on my way outside. I sat under the trees that grew through the deck, took in my magnificent view—the lawn to the pond and the weeping willows, Mrs. Gallagher's horses next door, and the distant mountainside—and savored every bite of my sandwiches.

For a restful half hour, I didn't think about the case.

Afterwards, however, I was eager to analyze the clues I'd gathered. I took the evidence bags into my home forensics laboratory, a converted photography darkroom, and dusted both the Links scorecard and the Altoids tin for fingerprints. Finding good prints on both, I photographed them, lifted them with tape and placed them on two labeled cards.

Next, I turned my attention to the shoe prints. I photographed the soles of the casts, then consulted a table in my shoe impressions reference book. A 13-inch shoe print translates to an American men's size 17. The book had photos of hundreds of different types and brands of shoes. I skimmed through it looking for a match. The closest I could find was a "watermoc" shoe, which had a similar grooved, segmented sole, and a staggered, blocky tread pattern. It also came in a men's size 17.

Finally, I made some calculations using the length of the shoe prints, the distance between them and the overall stride length. All three measurements pointed to the shoe prints belonging to a subject slightly over seven feet tall.

Satisfied with my work, I printed out photos from the bunker "crime scene" and the ones I took on the dirt road turnout, and put them and the fingerprint cards in a manila envelope. Then I grabbed the evidence bags containing the shoe print casts, and headed out. It was time to pay my buddy at Troop K a visit.

I stopped in the Village of Millbrook first, went to the library and checked out all of the books available on golfer Ben Hogan. Then I picked up my mail. One letter said I "might already be the Grand Prize Winner of a brand-new Range Rover or a tract of valuable land in Nevada." I threw it out and drove over to Washington Hollow, to State Police Troop K headquarters. There, I asked the desk sergeant to get Detective Lieutenant Brian Sutherland.

"Who are you?" he said.

"Dakota Stevens, P.I."

Ever since I'd seen *Magnum, P.I.* as a kid, I'd wanted to introduce myself that way.

"All right." He shoved a log book at me. "Sign in. I'll tell him you're here."

A moment later, the side door buzzed open and Brian, a quick, wiry guy with the same mustache he'd had since high school, appeared in the doorway. His eyes darted across my outfit. He snorted.

"Damn, must be nice being private—playing *golf* in the middle of the workweek. Did you get in a full eighteen, Dakota, or could you only squeeze in nine?"

"Hilarious," I said. "I was over at the Links—you know…following up on that case you refused to take."

"Some *case*," he said. "Missing greenskeeper, pile of rocks and a giant Indian. The so-called Indian was probably a ghost. Everybody knows that course was built on a burial ground."

"Ah, but I have photos, fingerprints and shoe print casts." I held up the manila envelope and the evidence bags.

He raised an eyebrow. "You've got my attention. Come on in."

In his office, he poured me some coffee. While he examined the evidence, I described my findings at the course.

"I'm pretty sure the prints from the Links scorecard belong to the Native American," I said. "I found it when I followed a trail of shoe prints he left—size seventeen shoe prints by the way."

Brian whistled. "Seventeen?"

"Yeah," I said, sipping some coffee, "and based on the length of the shoe prints, the distance between them and the overall stride length, I can say with confidence that the Native American man was seven feet tall, if not a couple inches taller."

"Big sonovabitch."

"After Brett spotted him," I continued, "he walked from a bunker, across the stream and through the woods to a dirt road. I found the scorecard in the weeds by a turnout, along with a matching shoe print and fresh tire tracks. It was a vehicle with a narrow stance, short wheel-base, and a tight turn radius. The tires were turned to the extreme left, as though the driver were making a U-turn to head towards Dover. There was no break in the tire tracks, so the vehicle didn't have to make a three-point turn. This all suggests to me that it was a compact car, and the shoe print indicates that the passenger was our seven-foot tall Native American."

"How do you know he was the passenger?" Brian said. "Maybe he parked there, went in and came back."

"I doubt it," I said. "The shoe print I found was on the passenger side of the car."

"Which you determined from the turned front wheel," he said.

"Exactly."

"Look who I'm talking to. Former FBI man—you've got game," he said. "Okay, I'm in. How can I help?"

"Could you run those fingerprints through AFIS?" I asked.

"Sure," he said. "Now, what's this second set? Card says, 'Altoids tin.'"

I explained where those prints had come from, and how I wasn't sure if the events on the course were connected to the ones in the clubhouse.

"If we can get IDs on the prints, that should tell us more," Brian said. "I'll see if I can get some kind of match on the shoe prints. To me, first glance…they look like a pair of swimming shoes."

"That was my first instinct, too," I said. "I looked them up in a reference book and the closest match I found was a shoe called a 'watermoc.'"

"Moccasin? Really?" Brian grinned. "Kind of playing on the stereotype, aren't you?" He carefully picked up the bag with the casts and pointed at the soles. "Clearly defined tread. Either these shoes are brand-new, or they haven't been worn on asphalt very long."

"Which suggests they might have been purchased recently," I said. "Good point."

"I'll have one of the boys call some of the sporting goods stores around. You never know—we might get lucky."

"It's worth a shot," I said.

"All right, I'll have to do this on the Q-T, and I've got other cases pending, so…how's tomorrow morning sound? We can meet for breakfast. You're buying."

"That's more than fair, Brian. Thanks."

From Troop K, I drove back toward the Links, then turned down the dirt road that ran along the south side of the course (it *was* Ridge Road). About a half mile in, I saw the turnout where I had found the scorecard, shoe print and the tire track. I kept driving east, in the direction the car had gone, towards Dover. The road wound downhill through dense woods and alongside a stream grandiosely named Mill River.

At first there were no houses whatsoever on the road, and then I drove past a couple of mobile homes with junked cars in the yards. Although it was midday now with crystal-clear skies, for a couple of miles the thick canopy of maples and old oaks blocked out the sun, making this section of the road feel shadowy and sinister, like I was in the movie *Deliverance*.

I followed the road until it terminated on Dover Furnace Road. From here, the car could have turned north towards Dover and Amenia, or south towards Wingdale and Pawling. Ever since they tore down my beloved Adams Diner on Route 22 (I'd stopped there many late nights driving up from the city), Wingdale had had a whole lot of nothing; just the abandoned psychiatric hospital. Dover, on the other hand, was an actual village—with gas stations, bars, restaurants, a motel and a train station—*and* it was closer. I headed north. I had no specific plan in mind, except to keep my eyes open and ask questions here and there. Dover is the kind of tiny rural community where seven-foot tall Indians don't go unnoticed. If he'd been through there recently, someone would have seen him.

My first stop, a Dunkin' Donuts, was a bust, as were a CVS pharmacy and a McDonald's. I passed the firehouse, and then, driving by the elementary school, I thought about dropping in on one of the teachers there—a woman I went to high school with named Dana. I'd once spoken to her class on Career Day. Dana knew people in the community, and if I asked her, she'd probably be willing to make some inquiries for me; but she also had her hands full—with like 100 fourth graders. I decided not to bother her.

I stopped at two gas station convenience stores; neither clerk had seen my suspect. Next, I drove to the train station. Across the tracks I saw a bar—The Four-Leaf Clover. It had a big picture window in front with a view of the train station and Mill Street down to Route 22.

Four-leaf clover? Maybe it'd bring me good luck.

I parked in front and went inside.

A bell on the door jingled when it closed behind me. Once beyond the front window, the bar was dim and cool. It was nearly empty at this hour. A couple of guys with beer bellies sat at a table in the corner. One wore a Tractor Supply cap, the other a Winchester cap, and they drank bottles of Budweiser. I was going to ask them about my seven-foot tall Indian, but the eleven beer bottles on the table made me question their potential reliability as witnesses. I pretended not to notice them and walked up to the bar.

The bartender was wiping down the counter, but I got his attention with a $20 bill. He had a bale of curly gray hair cinched in a ponytail and a pair of bushy eyebrows that would start attracting nesting sparrows soon if he didn't take some action.

"What can I get you, sir?" he asked.

"Information."

"You a cop?"

"Nope. You?"

He chuckled. "Let me guess…you're a P.I. For real?"

"For real." I took out a business card and laid it next to the $20 bill. "Both of these fine pieces of paper are yours, sir—*if* you can answer a couple questions for me."

"I'll see what I can do," he said.

"I'm looking for a Native American man. Oh, to hell with political correctitude—an Indian."

The bartender leaned over the counter and lowered his voice.

"He wouldn't be a huge one, would he?" he said. "I'm talking like seven feet tall, three hundred pounds."

"He might be," I said, trying to conceal my excitement. "What else can you tell me about him?"

"The guy I saw had long black braids, and a bowler hat."

"Sounds like my man. When'd you see him?"

"Came in the other afternoon, three, four days ago," the bartender said. "Asked me how to get to The Links at Chestnut Ridge. Did a couple shots of Wild Turkey while I gave him directions, then he paid and left. Scary looking guy, didn't exactly look like the *golfing* type, you know? But I wasn't about to ask him why he wanted directions there."

"Did he come in again?" I asked.

"Not that I know of," he said, "and I'm on twelve hours most days. Name's Kieran Lynch, by the way."

"Dakota Stevens." We shook hands. "Our big Indian friend—did he mention where he was staying?"

"Not a chance. And I wasn't about to ask him."

"You've got a good view up there," I said, pointing at the big picture window in front. "When he left, did you happen to notice what direction he went in?"

"Yeah, he had a buddy waiting in a car right outside. They turned around and went back out to Route Twenty-two."

"What did his buddy look like?" I said.

He shrugged. "I think he was an Indian, too, but much smaller. Hard to tell with him behind the wheel. He was wearing a baseball cap. That much I remember. Think it was a Hooters cap."

"At the light up there, did you see which way they turned?"

"They turned right," he said. "Positive of it. Watched that car all the way out."

"Notice anything about the car?" I asked. "Make, model, color?"

"Beige compact. Chevy, I think. One of those generic fiberglass deals. All of those things look the same to me. Nothing like the cars I had when I was a kid."

"I hear you. How about the license plate?"

"Hmm, that's tough." He squinted one eye. "Pretty sure it wasn't New York. That's all I can remember about it."

I slapped a second $20 bill on top of the first one. "Thanks, Kieran. Anything else occurs to you, please give me a call."

"I'm hopin' I was some help to 'ya." He picked up the money and the card.

"You were," I said. "Must be the luck of the Irish."

Back in the Cadillac, I went to the light, turned right and drove north on Route 22 for a couple miles until I saw the Royal Motel. I'd probably passed this place a thousand times over the years and never had a reason to check it out. Even from a quarter mile down the road, it looked like the kind of upstanding, quality establishment that would lodge anybody—including hulking, seven-foot tall Native Americans—no questions asked. My intuition about the place was immediately confirmed. The moment I turned in, the blinds moved in several of the rooms, and pairs of eyes stared out at me.

I got out of the car and opened the office door expecting to find a wide Formica counter, wood paneling and a TV set playing a Mets game. Instead, two feet inside the doorway, I was faced with a wall of one-way glass. At the bottom of the glass was a narrow slot, with a speaker-microphone just above the slot. The speaker crackled, there was a pause, and an Asian woman's voice blared out.

"Who you?" she said. "You cop?"

When the first question they ask is whether you're a cop, you know you're dealing with only the finest, most law-abiding elements of the citizenry.

"No, no cop," I said. "I'm looking for a seven-foot tall Native American man." I stared into the glass, trying to look stern and authoritative, yet friendly and sympathetic. It wasn't easy. "Do you have a very tall American Indian man staying here?"

Every time I spoke into the microphone, there was a pause, then a crackle from the speaker and another pause, and then her voice again. This protracted, awkward method of communication between us made me wish I could simply talk to her face to face, instead of face to mirror.

"Who calling?" she asked.

Clearly we were suffering from a language barrier here, so I switched to the universal language—cash. I pulled a $20 bill out of my pocket, snapped it twice in the mirror, and shoved it in the slot below the mirror, along with a business card.

"Ever see the TV show *Magnum, P.I.*?" I hummed the theme song for a few seconds.

Pause. Crackle. Pause.

"Yes, yes, he on TV, many year ago."

"Right," I said. "Well, that's me—a P.I."

"Okay."

"I'm looking for a *very* tall man with"—I cringed saying it—"red skin, long black hair and a round hat."

"He no here," she said. "He and other one leave this morning."

"Do you have their names?"

"No name. Pay cash."

"What about their car?" I asked. "A beige Chevy compact. Did you get their license plate number?"

"No," she said. "No get license."

I frowned at myself in the mirror. This was the weirdest motel lobby I'd ever been in.

"If they come back," I said, "call me at that number, okay?"

"I call."

I started to leave when the speaker crackled again.

"Hey, you Dakota, right?" she said.

"That's right."

"You good-looking, like Magnum."

"Thanks," I said.

Pause. Crackle. Pause.

"But no mustache. Why no mustache?"

I glanced at my reflection and imagined myself with a mustache. I didn't like it.

"Just not a mustache guy, I guess," I said. "Call if they come back, okay?"

"I call," she said. "Bye."

I shook my head at the bizarre setup—one-way mirror, speaker, slot at bottom—sighed and left.

Back in the car, I was unsure what to do next, so I continued north on 22 until I reached Tower Hill Road. I had just turned onto it, heading towards Javier's house, when my cell phone rang. It was Svetlana.

When I was a kid, my grandmother's favorite movie had been *Meet Me in St. Louis*, and every Christmas we'd seen it together at a theater near our Manhattan apartment. I answered the phone by singing the first lyric from the movie's title song.

"Dakota, darling?" Svetlana said.

"Yes, Champ?"

"Do not quit your day job."

"I've missed your rapier wit, Krüsh," I said. "How is beautiful St. Louis?"

"The chess center is state-of-the-art and my students are all master level or higher."

"So, basically, you're in chess heaven," I said.

"Correct."

"Did you have a chance to look into those photos I sent?"

"Yes," she said. "the person-shaped figure in the photos is a stone marker called an *'inuksuk.'* The plural is *'inuksuit.'* The Inuit—peoples indigenous to northern Canada and parts of Alaska—use *inuksuit* mostly for hunting and navigation. Each one is built by hand with stones locally available."

"Inuit...interesting," I said. "This coincides with another fact."

"Which is?"

As I drove up the twisty dirt road through the lush and shady woods, I told Svetlana about the Indian and the fingerprints.

"Perhaps your Native American is in fact an Inuit," Svetlana said.

"That's possible."

I turned a corner, and high up on a rocky bluff above the road was an old hunting cabin built on wooden scaffolding. The thing looked a hundred years old if it was a day.

"Thanks for looking into the stones for me," I said.

"There is one other point of interest," she said. "Once built, an *inuksuk* is considered sacred, and if a person disassembles or destroys it, it is said to be bad luck and will shorten the person's life."

"I'll have to relay that to Brett," I said. "I don't want the poor guy cursed."

"Call if you need anything else," she said. "I will be at the hotel, probably in the tub, all evening."

"I'll be reading, most likely."

She replied in a taunting tone: "Oh? Back issues of *Forensic Science Quarterly* perhaps?"

"No. Books about golf legend Ben Hogan."

"Why?"

"Another part of the case," I said. "Enjoy the rest of your day, Champ."

"And you, Dakota."

I hung up just as I reached a gravel driveway. Atop a knoll and set back from the road was a slate blue clapboard Cape, and a ramshackle gray barn. In the distance behind the house towered a high, grassy hill with horses grazing. I parked at the foot of a walkway that led to the front door and got out.

It was then that I noticed the front door was ajar. Somewhere behind the house, a car engine was idling. I pulled my gun and crept around the house. A beige Chevy compact was parked near the back stairs.

"Hey," I said, "hold it!"

I ran towards the car, but before I'd gotten ten feet, a huge figure leapt off the back porch stairs, landed on the lawn and got in the car. By his size and his long black braids, I knew it was the giant Indian. The car roared across the grass and around the house. I ran after it. When I got around front, the giant Indian was leaning out of the car passenger door, puncturing my car's front tire with a knife.

"Stop!" I said.

Calmly he pulled the knife blade out of the tire, folded it closed, and took a second to stare at me before slamming the car door shut. This annoyed me. I couldn't pump him and his driver full of lead, simply because they'd flattened one of my tires, but I *could* make things inconvenient for them. Also, if my shot was accurate, I'd have a nice detail to give the State Troopers for an APB.

I fired one round, shooting out the right-hand tail-light, and holstered my gun. Then, as the car fishtailed out of the driveway onto the road, I pulled out my note-book and jotted down a partial license plate number: State of Washington, "B4DS."

At least now I knew without a doubt that the seven-foot Indian wasn't a ghost; he'd just flattened my tire, the big jerk. Fortunately, Cadillac doesn't cut corners on things like spare tires—there was a full-size spare in the trunk—so I wouldn't have to suffer the ignominy of the donut spare. Frustrated, I stood there for a second, breathing heavily, looking around with my hands on my hips, and then I noticed a deep set of tire tracks in the driveway and a trail of flattened grass. I followed it up the driveway and behind the barn, where, directly against the barn wall, I found a long, rectangular patch of dead grass.

I got my tape measure out of the car and measured the patch. It was 32 feet long by 8 feet wide, and there were deep impressions on both ends, where tires would be. A giant RV had been parked here, clearly for a long time. As I walked back toward the house, I found a heavy-duty extension cord and a garden hose hastily slung against the side of the house. Svetlana's nickname for me might be Holmes, but it didn't take Sherlock to see the obvious: someone had recently charged a battery and filled a water tank for a trip.

I had no idea whether the Indian and his buddy had looked behind the barn and found the patch of dead grass, or, if they had, whether they would deduce the existence of an RV from it. However, there was one thing I now knew for certain: whoever the big Indian and his partner were, they were definitely looking for Javier. I called Svetlana back.

"Ah, let me guess," she said. "You solved it."

"Do I detect a soupçon of sarcasm in your voice, Miss Krüsh?"

"Yes."

"There's been a development here at *chez* Javier," I said. "I'm going to need your help."

As I gave her the rundown on what had just happened, I noticed a woman's blouse, still on its hanger, lying in the driveway. On the phone, Svetlana clucked her tongue.

"The bad man punctured your *tire*?" she said. "The poor Dakotamobile!"

"Your feigned sympathy is adorable," I said. "Can you do me a favor?"

"Certainly."

A water faucet was running on the other end of the line.

"Wait, where are you?" I asked.

"Taking a bath," she said.

"You're in the tub?"

"No." The faucet stopped and there was a sharp intake of breath from Svetlana. "*Now* I am in the tub."

I loved and hated when she did this: talked to me on the phone as she tried on clothes or soaked in a tub, and alluded tangentially to her state of undress. To imagine her nude and wet was discomfiting to say the least.

"Well, you might have to get out of the tub to do this," I said. "Here's what I need."

I asked her to find, within a 200 mile radius of Millbrook, all of the RV parks and campgrounds capable of providing power and water hookups to a large RV. Then I needed her to call each one and ask if a Mexican-American family had checked in recently.

"You're looking for Javier Rodriguez," I continued, "so do it in Spanish—with a Mexican accent if you can, okay? Say you're a friend and you haven't been able to reach them by cell phone."

Svetlana huffed. "All of the RV parks within *two hundred miles* of Millbrook, Dakota? I will be calling all night."

"No you won't," I said. "There aren't as many as you think. I'm going to say maybe twenty. Twenty calls. You can do that for me, right?"

"Of course."

"Hey, while you're out there, you should get yourself some spa treatments—on the agency. You know…a massage, salt rub, that hot rock thing…"

"I shall do all of the above," she said. "Okay, I start now. I will call you as soon as I find anything."

"I'll probably be home, so call the landline first," I said. "No matter how late, okay?"

"Yes. Goodbye."

I put my phone away. With Svetlana working that line of inquiry, I was free to focus on Javier's house. I went in the open front door and closed it behind me.

From the very first room—the entry hall—it was clear that Javier and his family had hurriedly packed, and that other people had tossed the place afterwards. I'd seen a lot of tossed places in my time, and this was one of the milder examples. In this case, so far as I could see, no one had ripped up the floorboards or bashed holes in the walls looking for something.

I needed to find any items that might tell me where Javier was headed, and, if possible, why a seven-foot Native American was after him. After the entry hall, I methodically searched the living room, the kitchen, the bathrooms, the bedrooms, and the attic crawl space. Mercifully there was no basement.

I found a few interesting items: an unopened box of .40 Smith & Wesson rounds, a knot of $20 bills under the master bathroom sink, and signs that more cash had been removed from the kitchen freezer. These things told me that Javier had a gun and ready cash, and that he'd been prepared to leave in a hurry. Next, I found a photo of Javier, a woman (presumably his wife) and a baby; there were snow-capped mountains in the background. Beside that photo was a more recent one of him and the family. In the background of this one, there was a lot of colorful foliage, an RV, and a portion of a sign that read, "OW TRAIL," with an arrow pointing left.

The photo with the snow-capped mountains looked like it was taken in the West—the Rockies, Sierra Nevadas, or perhaps Alaska. As for the photo with them and the RV, I was pretty sure it had been taken in the East; there was that colorful foliage and the hints of mountains that could be the Catskills, Adirondacks or Green Mountains. If Javier and his family had to leave in a hurry, chances are they would go to a familiar place first. I sent Svetlana a text message asking her to cross-reference the

RV parks against ones with trails, most importantly one including a trail name that ended in "ow"—low, row, bow, crow, meadow, etc.

Satisfied that I'd learned all I was going to learn here, I closed up the house and went out through the back door off the kitchen. I called Brian at Troop K and told him about the incident with the beige Chevy compact. I also told him about the car's partial Washington state plate, "B4DS," adding that if he were to put out an APB, the car now had a broken right taillight. Finally I asked him to find out if there was an RV registered to Javier Rodriguez or his wife. Then I hung up, walked around the house to the Cadillac, and sighed at my pathetically pancaked front tire.

⎯⎯⎯◆⎯⎯⎯

After I dropped off the punctured tire at J & J's garage in Millbrook, I went back to my place. There was no other detecting I could do until I heard back from Brian or Svetlana, so I read the books on Ben Hogan for a while, then went down to the tennis court and practiced ground strokes with the ball machine.

With the machine set to oscillate, firing balls to my left and right, I had to do a lot of running back and forth along the baseline to alternate my return shots: forehand down the line, backhand crosscourt; forehand crosscourt, backhand down the line. At first while I was skidding across the clay and hitting the ball, thoughts of the case crept in—*a vanished Mexican-American...an Inuit stone marker...an RV...a giant Indian*—but after a few shots, focusing on the ball took all of my concentration.

I was proud of how many of my shots were going where I'd aimed, and how close to the lines I was putting the ball. My grandfather, who'd once reveled in making me run back and forth chasing his infuriating spin shots, would have been proud too. By the time the first bin of a hundred balls ran out, I had worked up a sweat. I hopped the net and shut off the machine. As the high-pitched vacuum sound faded, replaced by rustling leaves and bird-song, I walked over to the sidelines, sat down on the bench and poured myself a cup of iced tea from the Thermos.

For the first time in a long time, I was able to bask in the peace and quiet of this place, this place I so seldom got a chance to enjoy. To my left, the waterfall from the stream splashed softly into the trout pond. Straight ahead, beyond the black rail fence outside the court, Mrs. Gallagher's horses grazed in the adjoining pasture, while Brush Hill, sharply steep and spring green, loomed in the distance behind them. And to my right and behind me, bullfrogs croaked in the bass pond. I sipped some iced tea and closed my eyes. I wanted to stay in this peaceful moment, to hold on to it and never leave it; but now that I didn't have a tennis ball forcing me to focus, my mind drifted to thoughts of the case again.

What was the meaning of that inuksuk *in the equipment shed? Why was a giant Indian looking for a Mexican-American man? Or was he possibly after Javier's wife? Maybe Javier knew him somehow. Or maybe he had something that belonged to the Indian—like money from a robbery. Which would mean that Javier was a fugitive.*

Then my phone chimed with a text message. I had no idea who it could be; Svetlana couldn't be done making her calls already. I checked the phone. The message was from Sherilyn Jones, my redheaded stylist extraordinaire:

> Howdy Dakota darlin'. A little birdie said you were in town. Want me 2 come over 2nite and give you some trim? Oops, I meant *a* trim. Or did I? ;) Text me. ♥ –Sher

I grinned. A message so brazenly flirtatious deserved a good reply. I thought about it for a moment and started to type:

> Sher: Tonight no good. Working a case. But if you're avail. tom. night, I'd ♥ your company for dinner and any kind of trim you want to give me. –Dakota.

Like a return off a fast serve, her RSVP came back with blistering speed:

> What *time* tomorrow nite?

I countered with a sliced drop shot:

> Sher, that depends on when you want to get off. Sorry, I meant "when you get off work." Or did I? –D

She lobbed this back to me:

> When I *want* to get off and when I can are totally different things. How about 7 o'clock, sugar? Now… where? –S

I ended the rally with a backhand overhead smash:

> La Puerta Azul 7 p.m. tom. night for spicy dinner, then over to my place for cooling swim and hot dessert. Bring toothbrush. Underwear optional. –D

Finally, she conceded the point—saucily:

Done. But I say we skip the swim, and get right to dessert. xoxo –Sher

I put down the phone with a grin. *Sherilyn Jones, I like your style.* I breathed a long, contented sigh, then started collecting the balls with the ball basket.

From across the pond I heard a car racing down the driveway beyond the trees. I put down the basket, ran over to the bench and grabbed my gun. A black BMW convertible with its top down zoomed under the weeping willow tree and around the trout pond. It was Brett. I put my gun down and went back over to the ball basket.

The car ground to a halt just outside the tennis court gate. Brett got out, opened the court gate door and started talking to me as he came inside.

"Dakota, I think I've figured it out."

"Figured what out?"

"The partial course map—the one we found in the tin, remember?

"Sure."

I picked up balls with the basket.

"Get this—the course is Shady Oaks, in Texas," he said. "I've played it a couple times. I looked it up, and the yardage, the pars and the hole layouts all match. And get this. Remember the quote on that slip of paper—'I dug it out of the dirt'?"

"Yeah, what about it?"

"Well, I checked, and Ben Hogan *did* say that. And guess what his home course was?"

"Shady Oaks," I said.

Brett frowned.

"Sorry," I said. "I started reading some books on Hogan. Do you have the map and the paper with the handwriting on it?"

"I do. Here."

He pulled them out of his pocket and handed them to me.

"Thanks. I'll check them out more closely later."

"How goes the rest of the case?" Brett asked.

"I'm making progress," I said. "I saw our mysterious Indian friend."

His eyes shot open. "Seriously? Was he as huge as I said?"

"Yup, and sneaky, too."

I recounted tracking him into Dover, asking around about him and finally stumbling upon him and his buddy at Javier's house.

"Why didn't you shoot him?" Brett said.

"Excuse me?"

"If you'd shot him—you know…like wounded him in the leg or something—we could find out where Javier is."

"Brett, you've been watching too many movies," I said. "First of all, if I'd shot him, I could be prosecuted for attempted murder. There was no self-defense. Besides, I don't think he knows where Javier is, which is why…"

In the distance, I heard a second vehicle coming down the driveway. I ran over and got my gun, and when I turned around, an unmarked gray police cruiser parked behind Brett's convertible. Brian got out. As I was putting my gun back, Brian walked through the fence gate and shook hands with Brett.

"Good to see you," he said. "Hey, turns out I was wrong. You've got yourself a *gen-u-ine* case here."

"Yeah?" Brett said. "What'd you find out?"

I grabbed the ball basket and walked along the fence picking up balls.

"Well, Dakota gave me those fingerprints to look into." Brian looked at me. "Wanted to give you the good news in person. You'll never guess who the Indian is and where he's from."

"I have no idea what his name is," I said, "but I think he's an Inuit Native American, from Alaska or Canada."

Brian frowned. "Alaska. And how the hell did you know he was Inuit?"

"The *inuksuk* I found in Brett's maintenance shed."

"The *what*?" Brian said.

"An Inuit stone marker." I dumped the full basket of balls in the machine hopper. "Never mind that. Who is he?"

"We ran the fingerprints through AFIS," Brett said. "Guy's an Alaskan felon with priors—aggravated assault, assault with a deadly weapon, burglary, possession with intent to distribute. Six outstanding warrants, including one for assaulting a police officer. We're talking one seriously bad dude here. Legal name is Tecumseh Bridger, but he goes by his Indian name, Kodiak. As in a Kodiak grizzly bear."

"I'll say this," I said. " 'Kodiak' is a hell of a lot better than 'Tecumseh.' And as far as his warrants go, you can add slashing the tire of a fine luxury automobile to the list. How about the Chevy? Find anything on it?"

"Yep."

He pulled a printout from his pocket and handed it to me. I glanced at it and gave it back to him.

"What is it?" Brett asked.

"Seattle police report," I said.

"The car was reported stolen ten days ago," Brian said. "What bugs me is, why the heck would an Inuit from Alaska drive all the way out to New York to stalk some Mexican immigrant and his family?"

"Good point," Brett said. "It doesn't make sense."

"Actually, it does," I said, "*if* Javier isn't Javier from Mexico at all."

"What are you saying?" Brian asked.

"What if Javier is actually an Inuit who pretended to be Mexican to throw Kodiak off his scent?" I picked up the last of the balls and dumped them in the hopper. "If we look into Javier's background, I think we're going to find he's connected to Kodiak in some way. Brian, were you able to run a search for an RV registered under Rodriguez?"

"We did a search," Brian said, "but there's nothing in the New York DMV registry under the name Rodriguez. If Javier or his wife has an RV, they did it under a false name, or it might be registered in another state."

"RV?" Brett said. "I didn't know Javier had an RV."

"You wouldn't have known," I said. "He kept it hidden behind that old barn on the property. I'm pretty certain it's what he used to get his family out of Dodge." I unplugged the ball machine. "Help me put this in the shed, would you, Brett?"

Brett and I carried the ball machine into the shed, put it down and covered it with a tarp. When we were all outside the shed, I locked it up again.

"Brian," I said, "anything on the other fingerprints?"

"Yes. The ones from the Altoids box belong to a Fort Worth, Texas businessman named Davis Kinney Granger. Went by the nickname 'Deek.'"

"Went by?" I said.

"Died three days ago."

"Weird," Brett said. "Guy forgets his clubs at my course, then dies, and somebody breaks in to my clubhouse to get them. Think any of this is related to Javier?"

"I doubt it," I said.

I picked up my tennis racquet, gun and Thermos of iced tea, and the three of us went out the court gate.

"Brian," I said, "you didn't put out an APB on Kodiak yet, did you?"

"Yeah, him and the car. Soon as I read his sheet."

"How long ago?"

"Maybe an hour."

"I doubt it will do any good," I said. "After I shot that taillight out, they probably dumped the car for a new one. But I think I know how we can bring him to us." I waved my tennis racquet at Brian and Brett. "What are you guys doing tonight? I mean *late* tonight."

"Why?" Brian said. "What'd you have in mind?"

"A road trip."

"Where?" Brett said.

"Not sure yet," I said. "Come up to the house with me and have a beer while I change, then I'll take you out to dinner and explain."

"I'll have to call my wife and tell her," Brian said.

"Me, too, Dakota," Brett said. "We can't all be freewheeling bachelors like you."

I smiled thinking about Sherilyn's text messages from earlier.

"Sadly, no," I said, "you can't."

We went into the village for dinner, to the Millbrook Café, where the Belgian owners knew me. I'd been there a couple times with Svetlana, who had impressed them by talking with them in fluent French about their native country. Brett, Brian and I had rotisserie chicken cooked in their brick oven. I told the guys how Svetlana was tracking down RV parks where Javier might be, and about my plan to go there and lure in Kodiak. By ten o'clock, the three of us were back at my place, sipping coffee on the deck beneath the trees, listening to the crickets. My cell phone rang. It was Svetlana.

"My associate, guys," I said. "Be right back."

I went inside and sat on the leather sofa in the library, beneath a fox hunt painting that had perplexed me since I was a child. My grandparents hadn't cared for horses *or* fox hunts, so where did it come from and why did they keep it?

"Hey, Champ," I said. "What'd you find out?"

"There are two RV parks within two hundred miles of you where a Latino man and his family checked in very recently," she said. "The first is a KOA campground in the Catskills, and the other is called Placid RV Park. It is outside of Lake Placid, near the Canadian border. I will text you the exact addresses when we hang up."

"Good work, Svetlana. How many phone calls did it take?"

"Twenty-nine."

"And how many did you make from the tub?" I asked. "Just curious."

"All of them. It took an hour."

In my mind's eye, I could see her—covered to her pretty neck in bubbles, her long hair piled on her head, her phone held gracefully to her ear. The thought of her in a tub all that time making phone calls was strangely tantalizing.

"An hour? Really?" I said. "Your skin must have gotten pruney."

"I do not prune," she said. "So, of the two campgrounds, which one will you visit?"

"Both. We'll try the Catskills one first, then make the long drive up to Lake Placid. My instincts tell me that's where Javier and his family are. They might be trying to make a break for it to Quebec."

"We?" she said. "Who is joining you on this?"

"Lt. Sutherland—you know, Brian from Troop K?"

"Yes."

"And Brett Vaughn—guy who owns the golf course up the road from me. It's his employee we're looking for."

"I see," she said. "Well, drive carefully, Dakota. Knowing your bloodhound nature, I assume you will head out immediately."

"That's the idea."

"I am going to bed. I have an early class."

"Make sure you have some seaweed treatments, or whatever they are."

"*Zadnitza*," she said. "Good night, Dakota."

III

It was four o'clock in the morning, and Brian, Brett and I were rocketing up the Northway at 90 mph in my Cadillac, somewhere north of Saratoga. The Catskills KOA had been a dead end, so I needed to make up for lost time. A red police light flashed on the car roof, and in the event that we got stopped, Brian had his police badge with him. I nudged him in the passenger seat.

"Why don't you call Troop K? Tell them to get some chatter going on the radio. State-wide."

"Good idea." He took out his cell phone.

Brett spoke up from the back seat. "Dakota, what do you mean by 'chatter'?"

A "MOOSE CROSSING" sign flashed by. Hit one of those and it's Game Over. I slowed the car to 70 mph.

"Well," I said, "if Kodiak is like any other career criminal, he and his partner have a police scanner with them. So, we're going to lure them to us."

"How?"

"By putting out info that we've found Javier."

"Isn't that dangerous?" Brett said. "For him and his family, I mean. What if Kodiak gets there first?"

"I don't think that will happen," I said. "Unless he found some clue at Javier's house that said explicitly where he and his family were headed, it's doubtful Kodiak knows where he is."

Brian hung up. "Okay, it's done. Just some light chatter for now about his general whereabouts. When we get there, I'll call back and have them announce the exact location. We should also get some backup. Have them just in the woods surrounding the campsite. You know, to help with our big Indian buddy." He yawned and shook his empty coffee cup. "I could use a refill, Dakota."

"Yeah, let's pull over for a few minutes," I said.

We picked up fresh coffees, and, cliché or no, a dozen donuts to finish our drive. Then we made the final push to Placid RV Park. The first pink and gray hints of dawn glowed behind the hillsides when we turned off the Northway again. As I turned in at the park entrance, I shut off the headlights. The office was dark.

"My associate said they checked into camp thirty-two," I said. "Let's drive until we get close and walk from there."

"Sounds good," Brian said.

With only the faint amber of the parking lights to see by, we crept down the dirt road, passing a sign that read, "ARROW TRAIL." Camp number 29 was empty, so I pulled in and parked. The three of us got out and walked down the road. Brian and I took out our pistols.

"Guys, I'm pretty sure Javier's got a forty-cal Smith and Wesson," I said. "Be careful. He's bound to be jumpy."

"I've got an idea," Brett said. "He knows my voice and he trusts me. Why don't I do the knocking on the door? Then the three of us can go in."

"That's not a bad idea, actually," Brian said. "Just make sure you're standing well off to the side of the door when you knock. He's liable to shoot right through the door."

"Okay," I said, "here we are."

The RV, with a small SUV in tow, was parked along the treeline at the edge of the campground. As we passed a picnic table and then a fire pit, I looked at the RV tires and got an idea. I grabbed a couple large stones from the ring around the fire pit and wedged them under the tires. Brian and Brett nodded at me in the half-light and did the same. When we had wedged stones in front of and behind all of the tires, we squatted by the side of the door. Brett knocked.

"Javier? Javier, it's me, Brett. You in there, *amigo*?"

There was stirring inside the RV, and then a voice near the door.

"Brett? Is that you?"

"Sure is, *amigo*. Can I come in?"

"What are you doing here?"

"I tracked you down. Listen, can I come in and talk?"

"Who's with you?" Javier asked.

"No one. I'm alone."

Just as I'd predicted, the RV started up and went into gear. The engine revved as it tried to go over the rocks, then the RV went into reverse and tried to move that way. It was stuck.

"Stop, Javier!" Brett shouted. "We know about Kodiak! We're here to help you!"

A moment later, the engine shut off. Lights went on inside and the door opened.

"Come in," Javier said.

When we were all inside, Brett said, "These are friends of mine. This is Lieutenant Brian Sutherland, a detective with the state police."

"Sorry to barge in so early like this," Brian said. "But we were concerned for your safety. Excuse me while I make a call."

Brian stepped outside. Brett motioned to me.

"And this is my friend Dakota Stevens," he said. "He's a private investigator. Lives right down the road from the Links."

"*Hola*," Javier said. "*Mucho gusto*."

"Yeah, that's another thing," I said. "It's time to drop the whole Mexican act. We all know you're an Inuit from Alaska."

"I don't understand," he said.

"Let's sit down and discuss it."

I noticed a .40 Smith and Wesson semiautomatic on the table. As Brian came back in the RV, I nodded at the gun, and he unloaded it. The four of us sat in a booth around a small dining table with the gray dawn light coming in through the front windshield.

"Let's get started," I said. "We don't have much time."

"Time until what?" Javier asked.

"Until Kodiak shows up," Brian said, coming back inside. "We just announced your location over the radio."

The door at the far end of the RV opened, and a woman in a bathrobe holding a toddler peeked out. Javier spoke to her, waved her away, and she closed the door.

"Now," I said, "why don't you start by telling us your real name."

"It's Grant Taylor."

"All right, Grant. You're running from Kodiak. Did you know him in Alaska?"

Grant nodded and took a deep breath. Brian patted him on the arm.

"Don't worry," he said, "there are more state police outside backing us up. You and your family are safe. Why don't you tell us your story?"

"Put this all behind you, Javi—sorry, Grant," Brett said.

"Water?" Grant said. "In the fridge."

I went to the fridge, pulled out a bottle of spring water, opened it and handed it to him. He chugged half the bottle and set it down on the table.

"It was three years ago," Grant said. "I'm at this bar in Fairbanks. Bathroom's out of order, so I go out back to take a piss, and I hear someone making croaking noises around the corner of the building." He gulped. "So I go around the corner and there's Kodiak, strangling some guy. I see him and a couple other guys dumping a body in a pickup bed, so I start to run and Kodiak hears me and comes after me.

"Now the way this bar is, it's in a hollow off the main road, and there's two places to park—in a lot up by the road or behind the bar. Kodiak's truck is behind the bar, but I'm parked up by the road, you see? So I run up this embankment, and the whole time Kodiak's chasing me with this huge hunting knife. I'm scared out of my mind. Finally I get in my car, start it up and floor it. Kodiak's standing under a street light, just as calm as can be, staring at my license plate.

"I'll never forget the look he gave me as I drove by— his eyes were totally dead, the guy looked right through me. I knew that as soon as he found out who I was, he would kill me and my family. So I went home and packed us up, and we left that night. When we got to California, I bought fake green cards with Mexican names. I got a job at a golf course, then another one, and we kept moving east until"—he nodded at Brett—"I met you, Brett, and you gave me the head greenskeeper job. And everything was great until the other day, when I saw that *inuksuk* in the maintenance shed. I knew it was a message for me. So when I saw Kodiak that morning, I just took off."

Brian's cell phone rang. He got up from the table, walked into the galley and answered it.

"What I'm curious about," Brett said, turning to me, "is why Kodiak bothered to build that stone thing and didn't just kill Grant on the spot?"

"My guess is," I said, "he was trying to provoke Grant into running, so he could kill him someplace more isolated. Less chance of being caught."

"But how did he find me there?" Grant asked. "I mean, how did he track me all the way across the continent?"

I shrugged. "Beats me. Indian magic?"

Brian walked over and sat down again.

"Our backup's here," he said. "They're in the woods around the campsite. Got their cars parked all the way in back, out of sight, and one Trooper's hiding out at the main road. When Kodiak comes in, he'll block off the exit with a spike strip."

"I don't understand," Grant said. "What the heck is going on?"

"We're bringing in Kodiak," Brian said. "There are half a dozen warrants for his arrest, and once we take your affidavit, he'll have a murder charge as well."

"Oh," Grant said. "But...my family."

"You're all safe," I said. "We're not going anywhere. But we should probably get ready. He'll be here soon."

The four of us sat on the floor out of sight of the windows, and we waited. The lights were off, the door was unlocked, and Brian and I had our guns ready. Birdsong from the woods outside poured through the screen window on the door.

It was seven o'clock, and the treetops glowed a radioactive green in the golden light. There was an almost imperceptible lull in the birdsong, and a moment later a car crept into the campsite and its engine shut off. Brian and I nodded to each other. We motioned to Brett and Grant to stay down in the booth, while the two of us got up on one knee with our guns steadied at the door.

Outside, two car doors opened, but I didn't hear them shut. A moment later the RV door creaked and

Kodiak, his massive body squeezing through the door frame, entered first wielding a long hunting knife. He was followed by a second, much smaller, Native American man wearing a Seattle Seahawks football jersey and a Hooters baseball cap. The door creaked shut behind them. Just as they turned toward the back of the RV, Brian got to his feet.

"Freeze, Kodiak! Drop the knife!"

The smaller guy put his hands in the air, then jumped for the door and ran out. Kodiak moved toward us. I eased out of the booth, steadying my Sig Sauer dead-center on his chest.

"I'd rethink that if I were you."

"You're a huge target with two guns leveled on you," Brian said. "Toss the knife over there, and lie face-down on the floor with your hands on your head."

Kodiak glared at me, then Brian, before finally tossing the knife aside and lying on the floor. And then, while I held my gun on Kodiak, Brian stepped forward and handcuffed him.

———◆•◆•◆———

A week later—after Kodiak was extradited to Alaska, after Grant gave a sworn affidavit and returned to work, and after Brett's celebrity-veteran charity tournament went off without a hitch—Brett and I caught a flight to Fort Worth, Texas. It was time to solve the second, unrelated mystery from Brett's golf course: the meaning of the tossed storage room, where we'd found the partial Shady Oaks map and the cryptic message, *"It's in the dirt. Max watched for hours."*

We met Svetlana, checked into a hotel, and drove to Shady Oaks Golf Club. Brett had used his clout as a U.S. Open champion to wrangle us a lunch reservation in the dining room, next to Ben Hogan's legendary table, then a walking threesome for 18 holes. Ever the chameleon, Svetlana had dressed in the perfect golf outfit—pink polo shirt, white golf skirt, ankle socks, golf shoes—but she had to get an impromptu lesson from Brett on her grip, stance and swing before we could tee off. To make our round go faster, we all teed-off from the white tees.

The Shady Oaks course is so beautiful, the fairways and greens so lush and luxuriant, that I felt a twinge of guilt about Svetlana and me defiling them with our mediocre play. Meanwhile, Svetlana took so many strokes that, by the seventh hole, she stopped keeping track of her score. But that didn't stop her from garnering attention on the course; men on the adjoining fairways halted their games to watch long-legged Svetlana take ungainly swipes at the ball and to help her find her ball when it ended up in the rough. The men behind us weren't in any hurry to pass, so we were able to take our time. I was glad for this, because the entire reason why we were down here at Shady Oaks had to do with something I'd read about Ben Hogan.

Hogan's favorite spot on the course, the spot where he spent hours hitting balls for pleasure, was a little hilltop east of the 18th fairway. The hilltop was actually on the club's "Little Nine" course—a small nine-hole course built inside the loop of the main course. On the 18th tee, I spotted the hilltop, aimed at an angle, and drove my ball there. It was my best shot of the day.

While Brett helped Svetlana on the other side of the fairway, I hiked east and climbed the hill to find my ball. It was here that I found a rock with a plaque on it that read simply, "MAX—BELOVED FRIEND." This was where the club's unofficial mascot, a border collie-mutt named Max, had attentively watched Hogan hit balls "for hours." According to one of the Hogan biographies, Max was buried beneath the plaque.

Reputedly, this was the place where Hogan "dug in the dirt" to discover the secrets of his swing. In addition to the plaque for Max, there was a young oak planted here. This was a perfect spot to bury something else.

With a nod of satisfaction to myself, I approached my ball with a hybrid club. I was standing where the great Ben Hogan had once stood, and I wanted my next shot to do him justice. I took my time lining up the shot and easing into my stance. I made a couple practice swings, then stepped up and swiped the ball cleanly off the turf, kicking up the slightest sliver of grass as a divot, sending the ball sailing. When it finally landed, it hit the fairway, bounced twice and rolled to the apron of the 18th green. I caught up with Brett and Svetlana at the apron, chipped my ball and two-putted.

"What kept you?" Brett said. "You were up on that hill for quite a while."

"I think I just found it."

"Found what?"

"You'll see tonight," I said.

Brett frowned. "Come on, Dakota—tell me now."

"Be patient, Brett," Svetlana said, replacing her putter in the bag. "Dakota will reveal all, when the time is right."

At one in the morning, the three of us drove from the hotel to a road bordering the east fence of Shady Oaks. Svetlana stayed in the car, behind the wheel, while Brett and I got out and hopped the fence.

"I can't believe I'm doing this," Brett said. "Breaking into Shady Oaks in the middle of the night. Dakota, if we get caught, I could get kicked out of the PGA, for Pete's sake."

"We're not going to get caught," I said. "Come on."

I carried a bundle comprised of two flashlights, an Army collapsible spade shovel, a gallon of water and a turf-cutter, all wrapped up in a tarp. We stole across the 9-hole course in the clear starry night and climbed the hill to Hogan's spot and Max's grave. With no moon tonight, it was very dark. I handed Brett a flashlight and shone the other one on the grass myself.

"Find the flattest spot here on the hill," I said. "If you were Ben Hogan, and you came up here every day to hit balls, where would you hit them from?"

Brett switched on his flashlight and painstakingly moved the beam across the small plateau, away from the young oak tree.

"Right…*there*," he said.

"Okay, I'll mark it. Now shut the lights off."

"I don't understand what you brought the shovel for."

"Hogan always said that the secret of his swing is *in the dirt*, right?" I said.

"Are you saying…?"

"That's what we're about to find out."

With the turf-cutter, I cut four squares of turf, dug underneath the edges and peeled them up. Then I dug into the dirt with the spade and carefully dumped each shovelful of soil onto the tarp. Once I'd gone down about a foot, the shovel hit metal. I dropped the shovel, dug with my hands, and pulled out a small metal cash box. I held it under the flashlight. The lock was mottled with rust, but I used my pocketknife to jigger it. Inside, sealed in a plastic bag, was an envelope. I handed it to Brett.

"Holy crap," he said, "is this what I think it is?"

"Yup. Read it."

"Don't you want to first?" Brett said.

"Nope. This is all for you."

I watched him as he opened the plastic bag and the envelope, and read a one-page letter inside. When he finished the letter, his eyes were misty. He shook his head in a daze.

"Well, I'll be damned. *That's* the secret."

"Okay," I said, "let's put it back."

"What?"

"You're a fisherman, Brett," I said. "It's like catching a big trout. You put it back out of respect for the fish, and to give someone else the thrill of catching it."

After a moment, he nodded, put the letter back in the plastic and gave it to me. I replaced it in the box, reburied the box, refilled the hole and smoothed out the soil. I poured some water on the soil, laid the turf squares back in place and poured the rest of water over the turf. Once I'd tamped down the area with the spade, it was as if we'd never been here. I wrapped everything in the tarp and stood up.

"Ready?"

"Yeah," Brett said. "Thanks, Dakota—for everything."

"Don't mention it. Now let's get out of here before someone catches us."

We jogged down the hill and faded into the starry Texas night.

THE CASE OF
THE FAKE REALITY TV SHOW

Ah, hazy L.A.

Anytime you see Los Angeles in movies or TV shows, it's presented as a sunny wonderland where the sky is so blue it cuts your soul. And maybe the place really is like that most of the time.

But never when I visited.

I'd been to L.A. twice before—on Bureau business—and both times the so-called sun appeared only as a light gray orb through the haze. And when I say "haze," what I really mean is *smog*—a choking, eye-smarting smog denser than cappuccino foam. A smog that, for the entirety of my two stays here, had sprawled across the city as immovably as a drunk man on a waterbed.

When Svetlana and I alighted from the LAX terminal with the studio driver carrying our bags, I glanced at the gray February skies and knew this trip would be no exception. While the driver loaded our luggage in the car trunk, I opened the door for Svetlana.

"Why the sunglasses?" I asked. "It's not that bright out."

"U-V rays," she said. "You should wear some too."

"I brought some, but I doubt I'll wear them."

"Why not?" she said, sliding into the car.

I got in and shut the door.

"Because the ones I have make me look too damn good. I can't have starlets attacking me, Svetlana. It may be Valentine's Day, but we *are* here on business."

She muttered something in Ukrainian or Russian. Up front, the driver got in and we pulled away. After an hour on a confusing array of freeways and surface streets, we finally turned in to the Warner Brothers studios lot.

Our client, Theodore Vance, was the Vice President of Development and a famous movie producer in his own right. Gazing out at the palm-lined entrance and the mammoth studio buildings, I thought about how many of my favorite movies were WB productions: *Casablanca*, *Sunset Boulevard*, *Dirty Harry*, *The Dirty Dozen*, and *L.A. Confidential*. A clique of actors smoked outside a studio door. A man in an L.A. Dodgers cap made a picture frame with his fingers and talked to a skeptical group of suits. And beside me, Svetlana sat with her legs crossed, reading a book on classic Hollywood she had picked up at the airport.

The car stopped at a sprawling single-story building with a red tile roof. Flower gardens, a peeing cherub fountain, and a hedge in the shape of "WB" festooned the front of the building.

"Mr. Vance's office is right in there," our driver said. He reached over the seat and handed us business cards. "Name's Coltrane, like the saxophonist. Anywhere you want to go, day or night, call me. And don't worry—I'm not one of those *aspiring actors* working an angle. I drive. That's what I do. I'm about the best there is in L.A. I get people where they need to go—fast."

"Thank you, Coltrane," Svetlana said.

"*De nada.*"

"*Habla español?*"

"*Si, señorita.* Helps a lot in L.A."

"Tell me, Coltrane," I said, "what kind of guy is Mr. Vance?"

"Well, he can come off kind of rude—you know, brusque-like—but that's just 'cause he's so busy all the time, and he's used to getting what he wants. What he really is, is decisive. Know what I mean?"

"I do." I reached for my wallet.

"Keep your money, Mr. Stevens," he said.

"Dakota," I said. "And this is Svetlana."

"Thanks, Dakota, but Mr. Vance already pays me real good." He unlocked the doors. "You two had better get in there. I'll see you later. Remember—just call."

I slid out of the car and walked inside with Svetlana. Mr. Vance's assistant, Nancy, led us down a hallway lined with movie posters to his office. Upon entering, my first impression was that I'd been in warehouses smaller than this. Nancy put a finger to her lips, and we waited silently by the door.

At the far end of the room, near a mahogany desk, a bronzed silver-haired man leaned over a golf ball with a putter. Behind the desk was a massive picture window, and flanking either side of the window were a round conference table and chairs, and a trickling stone waterfall. Nearer to us by the door was a cluster of sofas and armchairs, where three men sat watching the silver-haired man. They watched with a sycophantic level of interest. Finally, after several practice swings, he tapped the golf ball. It rolled down a long, undulating putting green towards the door and dropped into the hole. The men on the sofas clapped.

"Nice shot, T.V.!" one of them said.

"Mr. Vance?" Nancy said.

"One sec." Vance turned to the men on the sofas. "Okay, fellas…cut to the chase already. What's your second act reversal?"

"Right. So here's the deal…she *thinks* he's normal, but it turns out, he's really a zombie—"

"But a totally healthy one," the man beside him interrupted. "T.V., listen to this—it turns out he's actually got a new strain of the plague. A strain that makes him even *better* looking."

"We're thinking McConaughey or DiCaprio in the part, and—"

"I'm gonna stop you right there," Vance said. He leaned the putter against the wall. "Gentlemen, I've been in pictures for almost fifty years, and that is the goddamn *dumbest* idea I've ever heard. Thanks for coming in. We'll be in touch."

The men looked at each other in shock for a second, then picked up some papers and filed out.

"Nancy," Vance said to the receptionist, "that's the fourth stupid pitch I've heard from those jokers. I don't want to see them on this lot again. They're banned. Make sure security knows."

"Yes, Mr. Vance. And here are Dakota Stevens and Svetlana Krüsh, sir."

Vance gave me a firm handshake and cupped Svetlana's hand gently in both of his. He waved at the sofas.

"Sit. You two must be exhausted from that early flight. Nancy—coffee, please. And hold my calls."

"Yes, sir."

The moment we sat down, Vance started right in.

"So, what do you know?"

"About the case?" I said. "Just that you require our services. Nancy called Svetlana at three o'clock this morning, we boarded your jet at four, and now we're here."

"Mr. Vance," Svetlana said. "All Nancy told us was that the case involves your daughter, and that you would fill us in on the details when we arrived."

"Before we start, sir," I said, "I'm curious how you heard of us. I've never done any private work in Hollywood."

"A friend of mine at the FBI recommended you," he said.

"Who?"

"Your old boss, Director Reeves," he said. "I asked him the name of the best private agency he knew and told him I wanted somebody who wasn't in the business— you know, show business—someone unknown in L.A. He said, 'Dakota Stevens Investigations in Manhattan.'"

"That was nice of him," I said.

"He also said you could be a hotshot at times, but that you and Miss Krüsh did a good job solving a case for a friend of his."

I tapped Svetlana's knee. "Our first case together. Remember? Mr. Brookhiser's daughter at Harvard?"

"Ah, yes…'A Study in Crimson.'" She sighed and flapped a hand. "Our salad days."

"The reason Nancy didn't tell you anything," Vance said, "is because I've purposely left her in the—"

The door opened and Nancy brought in coffee service. She placed the tray on the coffee table.

"Anything else, Mr. Vance?"

"Coverage on that new script, please, Nancy," he said. "The one my dog trainer gave me."

"Already on it, Mr. Vance."

"Thanks."

She left. Mr. Vance poured cups of coffee for Svetlana and me and placed them in front of us.

"Help yourselves to cream and sugar," he said.

He took a sip and sighed. It was the first moment of non-composure I'd seen on the man since we walked in. After a moment, he gathered himself, sat up tall in the armchair and spoke with a pained expression on his face.

"It's my youngest daughter, Hailey, from my second marriage," he said. "She's always been a handful, and she's become something of a wild child. A couple of years ago—when she was underage—she did some nude modeling and I had to pay off the photographer. Then, last year, she was busted in Miami on drunk and disorderly and possession charges. She has a group of C-list friends, and for the past year she's been trying to break into the business. I wanted her to make her own way, so I told her to go on some cattle calls, get some extra work, and *then* I'd help her get a few bit parts with lines so she could get in the union."

"Pardon me, Mr. Vance." Svetlana poured cream into her coffee. "The *union*?"

"Screen Actors Guild." He put down the cup and saucer. "Bottom line is, I wanted her to start at the bottom, like I did, and work her way up."

"Makes sense," I said.

"But these millennials," he said, "they expect instant gratification. Hailey's mad at me because she's been auditioning a lot and hasn't booked anything yet." Vance picked up his cup and saucer again. "Then, about two weeks ago, she bursts in here bubbly and smiling and says how she just got offered the lead on a new reality TV show. I ask her about the show, but she won't tell me anything. So then I say, 'At least tell me who's producing,' and she says, 'Second Story Productions.' I'd never heard of them. She asks me for some money and leaves. Then, last night, I get a call from our studio dick—excuse me, our head of studio security, Barbara Soames. Barb says Hailey's been arrested for armed robbery. I nearly had a stroke. Some jewelry store over in Industrial City."

He sipped his coffee. "Apparently, Hailey was with another woman and two men. One of the men was shot dead by the owner. Hailey wasn't hurt, thank God, but she was the only one arrested, and the other man and the other woman got away. Barb and my attorney are bailing her out now and then Barb's going to hide her someplace to give this time to cool off."

"Mr. Vance, based on my experience—"

"One second," he said. "Something you have to know about Barb. She can be a bitch on wheels, but she's connected up the wazoo in this town. I need the three of you to work together on this. Her priority is to keep the studio insulated from any blowback." He waved a hand at the big picture window. "Hundreds of millions of dollars are on the line out there."

"Sir," I said, "based on my experience, if your daughter was caught participating in a crime in which someone was killed, your number-one priority should be securing the best defense counsel you can for her."

"I've already done that," he said.

"Then," Svetlana said, "exactly what is it that you wish us to do?"

"Okay, here's the second-act reversal," Vance said. "Hailey insists this was a set-up. She says the jewelry store was a location for the reality show, and that they were filming a mock burglary. The problem is, when the police arrived, there was no camera crew on the scene, and no evidence that any cameras had been there. Hailey was arrested with a body cam strapped to her, so the police have it. You'll have to get a copy of the footage, and of course speak to Barb and Hailey."

"Does the jewelry store have security cameras?" Svetlana asked.

"I assume so," Vance said. "Barb will know. Mr. Stevens, Miss Krüsh, I know she's a little wild, but I have to believe that Hailey didn't know she was committing armed robbery. I want you to clear my daughter."

"And if it turns out she's guilty?" I asked.

"Let's burn that bridge when we get to it," he said.

"Before we speak with your head of security—"

"*Barb*," Svetlana interjected.

"Yes, Barb," I said. "Before we speak with her and Hailey, I'd like to talk to some people around the studio. The day Hailey came in and spoke with you, she might have said something to someone else."

Vance nodded.

"Whatever you need," he said. "Nancy will give you all-access passes. Check with the stage managers, the commissary, the props and costume departments, and definitely the writers' offices. I've seen Hailey with a crackerjack young screenwriter I've got over there, Blaze Gerard."

"Mr. Vance," Svetlana said. "About our fee."

"Yes." He reached in his shirt pocket and pulled out a check. I pointed to Svetlana.

"I trust this will cover me for a week," he said.

With a glance at the check, Svetlana smiled faintly and nodded. She put the check in her handbag.

"It most certainly will."

"I need this wrapped up in a week, Mr. Stevens. Or less."

"We'll do our best," I said. "It might take us a couple of days to get the lay of the land, but we always get results."

"You're booked at the Peninsula. Two suites."

"That's great, Mr. Vance, but if the case is going well, we won't be spending much time at the hotel."

"Good to hear." Vance stood. We stood up with him, and he walked us to the door. "Nancy will have an intern drive you around the lot, and Coltrane is at your disposal." He handed each of us a business card. "Call Nancy anytime and she'll put you straight through to me."

We shook hands with him and left.

———— ❖ ————

After visiting Studio 1 together and asking if anyone remembered seeing Hailey Vance (no one did), Svetlana and I walked outside the studio door and frowned at each other.

"This is going to take forever," I said.

"Yes," she said.

"We should split up. You take the even-numbered studios and the costume department," I said. "I'll do the other studios, the props department and the writers' offices. Let's meet at the commissary at one for lunch. Okay?"

"D'accord," she said.

Svetlana climbed into a golf cart (the one with an attractive male intern) and made a deft forward gesture with her hand. The golf cart sped away. I had my intern, an equally attractive Rubenesque young woman, drive me to Studio 3. Walking in, I flashed my pass and made the mistake of asking where I could find the stage manager.

"Shh!" a woman said. "They're about to start shooting. Go *that* way."

I walked past craft services and some rolling costume racks to the edge of a set. It was a living room on Christmas Day. The director called "action," and a middle-aged man raced two little kids down the stairs to the Christmas tree. The man and the kids shoved and tripped each other to be the first to open presents. The scene was surprisingly funny. As soon as the director called "cut," I turned to an elegant older woman and asked her where I could find the stage manager. She glanced at me, started to point, and did a double-take.

"Excuse me," she said, "where have I seen you before? Did you audition for Ridley's new feature?"

"I'm not in movies, ma'am. I'm a private detective."

"You're *kidding*!"

She eyeballed me up and down like she was going to guess my weight at a carnival.

"You have the perfect look for a TV pilot I'm casting," she said. "Would you consider coming in to read for it?"

She dug into her purse and handed me a business card: "ELOISE TRUNCHEON, CASTING DIRECTOR."

"I'll think about it, Eloise," I said. "Now can you tell me where the stage manager is, and his name?"

"Jeff Dougherty," she said. "He's the young man over there with the mustache and fedora."

"Thank you."

"I hope to see you soon, Mr…"

"Stevens. Dakota Stevens."

"Darling," she said as I walked away, "you should be a *star* with that name! Call me!"

Mr. Dougherty was surrounded by technicians as I approached. He was young, maybe in his late twenties, and the brim of his fedora was canted low over one eye, as if he'd just watched a YouTube video on how to look like a noir movie gangster. He was flipping through a script. When the technicians dispersed, I stepped forward.

"Jeff Dougherty? I'm Dakota Stevens, a private detective from New York. I need to ask you some questions about Hailey Vance."

"Who?" His eyes flashed as he looked up from the script. "How did you get in here?" He glanced at a burly man standing by the set curtain and snapped his fingers. "Pete?"

I showed Jeff my pass. "Mr. Vance hired me. I don't think he'd appreciate your throwing me out."

"Vance can't do anything to me. I'm union, idiot."

"Kid," I said, "I'm starting to lose my patience with you. I have half a mind to take your fedora away."

I yanked it down over his eyes. Take *that*, punk.

By now, Pete was on the scene. I noticed a couple of jailhouse tattoos on his neck and forearm. He'd probably been a bouncer, maybe a half-assed bodyguard. It was just a matter of time before he'd try to muscle me; the only question was how.

"Pete," Jeff said, fixing his hat, "please escort this man off the set."

I gave Pete a weary stare. "Look, Pete, I'm sure you were a tough guy inside, but I'm out of your league. Just go back to your corner and practice your reading."

My last comment was meant to provoke a response from him. Intuition told me he'd be an arm-grabber (most of the burly bouncer-types are), so when he tried to grab mine, I pushed his arm to the side and across his chest, exposing his rib cage to me. Shielded from view by Jeff and my own body, I pivoted and drove a stiff punch into his kidney. His entire midsection bowed against my fist. Pete let out a puff of air like a tire being punctured, and he buckled to the ground, where he remained on his hands and knees, catching his breath. People walking by ignored him; maybe because he looked like he'd simply lost a contact lens.

"We were discussing Hailey Vance," I said to Jeff. "I was told she was on your set last week."

This last bit was pure fishing on my part. Most of the time, fishing catches you a whole lot of nothing; but once in a while, like today, you hook into something big.

"All right, fine," he said. "She was here two or three weeks ago, talking with a couple of guys Pete brought by." Jeff helped Pete to his feet. "Pete, you know what they talked about?"

I watched him warily. "Yeah, Pete…how about it?"

"Screw you," he said. "You mighta ruptured my kidney, jerk. Or my spleen."

"Pete, if I'd done either of those things, blood would be gushing out of your mouth right now. Start talking, or I guarantee you, Mr. Vance is going to put your ass in a sling."

"They're some guys I knew inside, got out maybe a month ago," he said. "They said a producer wanted them for a new reality show, and they needed to find a couple women to round out the cast. They were looking for a young, attractive one—an on-something or other."

"An ingénue?" Jeff said.

"Yeah," Pete said. "I seen Vance's daughter around— hot little number—and I heard she was looking for work."

"These friends of yours," I said. "What are their names?"

"Val Veliz and Dan Duran. Damnedest thing, though. I heard this morning that Dan was shot and killed last night."

"'Val' and 'Dan'—are those their full names?"

"What do you mean?" he asked.

"I mean, are they truncated versions of their names or are they nicknames?"

"Okay, I get you…Val's full name is 'Valentino,' and Dan's is 'Daniel.'"

"Valentino—where can I find him?"

Pete shrugged. "Try Googling him."

"Hey, be nice," I said. "You're telling me you don't have his phone number?"

"That's what I'm telling you."

"How about the reality show?" I asked. "They mention the producer?"

"No, all they told me was the title—*The Score*," Pete said. "Now I'm *done* answering questions, jerkoff. Don't let the door hit you in the ass on your way out."

"Oh, Pete." I shook my head. "I hope that's not part of your audition monologue. *Pretty* shopworn, my friend." I slapped Jeff on the back—hard—like I thought he was choking. "Happy Valentine's Day, Jeffy!"

From the soundstage, I went over to the writers' offices. They were housed in a white stucco, single-story building (apparently no one believed in stairs out here). I walked past a fountain adorned with water lilies, up two steps and through a pair of French doors to the receptionist's desk. No one was around, and the desk was covered with leaning towers of screenplays. I picked one up and snickered at the title: *The Elephant in My Pajamas*. I skimmed it and determined that the title—a blatant rip-off of a Groucho Marx line—was the best thing about it. I put it back on the desk.

Down a long hallway, a door opened and a head of shiny gold hair leaned out. The woman wore lilac-colored eyeglasses, and for about a millisecond I found her very attractive—in a harried, overworked sort of way. Attractive, that is, until she frowned at me.

"Well, come on," she said. "We don't have all day."

"Me?" I said.

"Yes, *you*. Blaze is waiting. You're the rewrite guy, aren't you?"

"Sure am."

She gave me a quizzical look. "I thought you were British."

"No," I said, striding down the hall, "I'm Native American, actually."

"Really?"

She leaned back and watched me walk, as if she were witnessing something exotic.

"Really," I said. "Don't be fooled by my skin color."

"Okay," she said as I entered a conference room. "Blaze, everybody, this is—"

"Dexter Price," I said.

"Wait," the blonde woman said, "I thought your name was Harold Smith."

"No, that's my name for full-length scripts," I said. "For my rewrite work, I go by Dexter Price."

Across a conference table, a light-skinned, 20-something African-American man leaned back in his chair. He crossed his feet on the table and opened a script on his lap.

"Dexter, Harold," he said, "whatever your name is—take a seat."

I sat alone on the side of the table nearest the door. Across from me were the blonde, Blaze, two men in suits and another woman—a near-anorexic brunette. The blonde slung a script across the table to me.

"Before we do a line by line," Blaze said, "I'd like to get your general impression of the script as a whole. What works, what doesn't, you know?"

"Blaze," I said. "Could I talk to you in private for a second?"

"Sorry, Dex, no time," he said. "We gotta hustle, brother. Director's breathing down my neck. Now… what are your first thoughts?"

"It's too long," I said.

"Which scene?" the brunette asked.

"All of them."

"Come again?" one of the suits said.

"Here's the deal." I zipped my thumb across the script pages. "With every script I work on, I like to use Fred Astaire's maxim. He used to tell his editor, 'Make it as good as you can, then cut it by ten percent.' So…I think we should cut the entire thing by"—I flipped to the last page (120) and did a quick calculation—"twelve pages. Yeah, twelve oughta do it."

"Who the hell is Fred Astaire?" Blaze said.

"A song and dance man—from the golden age of Hollywood."

"What?" Blaze shook his head like a cartoon character that had just run into a wall. He peered over his shoes at me. "Forget it…let's do the read-through. Any questions before we start, Dex?"

"Just one," I said. "I hear you're Hailey Vance's boyfriend."

He shrugged.

"Here's my question," I said. "When she visited you the other day, what did she tell you about the new reality show she was doing?"

"What the hell is this?" Blaze put his feet down and glared at me. "Who are you?"

"Dakota Stevens." I showed them my all-access pass. "I'm a private detective. Hailey Vance got into some trouble last night, and her father has hired my firm to look into it."

"Get out of here or I'm calling security," he said.

"Seriously? Why does everyone always say that? Like they're a platoon of Navy SEALs." I leaned across the table. "Blaze, do I look like somebody easily intimidated by rent-a-cops?"

"No, I guess not."

"Then can the two of us talk privately for a minute?" I said. "You've got time. Harold's not here yet. Besides, it's Valentine's Day. Have a heart."

He glanced at his phone. "Sure. Take five, everybody."

Blaze led me across the hall to a sunny office. One entire wall was a bulletin board covered with colored note cards. I shut the door and was about to ask what the various colors meant when Blaze made a fist and drew back his arm. The kid didn't telegraph his punches; he emailed them to me ahead of time. As he swung, I slipped the punch and slapped him three times fast across the cheeks.

"Ow!" he said. "I'll sue you for that."

"Self-defense, brother," I said. "We can keep doing this, but my guess is you're a better writer than you are a boxer."

"Fine." He plopped onto the sofa. "What do you want to know?"

"When did you last see Hailey?" I asked.

"Last week, man. She broke it off. Said she was gonna be too busy to see me anymore."

"What did she tell you about her new reality show?"

"Nothing." He rubbed his cheeks.

"Ever heard her mention Valentino Veliz or Daniel Duran?" I asked.

"No. Who are they?"

"Couple of friends of Pete something, an ex-con who does security for Jeff Dougherty over on Studio One."

"Never heard of him. Jeff I have, but not the other guy."

"Sounds like they recruited Hailey for the new show," I said.

"Yeah, whatever," Blaze said. "Girl's a total hot mess. She can self-destruct someplace else. Listen…you're a PI, huh?"

"That's right."

"Were you ever a cop?" he asked.

"I was with the Bureau for eleven years."

"*Bureau*? You mean like the FBI?"

"Yes."

"For realz, dude?" He sat up straight and gaped at me. "Hey, you ever do any writing? No, forget I even asked—it doesn't matter. Look, I've got a proposition for you."

"I'm not—"

"Hear me out," Blaze said. "That script we were gonna talk about in there? My protagonist's a rogue FBI agent, going after a killer against orders. His superiors say he's got the wrong guy, but he knows he's right. Anything like that ever happen to you?"

"Sure," I said. "A major kidnapping case."

He sprang out of his seat and grabbed my shoulders.

"You're the man I need," he said. "A script rewrite ain't gonna cut it. There are *technical* problems with it— procedural crap, you know? I need your help. Please?"

"Even if I wanted to—and I don't want to—I can't," I said. "I'm out here to solve the Hailey Vance case, not to be a technical advisor on a film."

"Dakota." He stared at me with a pair of amber eyes that were, frankly, mesmerizing. "Do this for me. Do it, and I'll throw you a few grand—cash—*and* get you an associate producer credit. All you have to do is read the script and give me notes. You know, stuff like, 'Bureau guys wouldn't say that.' 'That's not correct procedure.' Or, 'That's not the kind of gun he'd use.' Easy as pie. What do you say?"

I thought about what Svetlana would say.

"Okay," I said, "five grand, cash. Send the script to the Peninsula."

I handed him a business card.

"Dakota your real name?" he asked.

"Yup," I said. "Look, Blaze, it's been scintillating, but I have to go."

"*Scintillating?*" he said, grinning and shaking his head. "Brother, we'll make a screenwriter of you yet."

———◆———

When I got back in the golf cart, I had my intern take me to the props department, where the property master confessed that he'd recently given Hailey half a dozen prop pistols; Hailey had said they were for her father. The guns weren't a danger to anyone, however, because they could only fire blanks.

I stopped at two more soundstages but found them empty, and by this time it was one o'clock. The intern dropped me at the commissary. Thinking she was a typical poor college kid I gave her a $20 tip, and it was only after I got inside that I realized she was more likely the rich daughter of a WB executive, and didn't need the twenty bucks.

In the dining room, I saw Svetlana, alone at a big table reading something on her phone. I got a tray of food—coffee, club sandwich, matzo ball soup, Caesar salad and chocolate cake—and sat down across from her.

She glanced at my tray. "Hungry?"

There was only a cup of tea in front of her.

"Starved," I said.

I had some of the matzo ball soup. It was as good as any I'd had in New York.

"Guess what happened to me?" I said.

"You solved the case so we can go home," she said.

"Not quite. A casting director thought I was an actor. She invited me to do a reading for her. I'm not going to of course, but—"

"I was invited to do a screen test," Svetlana said. "It's a Cold War submarine movie, and they need a female crew member who speaks fluent Russian. The director saw me and said I have a quote 'watchable quality' unquote."

"I bet he did." I bit into my club sandwich. "So, besides the fact that you have a 'watchable quality,' what else did you learn?"

She sipped her tea. "That Hailey borrowed six black-ops costumes from the costume department and said they were for one of her father's productions."

"*Black ops*?" I said. "You mean all-black outfits with ski masks, like what burglars would wear?"

"Precisely."

"Interesting."

"What is interesting?" Svetlana asked.

"Well, Hailey also borrowed some fake guns from the property master."

"Ah. Sounds like a clue, yes?"

"Yes," I said. "In other news, Hailey's sort-of boy-friend—a writer named Blaze—hired me to advise on his script about an FBI agent. *And*, I met an ex-con who knows a couple of the cast members on the reality show, including the one that was killed. When we meet Hailey, we'll want to ask her about the rest of the cast, as well as the producers."

"I am wondering," Svetlana said. "What kind of television producers rely on their talent to procure props and costumes?"

I shrugged and took another bite of my sandwich. "Poorly financed ones?"

"Or perhaps ones that have never produced anything before," she said.

"Or...," said a woman's voice behind me.

I turned around. She was a tall blonde of indeterminate middle age, with taut skin on her face, neck and jaw. She wore black high heels, a gray power suit with trousers that fit her commendably in the seat, and a simple white cotton blouse with enough buttons undone to make the view interesting. From the complete lack of attention she gave Svetlana, my brilliant and gorgeous associate might as well have been a condiment caddy.

"Or...," the blonde continued, "they weren't *producers* at all, but criminals. Barb Soames. Head of studio security. Mr. Vance wants us to work together to resolve this situation."

"Nice to meet you, Barb." I stood and shook her hand. "Hailey—we need to see her as soon as possible."

Pulling out a chair, she spun it around, straddled it, and draped her arms over the chair back. She flipped her hair off her shoulders in a gesture of slight annoyance, and eyed me unwaveringly.

"Listen, New York," she said. "We need to set some ground rules first."

"The name's Dakota Stevens," I said, sitting back down. "And this is my associate—"

She glanced at Svetlana and said, "Yes, the *chess* player," and turned back to me. "Have you ever worked cases in L.A. before, New York?"

"Again, it's Dakota, and yes, I have."

"Good." She moistened her thumb and forefinger and plucked a piece of lint off her jacket sleeve. Then you know you have to tone things down out here. Okay, New York?"

"If you call me 'New York' one more time," I said, "I'm going to start using my nickname for you. And since it starts with 'B' and rhymes with 'itch,' I doubt you'll like it."

"Fine, Dakota…Svetlana…here's the bottom line," she said. "I've been here my whole life. I grew up on this lot, and I'm not going to have a couple of *New Yorkers* who don't know how things are done screw up important relationships for me, all right? If you want to question certain people—connected people—you need to go through me. Besides, without me, the people you want to talk to aren't going to give you the time of day."

"Agreed," I said. "Now take us to Hailey, please."

"I'll drive you," she said.

I gave the rest of my lunch a regretful glance. Story of my life as a crime-fighter: so many good meals left behind.

"No, we have a driver," I said. "Just lead the way."

Somehow Coltrane knew we were in the commissary, because we found him parked right outside. By the time Svetlana and I got into the car, Barb was already in her silver Mercedes convertible racing for the lot exit ahead.

"Coltrane," I said.

"Yeah, Dakota?"

"See Barb Soames' car up there? The convertible?"

"Yup."

"Follow that car."

"You got it."

The car surged forward.

"*Barb*," Svetlana muttered to me. "What a delight she is."

"Lives up to her name anyway."

"Dakota," Coltrane said, "when I dropped your bags at the hotel, this package was waiting for you."

He handed me a manila envelope over the seat back. I opened it and pulled out a screenplay and a bundle of cash. Svetlana took the bundle and weighed it in her hand.

"Hmm…fifty-dollar bills?" she said. "This is…seven thousand dollars."

She handed it back to me.

"Nice," I said. "We'd agreed on five. Coltrane—any idea where Barb's leading us?"

"Can't be a hundred percent sure 'cause she's got a few hideout spots, but if I had to guess, I'd say the Victory Motel. That's in Culver City, near the Baldwin Hill oil fields."

"What kind of place is it?"

"Honestly, a dump," Coltrane said. "Abandoned like. Lot of junkies and fugitives."

"What do you know about her?" I asked.

"Barb?" he said.

"Yes, your honest insights. They'll stay between us."

"She's ruthless, man. Watch yourself. Just sayin'."

"Message received," I said. "If she *is* leading us to the Victory, how much time do we have?"

"Half an hour. About."

"Thanks."

I read the script cover page. The title was *Gone Rogue,* and there was a note in the margin: *"Dakota, please give this a look and call us with any notes you might have. Number's below. Here's seven grand for your trouble (my own money). Thanks, brother. Blaze."*

"The script you mentioned?" Svetlana said.

"Yeah." I removed the cash from the envelope and divided it. I put half in my wallet and gave Svetlana the other half. "A little walking-around money, my dear." I winked. "You know, in case our investigation leads to Rodeo Drive."

"I am liking our first case in Hollywood." She smiled, slipped the bills into her magic handbag and went back to reading her Hollywood book.

"Now," I said, "please excuse me while I earn my technical consultant fee."

She patted my hand.

Within the first twenty pages, it was clear that while the screenwriters were good at writing—much of the dialogue, for example, was quite funny—they didn't seem to know much about criminal investigation or the FBI, and I was certain they'd never fired a gun before. I took out my phone and called Blaze. He answered immediately.

"So, you got it?" he said.

"Yeah."

"Good. You're on speaker, Dakota."

"Okay," I said. "Page one…the hero's name is 'Brock Tangier'? *Brock?* Seriously? Doesn't this bother anybody? Come up with a real name, okay? Next, you've got this guy at the range shooting bullseyes at a hundred and fifty yards with a forty-five ACP? I don't know any law enforcement person that can make that shot. Fifty yards, sure, but most encounters with handguns happen within twenty *feet*."

"Good, good, Dakota. We're listening. What else?"

"Well…the hero shouldn't be a SAC—Special Agent in Charge—or even an ASAC. Too much administrative work, too much responsibility. He should be a mid-level agent, maybe eight, ten years' experience. Single guy. Workaholic, but hates paperwork. Gets all the cases no one else wants, so he's almost never in the office. And make it the L.A. field office, not New York, because you clearly don't know New York."

"Okay. This is good, brother. Keep going."

"All right, the title," I said. "*Gone Rogue* is okay, but it's a bit on the nose, don't you think? What about *The Rogue* or just *Rogue* or…*Agent of Death*?"

"Damn, bro," Blaze said, "you're good. *'Agent of Death'*—I like it."

"I think *Rogue* is better. Oh, another thing—the forty-five ACP is *not* FBI issue. Depending on when this is supposed to take place, he should have a forty Smith and Wesson or a nine mil. Now, what about casting? Who are you considering?"

"Well…"

"I think you need a hunk—mid-thirties." I glanced at Svetlana when I said this. "I'm seeing Matthew McConaughey, or that guy who played Batman."

Svetlana rolled her eyes and went back to her Hollywood book.

"Christian Bale?" Blaze said. "Maybe. If we can get him."

"Okay, I have to go, but I'll keep reading and call you later. Goodbye, Blaze."

I hung up and put my phone away. Coltrane glanced at me in the rear-view mirror.

"Almost there, Dakota," he said. "It's the Victory all right."

"Thanks, Coltrane."

We were driving down a dirt road between fields of slowly churning horse head oil jacks. Ahead, a thick dust cloud streamed behind Barb's Mercedes.

"When we get there," I said to Svetlana, "I'd like *you* to ask Hailey most of the questions."

She dropped her book on the seat between us. "Why, may I ask?"

"I want to watch her and Barb," I said, "to see if either of them is lying. I'll jump in when I think it's appropriate."

"As you wish." She put on her Dolce & Gabanna sunglasses and gazed out at the brown landscape.

II

The Victory Motel was actually the Victory Motor Court—a collection of two dozen cottages around an office with a collapsed porte cochère. The asphalt—what was left of it anyway—was cracked all over and weeds sprouted through the cracks. Ahead, Barb steered around the office altogether, and went up a hill, beneath a canopy of eucalyptus trees. She passed several dilapidated cottages and ground to a halt in front of one with curtains in the windows. A man appeared briefly in the doorway behind a torn screen door, then disappeared into the shadows again.

I helped Svetlana out of the car. Barb leaned against her car and put her sunglasses on top of her head.

"It's a dump," she said, "but it's *very* out of the way. She's safe here."

"Makes sense," I said.

We followed her inside, the screen door creaking shut behind us. The one-room cottage was even less to look at on the inside: peeling paisley wallpaper, kitchenette, bathtub in the corner, rough wood floor, bureau, bed, night stand.

A muscular young man with high cheekbones and thick blonde hair sat in a ratty armchair facing the front door. He was reading a book: *Acting in Film*. A young woman—short blonde hair, white tank top, khaki short-shorts—was propped up on the bed listening to an iPod and painting her toenails. Presumably, this was Hailey. The room was heavy with the stench of nail polish. Barb opened two of the windows. There were no screens on them.

"Dakota, Svetlana…meet Hailey Vance," Barb said. "And my assistant, Knut Ibsen."

Knut rose out of the chair and kept rising until he stood in front of me—6'6" tall, 240 pounds to my six feet, 200. He looked like a Scandinavian Arnold Schwarzenegger. When I shook his hand, his grip was surprisingly light. It was the grip of someone aware of his own strength; a gentle giant.

"I am much pleased to be meeting," he said. "You are detectives?"

"We are," Svetlana said.

"Hailey," Barb said.

Hailey was leaning forward, meticulously painting one of her pinky toes one-handed. Her other hand was out of view between the wall and the mattress.

Barb snapped her fingers several times. "Hailey!"

"What? Can't you see I'm busy here?" Hailey's eyes flicked to me and Svetlana and gave us the once-over. "Barb, I thought you were bringing *detectives*, not a couple of Ralph Lauren models."

Svetlana and I looked at each other. I gave her the nod. Barb was about to say something when Svetlana, smiling faintly, walked over to the bed. She snatched the nail polish and brush from Hailey and tossed them out the window.

"Hey!"

"Silence," Svetlana said. "This is Dakota Stevens and my name is Svetlana Krüsh. We have been hired to prove your innocence in the criminal events of last night. You will answer our questions quickly and truthfully. You will hold nothing back. Is this understood?"

Hailey's eyes were wide. She nodded. "Yes."

"Good. Now sit up like a lady and look at us."

"I *can't*." She jerked her arm—the one between the wall and the mattress. The bed frame clanged. "Because *he*"—she jutted her chin at Knut—"locked me to this thing."

"Knut," Barb said, "what the hell'd you do that for?"

His face flushed. He pointed at Hailey.

"She tries to go out window!" he said.

Barb sighed. "Unlock her, please."

Knut reached across the bed and removed handcuffs from her wrist.

"You know, Hailey," Barb said, "I'm getting really tired of bailing out your ass."

Hailey glanced at the door. "You know what, *Barb*? Anytime you want to leave..."

A cell phone chimed. The sound was muffled. Hailey reached under the pillow behind her and glanced at a cell phone screen.

"Knut," Barb said, "you let her keep her *phone*?!"

Barb crossed to the bed and ripped the phone out of her hand. Hailey screeched.

"Barb! It's just a text! Come on!"

"Hailey, I don't care if it's a Brad Pitt sex video." Barb paused with the phone in her hand; she raised an eyebrow. "Wait…is it?"

"No," Hailey said

Barb snapped open the phone backing, removed the battery and dropped the phone and battery in her purse.

"Phones can be traced," she said.

"But *they* have phones," Hailey said.

"Enough," Svetlana said. "Hailey, tell us how you met the show producers. Leave nothing out. Every detail could be important."

"All right, all right, I get it. Pay attention, 'cause I'm only doing this once."

A hot breeze wafted through the cottage. It smelled of eucalyptus and crude oil. Knut stood in the corner, so I took the chair while Svetlana sat on the bed facing Hailey. Barb leaned against the wall near the front window and peeked out the curtains occasionally.

"Like two weeks ago, these two guys, Val and Dan, approached me on the lot at WB," she said. "They said they'd been approached by a couple of producers developing a new reality series. The producers' names were 'Bruce' and 'Davis,' and they wanted to meet me that night to discuss the series."

"Meet you *where*?" Svetlana asked.

"Double Indemnity," Hailey said.

I gave Barb a quizzical look.

"Noir-themed nightclub on Sunset," Barb said.

"Right," Hailey said.

"Okay…'Bruce' and 'Davis,'" Svetlana said. "Were those their first or last names?"

"Why does everybody keep asking me that?" Hailey said. "The cops and the lawyer asked me like fifty times. I don't know."

"We will come back to that," Svetlana said. "Please continue."

"So I'm at Double Indemnity, and Bruce and Davis come up to me and say, 'You're Theodore Vance's daughter, Hailey, right?' I tell them yeah, I am, and they talk about how they're developing this new reality series called *The Score*, and they want me to be a part of it. They tell me it's gonna be a crime reality show, where each week the crew plans a different job, then goes in and steals stuff. But the crimes would all be *staged*. Everything would be set up ahead of time for the owner to get"—she made air quotes—"*robbed*, and afterwards the crew goes back to the hideout."

"Barb," I said, "have you ever heard of Bruce or Davis?"

"No," she said. "I already scoured the trades. I haven't found a single mention of them, *The Score*, or their production company, Second Story Productions."

"Thanks," I said. "Sorry, Svetlana. Go on."

"Hailey," Svetlana said, "what exactly were you going to be doing on this show?"

"Well, I was the star *and* a producer. Bruce and Davis said they had limited resources, and they needed me to borrow some equipment from Warner Brothers so we could make and sell the pilot."

"*Borrow* equipment?" I said. "You mean like the costumes and prop guns?"

"Yeah, sure. And some cameras and lights and a van and—"

"You stole a *van*?!" Barb said.

"I didn't *steal* it, Barb," Hailey said. "I *borrowed* it."

"It's only *borrowing* if the studio gets it back," Barb said. Svetlana held up a hand to silence everyone.

"Hailey," she said, "what do you know about your fellow cast members?"

"Val, Dan and Regina? Not much. I know they were ex-cons, but Bruce and Davis said they were using them instead of actors for realism or something."

"Knut," Barb said, "tell them what the cops said."

He grinned and looked around; clearly Knut was surprised to get a line here.

"The two men serve three years for burglary," he said, "and woman is computer hacker."

"That's right," Hailey said. "She would take care of the alarms and stuff beforehand."

"Now," Svetlana said, "tell us exactly what transpired during last night's burglary."

"Right, Svetlana," I said. "And Hailey, we need to know more about Daniel getting shot, and especially what happened to all the jewelry."

"Alright," she said, "here's how it went down. Bruce and Davis came to the share house around nine o'clock, and we went over the plan one last time. Then they drove to the store in the van and stayed there, just like they had when I went in and cased the joint. From the beginning, they told us they'd be doing the establishing shots from the van, and that they had hidden cameras set up in each of the crime scenes."

"Everyone also wore body cams," Barb said. "But... when the cops arrested Hailey and tried to look at hers, there was no memory card in the camera."

"So...no footage," I said.

"Yeah," Hailey said. "Davis handed them to us right before the job. He told us they were already running and that we shouldn't touch them."

"Wait a second, "I said, "did you ever see *any* footage? As I understand it, actors usually get to see that day's filming."

"They're called *dailies*," Barb said.

"Right, dailies," I said.

"Yeah, I saw footage from the scene when I cased the jewelry store," Hailey said. "I was wearing a hidden camera, and afterwards we watched it and studied the store layout."

"Very good," Svetlana said. "Now tell us about the burglary itself."

"There's not much to say. Everything happened so fast. Regina bypassed the alarm, the guys broke in, and we smashed all the cases and put the jewelry in sacks. Meanwhile, Val cracked a safe in the office, and when he came out, he took all the sacks and put them in one big sack."

She pulled her knees to her chest and stared across the room.

"What next, Hailey?" Barb said.

"So…we're just about to leave, and the lights come on…and this fat guy puts a gun on us." She closed her eyes and shivered. "Dan pulled his prop gun…and the fat guy—he was the owner, I guess—he shot him."

"Hailey," Svetlana said, "listen closely. This is very important."

"Yeah, okay."

"Did the owner show any signs that he knew the robbery was being filmed?"

"No way," Hailey said. "That fat man looked scared to death. The second Dan got shot, Val and Regina took off. By the time I got outside, everybody was gone. The cops showed up literally thirty seconds later, and I was the only one arrested."

Hailey's face crinkled up and she started to cry.

"How stupid can you get, right?" She pounded the bed. "All because I wanted to be famous, and now I'm screwed…and I'm going to jail!"

"Easy, take a breath, Hailey," I said. "It's pretty clear this was a setup, and I think the cops will figure that out. Besides, you're not enough of a criminal mastermind to pull this off."

"I'm smarter than you think," she said, sniffling.

"Maybe," I said, "but you didn't realize you were being conned, did you? New question: how did Bruce and Davis know to approach you with this show opportunity?"

She shrugged. "Everybody knows I'm Theodore Vance's daughter, so maybe that was it."

"We need pictures of these people," I said. "Do you have any?"

"What people?" Hailey said.

"Well, Dan, Val and Regina for starters. And Bruce and Davis, too."

"I've got photos of everybody on my phone."

I looked at Barb. "Could you…?"

"Sure," she said, "I'll get the photos off her phone and send them to you and Svetlana."

"Great," I said. "Okay, Hailey, that's enough for now."

"What next?" Barb asked.

I stood and glanced out the back window. Nothing out there but a eucalyptus tree and a rusted car on cinder blocks.

"I want to talk to the jewelry store owner," I said.

Barb pulled out her phone, typed something and put it back in her suit pocket. My and Svetlana's phone's chimed.

"The address of the jewelry store," Barb said. "Owner's name's 'Goldman' by the way, if you can believe it. After him, where do you want to go?"

"This Double Indemnity club," I said. "We need to get a line on Bruce and Davis, as well as Valentino. I have a feeling he was in on the setup with them."

Barb scoffed. "Good luck getting in there tonight. It *is* Valentine's Day. But I know the doormen there, so—"

"Barb, I never have to worry about getting into places." I smiled at Svetlana. "I've got my secret weapon."

"I am able to jump tall rope lines in a single bound," Svetlana said.

"Barb," Hailey said, "can I get out of here, please? Let me hide at your place in Malibu? *Please*? I'll stay put and won't use a phone, I promise."

"If your arrest hasn't made it to TMZ tonight," Barb said, "then we can go. But I'll need to sneak you in my trunk."

"Fine by me," Hailey said. "The trunk of a Mercedes is better than this place."

———◆———

Back in the car, I asked Coltrane to take us to the jewelry store, and while Svetlana did some research on her phone, I continued reading Blaze's script. I got through another 20 pages and left him a voicemail with my notes.

When we reached the jewelry store, "Goldman's Fine Jewelry," I thought at first we had the wrong place. We were standing in front of a storefront flanked by a pet groomer and a consignment shop. The front door of the jewelry store was open, and a short fat man in a suit stood next to another man. Brilliant detective that I am, I deduced that the fat man was Mr. Goldman, the store owner, and that the other man, wearing coveralls and installing new locks on the doors, was a locksmith. Through the open doorway I noticed police tape inside. The locksmith glanced at Svetlana. His screwdriver slipped and poked the fat man in the arm.

"Ow! Jesus! Watch what the hell you're doing!"

"Sorry, Mr. Goldman." He gestured with his eyes at Svetlana.

"Hello?" Mr. Goldman said. "Who have we here?"

"Dakota Stevens, private investigator," I said. "This is my associate Svetlana Krüsh. We've been hired to look into the robbery. Could we ask you a few questions?"

"What the hell you think I been doin' all night?" he said. "Answering questions. And since I shot one of the robbers, the DA's talkin' about indicting me for manslaughter. I'm not in the mood. Go away."

I was about to reply when Svetlana stepped forward, removed her sunglasses and placed a hand on his arm.

"Mr. Goldman," she said, "I know that this experience has been very upsetting, so we promise to be brief."

"More than upsetting," he said. "It's a damn catastrophe. They took me for six or seven mil. You're not with the insurance company, are you? Because I had nothing to do with this."

"Sir," Svetlana said, "we are working on behalf of Hailey Vance, the young woman who was arrested last night. We believe she was a mere pawn in this whole affair. If we can recover your merchandise and catch the people behind the robbery, would that resolve your 'catastrophe'?"

"You bet it would," he said. "Hell, if you can do that, I'll give you a reward—a necklace to put around that beautiful neck of yours. Consider it a Valentine's gift, gorgeous."

I frowned. "That's a reward for her. What do I get?"

"You, buddy?" he said with a smirk. "You get virtue."

"Virtue's good," I said. "Not as good as a necklace."

"Yeah," he said, "but you don't got *her* neck, understand?"

"He understands," Svetlana said. "So tell us what happened last night. Not what you *think* happened, but what you actually saw and heard."

"Sure," he said. "I closed up at nine last night, then got home and realized I forgot some paperwork I needed—customs forms, they're a big pain in my ass—so I had to drive all the way back."

"Then what happened?" Svetlana asked.

"I park in the lot behind the building," Goldman said, "and go in the back door. The second I get the door open, I hear cases being smashed, but the alarm isn't going off. That's when I realize the alarm's disabled. So I call 911, and they tell me it'll be at least fifteen minutes."

"That's a long time," I said.

Goldman frowned. "Apparently there was an explosion under one of the freeway overpasses a couple of miles away. All the cops were tied up with that."

"Hmm," I said, "a possible decoy."

"What?" Goldman said.

"Never mind him," Svetlana said. "Continue, Mr. Goldman."

"Anyway," he said, "I say to myself, 'Fifteen minutes? I can't wait that long.' All I'm thinking is, 'These sons of bitches are going to clean me out!' That's when I got my piece out of the car and snuck inside. The cases were still being smashed, and flashlights were waving all over the place. So I sneak in, flick on the lights and put the gun on them. I yell for them to drop the stuff and get on the ground."

"Were they surprised by you?" Svetlana asked.

"Are you kidding? They were scared shitless," he said. "They all had ski masks on, but I heard two women's voices scream. Two of them—they were bigger, I'm sure they were both guys—those two were standing by the entrance, and one of them pulls a gun. So I shoot at him. Turns out I missed and hit the other guy. They all take off out the front. Except the guy I shot of course. Paramedics said he was dead instantly. And because he didn't have a gun on him, the cops and the DA don't believe me about the gun at all. They're saying I used excessive force and are going to try and pin the manslaughter charge on me."

"Wait a second, Mr. Goldman," I said. "What about the security footage? That should exonerate you."

He shook his head somberly. "Nope. In the footage, the guy with the gun was out of the frame. All you can see is me shooting an unarmed guy."

"The security footage," Svetlana said. "May we see it?"

"Sure, but I'll have to email it to you," he said. "Cops don't want anyone going in the store until tomorrow."

"Fine," she said, handing him a business card. "But the sooner the better."

"I'll email you what I got the second this guy finishes." He nodded at the locksmith.

"Almost done, Mr. Goldman," he said.

"Goldman," I said. "With that name, I guess you were fated to be a jeweler."

"Boy, that's a new one," Goldman said. He rolled his eyes and gently shook Svetlana's hand. "Solve this for me, goddess detective, and that necklace I promised is yours."

"We will," she said. "Email me the security footage. *Tout suite, s'il vous plait.*"

"Huh?"

"Right away, please."

<hr />

I wanted to go to Double Indemnity next, but it was late afternoon and, like any fashionable club, nobody arrived until midnight. To pass the time, we checked into the Peninsula and took a nap in our separate rooms.

When I woke up, I called Svetlana. She was about to get a facial and a massage, so we arranged to meet afterwards at the pool. I went to the fitness center and worked out while channel surfing on the TV for news about the robbery. Then I went upstairs to the pool, sweated in the sauna for half an hour, and swam twenty-five laps. When I finished, something happened that made the grueling workout worthwhile. Climbing out of the water, I caught the lifeguard, a flaxen-haired college girl, checking me out from her chair. I winked at her. She turned away smiling and spun her whistle around her finger.

I toweled off, saved a chaise for Svetlana and lay down in one beside it. I read another 20 pages of the script, called Blaze and gave him more notes. Then I wondered what time it was. I wasn't wearing a watch, but my stomach was a very reliable timekeeper and it said it was dinnertime. I looked around inquisitively. Two seconds later a pool attendant in an all-white uniform stood beside my chaise with her hands behind her back. Her nametag read, "JYLLE." With that spelling, she had to be an aspiring actress.

"How can I help you, sir?" she asked.

"Can I have food out here, Jylle?" I asked. "Is that allowed?"

"Of course. Shall I bring you a menu?"

"Thanks," I said. "And a bottle of Pellegrino and two glasses."

"Very good, sir."

Jylle returned in moments with my drink, then she waited while I ordered: shrimp cocktail for two, grilled mahi-mahi for myself, and filet mignon for Svetlana.

Just then, Svetlana walked in. A table of tanned, shirtless old men looked up at her from their card game. She walked along the pool deck toward me. She wore a sheer white kaftan, open-toed wedges and a white one-piece bathing suit that showed her preternaturally smooth legs clear up to her hips. Had I been eating something, I would have choked.

"The filet mignon," Jylle said. "Do you know how the lady likes it cooked?"

Without a hitch in her step, Svetlana eased onto the chaise, crossed her legs and spoke to Jylle.

"*Rare*," Svetlana said.

"Very good."

"Wait," Svetlana said. "Tell the chef to coax the cow through a warm room. *That* is what I mean by rare."

Jylle smiled. "Certainly."

When she left, I turned on my chaise to face Svetlana.

"Nice suit," I said. "Good thing you weren't wearing that little number this afternoon. Poor Mr. Goldman would be dead right now. How were your beauty treatments?"

"Adequate," she said.

"Oh, boo-hoo," I said. "Did our flight on a *private jet* this morning put a kink in your shoulders?"

She grinned. "I *do* have quite delicate shoulders, Dakota."

"Uh-huh. Well, we can rest a while longer, and then we'll hit Double Indemnity."

"Yes, I looked into that club," she said. "Apparently it is quite exclusive, with a very strict dress code. They only admit people in nineteen-forties attire."

"No problem."

I picked up my phone and called Nancy, who immediately put me through to Mr. Vance.

"Yes, Dakota?" he said.

"Svetlana and I need clothes to get into Double Indemnity tonight. It has to do with Hailey's case. Can you help us?"

"Sure, I'll have costumes for both of you sent to the hotel," Vance said. "What are your sizes?"

"Svetlana will text them to Nancy, okay?"

"Fine."

"And one other thing," I said. "Please make sure Svetlana's costume has a plunging neckline."

"Will do," he said. "How is the case going?"

"Making progress, sir."

"Good man. Tell Svetlana I appreciate all that she is doing as well."

"I will. Talk to you tomorrow." I hung up and tapped Svetlana with my foot. "Mr. Vance appreciates the work you're doing."

She picked up her mineral water and narrowed her eyes at me.

"A plunging neckline?" she said. "I assume that is for your benefit."

"Absolutely not," I said. "Verisimilitude, my dear. Verisimilitude. That, and to guarantee we get in tonight. Text Nancy our sizes, would you?"

She typed on her phone. "There. Oh, and it seems Mr. Goldman sent us the security footage."

"Let's take a look."

I got up and leaned over the back of Svetlana's chaise while she played the silent video. In it, four figures in all-black ran into the store. Wearing headlamps, they walked around smashing display cases and stuffing jewelry into sacks. Then the lights suddenly came on, and a moment later there was only one figure in the frame. He threw up his hands, and Goldman walked into the frame brandishing a revolver. It was unclear whether Goldman was aiming at the figure in the frame or someone outside the frame near the store entrance. Goldman gestured sharply with his gun several times, then fired. The figure in the frame collapsed to the ground. Then the video ended.

When Svetlana lowered her phone, I caught myself inadvertently gazing over her shoulder at her cleavage. This wouldn't do. I averted my eyes and stood up. Svetlana waggled her phone.

"Shall I play it again?" she asked.

"No, that's okay," I said. "The robbery went exactly like Goldman said. From the video it's pretty clear to me that he *was* aiming at somebody out of the frame when he fired. But there's no way to tell if that person had pulled a gun. Goldman's in a tough spot."

As I lay back down on my chaise, Jylle wheeled in a cart with our food. She placed a tray on Svetlana's lap, then one on mine.

"*Bon appétit*," she said.

"*Merci beaucoup*," Svetlana said.

Jylle walked away. I ate my shrimp cocktail while Svetlana glided her knife through her filet mignon.

"Rare enough for you?" I asked.

"Like they stood the cow in a lovely sun patch," she said.

"And I thought my grandfather liked *his* beef rare. He would have liked you, Svetlana. No—scratch that— he would have *loved* you. '*Hellooo*, gorgeous creature'— that's how he would have greeted you."

I swiped a shrimp through some cocktail sauce and ate it.

"This is your mother's father, correct?" she asked.

"Yes."

"He sounds like quite a charmer."

"He was," I said. "And he had the most amazing blue eyes. Better than Paul Newman's. They actually twinkled."

We ate in silence for a moment. Svetlana speared a piece of beef and admired it.

"Something about that footage seems off to me," she said.

"What's that?"

"I'm not sure," she said. "Right now I am bonding with this filet mignon."

"*Bonding*," I said.

I shook my head at her admiringly and cut into my mahi-mahi.

⸻

At midnight, Coltrane picked us up and drove us to Double Indemnity. The club was on Sunset Boulevard, in a converted Art Deco movie theater. The old-fashioned movie marquee glared over the entrance: "NOW PLAYING—DOUBLE INDEMNITY."

A line stretched down the block, but the moment I helped Svetlana out of the car—Svetlana in a regal purple velvet evening gown—she strutted directly toward the entrance without a word. A clipboard-wielding man, wearing a zoot suit and two-toned shoes, unhooked the rope line for her. A woman at the front of the line grabbed his arm.

"Hey!" she said. "My friend and me've been waiting two hours!"

"Sorry, baby," he said. "You and your friend don't look like *her*."

A doorman opened the club door and waved Svetlana inside.

"I'm with her," I said, palming him a twenty.

"Lucky man," he said.

"Yes, I am."

The lobby was dimly lit, but what I could see of it reminded me of Radio City Music Hall. Two sweeping staircases on either side of the lobby went up to a landing and a mezzanine level. Red carpet covered the floor. Instead of a concessions stand, there was a giant bar island in the center of the lobby, where men and women in gangster outfits and evening gowns drank and chatted.

"We should have drinks in our hands while we're asking questions," I said.

"I defer to you," she said.

She took my arm and we headed to the bar. Men, spotting Svetlana, cleared a path. I got the bartender's attention by tossing a $50 bill on the counter.

"Two club sodas with lemon."

The bartender tweaked his bow tie, glanced at the other customers and spoke loudly enough that people across the bar halted their conversations to listen.

" 'Hey look, mister,' " he said in a griping tone, leaning toward me. " 'We serve hard drinks in here for men who want to get drunk *fast*, and we don't need any characters around to give the joint *atmosphere*. Is that clear, or do I have to slip you my left for a convincer?'" He made a fist and held it up.

"Pretty good." I smiled. "But that's Nick from *It's a Wonderful Life*, not film noir. Two club sodas, Nick. Thanks."

He dragged the money off the bar. A moment later, he returned with our drinks and started to hand me our change.

"Wait," Svetlana said, "you may keep the change. We are looking for two men." She pulled out her phone and showed him pictures. "They go by the names Bruce and Davis. They are probably claiming to be movie producers with Second Story Productions. Do you know them?"

"Not personally," Nick said. "But *they* do."

He pointed at a pair of buxom platinum blondes made up to look like classic movie star Jayne Mansfield. They were sitting at a tall bar table with a couple of men old enough to be their grandfathers.

"The girls are Terri and Sherry," Nick said. "They're working girls, obviously."

"Obviously," I said. "Either that, or the men with them own Canada."

"I got no idea who the old guys are," Nick continued, "but *those* two guys, Bruce and Davis"—he pointed at Svetlana's phone—"I saw them leave with those girls a week or so ago."

Svetlana showed him more pictures. "How about these two? Their names are Valentino Veliz and Daniel Duran."

"They're ex-cons," I said.

"Sure, I know who you're talking about," he said. "Couple of tough guys, just out of the joint. Here two weeks ago maybe. Manager hired them to help with security—you know, bouncers—but they never showed. Must've gotten a new job or something."

"Yeah, or something," I said. "Thanks."

He walked away. I looked at Svetlana.

"Happy Valentine's, Champ. And that dress…purple velvet…*wow*." I leaned over and spoke in her ear. "You need to keep it, Svetlana. Let's tell Vance it was stolen."

"Ordinarily I would not," she said, "but—"

"—this is no ordinary dress," I said.

"Exactly."

We clinked glasses and sipped our drinks.

"You are looking rather dapper tonight yourself," Svetlana said. "A fedora and trench coat suit you."

"The coat's a little warm inside, but thanks," I said. "You know…this is probably conceited to say, but…I think we're the best looking couple in this joint."

"Tut, tut, Dakota," she said. "I *know* we are the best looking couple in this joint."

We shared a smile.

"I'm very grateful for you, Svetlana Krüsh," I said.

She looked away, then turned back to me with hooded eyes.

"And I am grateful to you, Dakota—for showing me I could be good at something besides chess."

"To us and our agency," I said.

We clinked glasses and drank. I gestured at the girls' table.

"Think I'll go talk with the Jaynes Mansfield," I said. "See what I did there…'Jaynes Mansfield'? It's like 'attorneys general.'"

"Remarkable," she said. "Shall I come with?"

"No way, not looking like *that*," I said. "You'll make them jealous, and they won't tell me a thing. Why don't you mosey into the main lounge and make a few discreet inquires? I'll join you in a second."

"Okay, *boss*," Svetlana said. "And if anyone refuses to talk, you want I should"—she made a fist—"feed them a knuckle sandwich?"

I laughed. "No, keep 'em on ice, doll, and we'll work 'em over together."

She sashayed across the lobby. A doorman opened the theater door and she went inside.

Club soda in hand, I walked over to the table with the two Jaynes and the noir movie fossils. Now that I saw the men up close, they looked like aging Mafiosos. But I knew they weren't real Mob guys because they spoke loudly and crudely, and every old school Mafioso I'd ever met had been paradoxically quiet and classy, still and dangerous. The women stirred their drinks and smiled uncomfortably as the guy on the right told a joke.

"So a priest, a rabbi, and a knockout blonde are on a plane," he said. "It's about to crash, and there's only one parachute. So the priest goes—"

"Excuse me, gentlemen," I said, "I need to speak with the ladies. Happy Valentine's Day, ladies."

The women smiled at me.

"Not now, kid," the man on the right said. "I'm telling a joke here."

"Yeah," said the other man. "Beat it."

"*Beat it?*"

I glanced over my shoulder, like they must have been talking to someone else.

"Guys," I said, "I'm not going to steal these ladies away from you. I just need to—"

"Hey, kid! We're not going to ask you again!"

These two were putting me in a tough spot. I'd been raised to respect my elders, but I'd also been raised not to take crap from anybody. However, if I so much as slapped one of them (I couldn't punch an old man), I'd look like the bad guy and probably get thrown out. My only option here was to embarrass them, to make them *want* to leave. A group of twenty-something guys and girls were standing near me. I tapped one of the guys on the arm and motioned at the old men.

"Check it out, dude," I said. "Father Time and Rip Van Winkle."

The guy chuckled.

"They're complaining about the cost of the drinks here," I said. "Remember, back in their day, drinks cost a *nickel.*"

The group laughed.

"Sir," I continued louder, looking at the one on the left, "the rest home called. They found your teeth."

More people laughed.

I turned to the one on the right and said, "And you, sir...it's time for your enema."

All of the nearby tables were laughing now. Even the blondes sniggered and covered their mouths. I was on a roll.

"Hey, you guys look like vets," I said. "Tell me, who'd you fight for...North or South?"

This entire side of the bar laughed. The men turned red, slid off their barstools and stormed away.

"Prick!" one of them shouted.

I waved goodbye and turned back to the Jaynes Mansfield.

"Great," said the one on the right. "There go our dates."

"Relax, ladies, there'll others." I pointed at a pair of men eyeing them from the bar. "Tell you what. I'll give you each a fifty if you answer my questions. But first… who's Terri and who's Sherry?"

"I'm Terri," said the one on the left. "Questions? What are you, vice?"

"No, but I'm a detective."

"You look like a cop," Sherry said.

"Yeah," Terri said.

Terri sipped her drink, got a maraschino cherry between her incisors and held it there.

"Terri, honey," I said, "unless you can tie that stem in a knot with your tongue, like the girl in *Twin Peaks*, I'm not impressed."

She plucked off the stem and ate the cherry. "What the hell is 'Twin Peaks'?"

"A nineties TV show," I said.

"Who cares," Sherry said. "Show us your badge."

"Can't. Suspended." I rested my elbows on the table and leaned toward them. "You know how in the movies, they make the detective turn in his gun and badge?"

They pouted in unison and dipped to show their cleavage.

Terri said, "Oh, how—"

"—sad for you," Sherry said.

The situation had already become tiresome. Reaching in my wallet, I pulled out a $100 bill and snapped it before their widening, avaricious eyes. Then I tore it in half and simultaneously stuffed both halves down their necklines, between their store-bought breasts. Terri and Sherry gaped at me in shock, stammering and coughing.

"Happy Valentine's, ladies," I said. "Sorry, but I don't have time tonight for the back and forth, the flirting, the negotiation—however it works with you gals."

"You mean you've never paid for it?" Terri said.

I just smiled.

"No," Sherry said, "I bet you haven't." She tapped Terri with her shoe. "Hell, who are we kidding? We'd do him for free."

"Yeah, probably," Terri said.

"Good to know," I said. "Ladies, I'm looking for two men. They go by Bruce and Davis." I pulled out my phone and looked for their picture. "Middle aged, probably telling people they're a couple of hotshot pro-ducers—Second Story Productions. Nick, the bartender over there, said he saw you two leave with them last week. Here." I showed them the pictures. "Were these two clients of yours?"

They looked at my phone, then each other.

"Yeah, we remember them," Terri said.

"Did they take you home?" I asked. "Would you remember where they lived?"

"They took us to the Standard," Sherry said. "Hate that place. I don't think they live around here."

"What makes you say that?

"Cause the one I was with—Davis," Sherry continued, "he said they were only in town for a few weeks. Just long enough to get production rolling on their new show."

"Did they tell you anything about the show?" I asked.

"Just the title," Terri said.

"*The Score*," they said together.

"Did they brag about a score they were going to make?" I asked.

"Nope," Terri said. "But we know something about them that you don't."

"What's that?"

"Their full, real names," Sherry said.

"So, what are they?" I asked.

"Hmm…" They tapped their lips with a finger and looked at each other.

"We forget," Sherry said.

"I've got a sure cure for amnesia," I said, reaching for my wallet. "Tell me, and I'll come across with another hundred. Each."

"The cash first," Sherry said.

"Forget it," I said. "I'm persistent. I'll figure it out eventually."

As I started to walk away, Terri grabbed my jacket sleeve.

"Alright, alright, wait," she said.

"Yes?" I said.

They looked at each other. Sherry nodded and sighed.

"Robert Bruce and Jefferson Davis," she said. "Can we have our money now?"

"Ladies," I said, shaking my head, "those might be their *full* names, but I seriously doubt they're their *real* names."

"What do you mean?" Sherry said. "We saw their licenses."

"Because Robert *the* Bruce was a Scottish king in the Middle Ages," I said, "and Jefferson Davis was President of the Confederacy. Get it? They're using aliases."

"*Confederacy?*" The girls looked at each other. "What?"

"Ask that thing," I said, nodding at a cell phone on the table. "Now, what about their addresses? Did you get them?"

"We can't remember their exact addresses." Sherry picked up her phone and turned to Terri. "We should probably start taking photos of their licenses."

"I know," Terri said. "Duh, right?"

"Ladies," I said, "if we could stick to the subject at hand. We were discussing where they lived."

"They had Nevada licenses," Sherry said. "I think one of them was from Vegas and the other one Reno."

"Narrows it down," I said.

"Hey now, sexy." Sherry bit her lip and tapped me with the toe of her pump. "It's a lot better than what *you* had, which is bupkis."

"True."

Sherry picked up her phone and started to scroll through text messages. I took it from her, clicked the search button and said into the phone, "Confederate States of America." I gave her back the phone. "There. It's kind of an important part of our history, girls, so read up—promise?"

"Yes, teacher," Sherry said. She tapped me with her toe again.

"So can we have our money now?" Terri asked.

"Sorry…I lied," I said. "I know this makes me a bit of a scoundrel, but if you think about it, it's the *scoundrel* in me that you're attracted to. It's the *scoundrel* you want to give a freebie."

"Not anymore," Terri muttered.

I grinned and shook my head. "No. Now you *really* want to sleep with me."

They glared at me.

"Have a good night, ladies."

I touched my hat brim and left them looking daggers in my back. I went through the theater doors, into the main section of the club. All of the movie seats had been torn out and a series of levels built on the down-sloping floor. Each level had a bar in the center, lounge areas on the ends, and a shallow set of stairs down to the next level. Svetlana was down below, questioning a group of men.

The movie *Double Indemnity* with Barbara Stanwyck and Fred MacMurray played loudly on the huge screen down in front. It was the scene where the two meet in a grocery store after murdering her husband, and Mac-Murray, an insurance agent, is having second thoughts about trying to collect the insurance claim. Just as Stanwyck removes her sunglasses and speaks to him, I heard a voice at my shoulder saying her lines along with her. I turned toward the voice at my shoulder. There was a jostling in the crowd, and Barb was shoved against me so our chests touched.

My, oh my, could this woman wear a gown—black, satin and strapless.

"Happy Valentine's Day, Barb," I said.

"That was yesterday," she said. "It's past midnight now."

I jutted my chin at the screen and said, "I take it you've seen *Double Indemnity* a few times."

"My mother was Barbara Stanwyck's makeup artist," Barb said. "So, yeah…I've seen her movies a few times."

More people surrounded us, crushing the two of us together. Barb looked down at her breasts, which were squashed against my ribs, then tossed her head back and scowled.

"Dakota, are you going to move or what?"

"You bumped into me," I said. "Besides, if I'm so unpleasant to be close to, why don't *you* move?"

"Fine," she said.

She waited for a lull in the crowd behind her, then eased backward and to her left until she was on the lee side of the bar, out of the line of traffic. I joined her there.

"Good girl," I said. "We don't have time for hanky-panky right now anyway. We've got a mystery to solve."

"You should be so lucky." She pulled up on her gown.

"Nice dress by the way," I said. "Get it from the studio?"

"No, I moonlight on the weekends as a gun moll," she said. "Of course it's from the studio. Stop fooling around. It's Val—I got a tip that he's at the Whiskey. If we leave right now, we can catch him. You and Knut can brace him."

"Barb, I don't need *Knut* to help me brace anyone," I said.

"Oooh, stop," she said, "you're making my panties steam up." She sneered. "Can we go already?"

"Not without Svetlana," I said. "Ah, here she comes."

She climbed the stairs holding up the train of her dress and leaned against the bar beside us.

"I have secured us a lead," Svetlana said.

"So have I," Barb said. "And we need to act on mine *now*. Let's go."

"Wait, Barb," I said. "A couple of call girls in the lobby said—"

"That the two producers are staying at the Standard?" Barb said. "Already on it. The concierge is a pal of mine.

He's looking for them now. The second those guys show themselves, we'll have them. C'mon!"

Barb marched toward the exit to the lobby.

"How utterly *delightful* she is," Svetlana said.

I watched Barb's shimmying backside until she disappeared through the doorway.

"Yeah, I know what you mean," I said. "So, what's your lead, Champ?"

"A coffee shop that Val always goes to," she said. "Two o'clock in the morning, every morning, he is there."

I checked my watch: it was one thirty. "No way Barb's going to catch him at the Whiskey."

"What?"

"Never mind," I said. "Let's find Coltrane and go. I'm hungry anyway."

———— ◆ ————

On our way to the Golden State coffee shop, I studied the photo of Val Veliz that Barb had sent me. Then the car stopped.

"Coltrane, are you familiar with this place?" I asked.

"Sure. Bring folks here all the time, why?"

"Park in back, would you? And if anyone runs out, especially anyone that looks like an ex-con trying to skedaddle—"

"Impede them?" he said.

"Exactly."

"You got it."

"Because in about ten minutes," I said, "I think we're going to have a runner."

"I'll be ready," Coltrane said. "And don't worry, you two. I like the action."

He held up his hands in driving gloves, made a fist with one, and punched it into the palm of the other.

Svetlana and I got out of the car smiling and went into the restaurant. I followed Svetlana into the dining area. Heads turned and tables of rowdy young men went silent. We were seated at the table I requested—one against the back wall with a view of the entrance. When we opened our menus, the young men across the aisle turned to face us.

"The waffles are good," one of them said.

"Are you kidding? The waffles are *great*," said another. "Where you guys from?"

Svetlana gave me an inquiring look. I shrugged.

"New York," she said.

"Yeah?" the first one said. "Well, it's a big menu, little lady, so lemme make a couple *sugjeshuns*."

"Thanks," I said, "but we can handle it."

"No, you don't unnerstan'," he continued. "This place…you can get anything, anytime. You want eggs and lasagna?" He pounded the table. "Boom—you got it! You can get lobster, pancakes, paninis, a—"

His buddy across the table slapped him in the arm. "Hey, didn't you hear them? They're from *New York*."

"Yeah, so?"

"Dude," he said wearily, "they got those *diners*."

"Yes, we do," Svetlana said. "Good *night*, gentlemen."

At first the young men just gaped at her in a stupor; they were too alcohol-sodden to process her command. Then she snapped her fingers—loudly enough to make the men jump in their seats. She pointed into their booth, and they spun around without a word. I leaned across the table.

"Have you ever considered becoming a dog trainer? No—a lion tamer. Well played, my dear."

The waitress took our order and delivered it inside of a minute. Not hard to do when the order is two coffees, lemon meringue pie (for Svetlana), and coconut cream pie (for me). Before she left, the waitress totaled our check, slapped it on the table and walked away. Svetlana, a forkful of pie halfway to her mouth, paused and blinked.

"And I was about to say, '*L'addition, madame. Tout suite, s'il vous plait.*'"

"*Oui,*" I said.

Her lips pursed in amusement. "You have no idea what I just said, do you?"

"*Oui.*"

She glanced at her phone. "Two minutes to two. Do you think he will show?"

"Yes," I said. "People are creatures of habit. Particularly recidivistic felons."

We detectives tend to eat fast because our meals are so often interrupted. I finished my slice of pie and drank half of my coffee, and when it turned two o'clock sharp, I looked up to see a skinny brown-haired guy with a goatee enter the restaurant alone. He took a stool at the counter. I checked the picture on my phone one last time to be sure. It was Val all right. Tossing a twenty on the table next to our check, I stood up and put on my fedora. When Svetlana was looking at me, I motioned with my eyes at Val across the restaurant.

"He's here," I said. "Would you be willing to do a little gambit with me?"

"With pleasure."

"Good. I want you to walk by him, putting a lot of swing in those hypnotic hips of yours."

"And why exactly am I doing this?"

"To create a distraction."

She tilted her head. "Is that all I am to you—a distraction?"

"No," I said, "but think of it this way. In chess, the Queen is the most devastating piece, right?"

"Most of the time, yes."

"Well, if you had a Queen and I didn't, wouldn't you be nuts not to use it?"

"Yes," she said. "So, what will you contribute to the gambit?"

"I will disable him. We'll call this the Distract and Disable Gambit."

"Ah, the D and D. And how does this gambit work, pray tell?"

"As you head toward the front door," I said, "look over your shoulder and smile at him. But for God's sake, not your full-power smile. We don't want the guy to spontaneously combust."

"Of course not." She held out a hand. As I helped her out of the booth, she glanced at him. "That so-called *goatee* of his looks like dried brownie batter."

"That's sharp, kid," I said. "Now put that tongue away before you cut somebody."

She winked at me and set off toward the entrance swaying her hips, applying lipstick as she went. By the time she passed Val's stool at the counter, he was gawking at her with a coffee cup dangling from his fingers. The waitress dropped a slice of open-faced blueberry pie on his placemat.

Svetlana paused near him and leaned over the counter to see herself in the big mirror behind the coffeemaker. With Val still watching her, she finished applying her lipstick, snapped a napkin out of the dispenser and blotted her lips on it. She dropped the napkin next to his saucer and walked away. At the door, she smiled at him over her shoulder and tossed her hair. While Val's back was turned and he stared at Svetlana—clearly unsure whether to follow her out—I slid onto the stool beside him and tapped him on the shoulder.

"Excuse me, pal," I said. "Pass the salt, will 'ya?"

"Not now," Val said, staring at Svetlana. "I'm busy with this broad. I think she wants to nail me."

"No, she doesn't," I said. "But I *do*."

With my left hand, I pulled hard on the bottom of his stool, swiveling him around fast to face me. His eyes were still dilated from watching Svetlana when I cracked him in the jaw with a hooking right uppercut. He and his coffee spilled across the counter.

"Happy Valentine's, Val!" I said.

The waitress gasped.

"I'm calling the cops," she said, removing a phone from her apron.

In my periphery I saw several patrons pull out phones—probably starting to record me already (what a world we live in today)—but I wasn't finished with Val yet. I pounded his face into his blueberry pie three times—*Dakota, you know that's going on YouTube*—then, wrenching his arm behind his back, I yanked him off the stool and shoved him through the kitchen double doors.

Blueberry pie filling dripped off his face. Svetlana clip-clopped ahead, clearing a path for us, calming the kitchen workers in Spanish.

"Svetlana," I said, "ask them where the nearest back exit is."

"I already have. This way."

I kept Val's arm wrenched behind his back and his hair clutched in my other hand. It was then that I noticed his haircut. He had a mullet.

"Ugh, Val…a *mullet*?" I said. "Like they say, 'Business in the front, party in the back.'"

Svetlana led us down a hallway and pointed at a door at the end. As soon as she stepped out of the way, I pushed Val, aka Mullet Man, toward the door, accelerating with every step. He grunted and cursed.

"You sonovabitch! I'll friggen kill—hey, stop!"

When I was nearly on top of the door, I gave him a final heave, launching him at the bar latch. He banged into it, the door flew open, and he stumbled outside. As the door creaked closed, I caught a glimpse of Coltrane outside punching him between the eyes. Svetlana minced up beside me. I pointed at the door.

"Now *that's* dedication to your job," I said. "We need to give Coltrane a nice tip before we leave."

"Agreed," she said.

I glanced at my shirt cuffs. There were tiny blueberry stains on the white fabric.

"Oh, crap," I said. "Look."

She patted my back. "Occupational hazard, Dakota."

"Yeah, I guess." Frowning, I opened the door for her.

Outside, Coltrane had leaned Val against the car. Our punching bag was slumped over, wiping blueberry pie filling off his face with one hand and rubbing his jaw with the other. His nose was bleeding too. Maybe I'd behaved excessively. Then I thought about the charges facing Hailey because she was set up for this, and you know what I decided?

Nah.

"Look," he said as I approached, "tell Mr. Race I'll have his money in a couple days. I got a cut of something big coming to me." He stood up, and that's when he noticed Svetlana. "What? She's with *you*? What the hell's going on? Who are you guys?"

"You're over your head, Val," I said. "We're detectives working for Hailey's father. You know who he is, right? Hailey had no idea the heist was real, but you *did*, didn't you? When the owner barged in, you pulled a gun—a real gun—and when you guys ran out, *you* had all the jewels. So, there's only one thing we want to know."

Svetlana stepped forward. "Where are the jewels?"

"I have no idea," Val said. "Piss off."

"Wrong answer."

I kicked him in the shin. He yelped.

"All right, all right! Stop! I'll tell you what I know."

Val was still trying to wipe the blueberry pie filling off his face, but now, with blood mixed in, it was so epically disgusting that it was funny. Svetlana looked away. I chuckled and tossed him my pocket square. It started to rain. Coltrane dipped inside the car and pulled out an umbrella. He opened it and handed it to Svetlana. Val leaned against the car door, tilting his head back.

"Start talking, Val," I said. "Right after the robbery, what happened? You left with Bruce and Davis, correct?"

"So I left with them," he said. "So what?"

"Look, sonny," I said, "drop the surly routine and we'll get along fine. The three of you—where'd you go afterwards?"

"Second we left," he said, "Davis got on the phone and talked to who."

"We don't know *who* he talked to," I said. "That's the point, dipstick."

"No, *you're* the dipstick, buddy." He held the pocket square under his nose. "Not 'who' like W-H-O, but 'Hu' like H-U. I'm talking about a *guy* named Hu."

"All right, fine." Rain dripped off my hat brim. "This *guy* named Hu…who is he?"

"I don't know."

Svetlana stepped forward holding the umbrella. "Where did you drive after the score?"

"Chinatown," Val said.

There were police sirens in the distance. Svetlana frowned at me.

"The waitress," she said.

"Dakota," Coltrane said, "we gotta boogie!"

I opened the rear door, shoved Val inside and got in beside him. As soon as Svetlana got in and shut the door, Coltrane sped us out of the alley with the headlights off and made a series of turns down back streets.

"You mentioned Chinatown, Val," I said. "*Where* in Chinatown?"

"I don't know streets," he said. "But I could find the place again easy enough."

"Coltrane?" I said.

"Yeah?"

"Chinatown, please."

"You got it," Coltrane said.

Beside me, Svetlana crossed her legs and peered over at Val.

"Chinatown," she said. "What happened there?"

"I don't know. Bruce and Davis went inside for a minute and came out with a duffel bag."

"What was in the duffel bag?" I asked.

"No idea," he said. "Sounded like stuff clanking together—tools, crap like that. Might've been a chain in there too."

"Where was the sack of jewels at this time?" Svetlana asked. "Did they leave it in the van?"

"No, they took the sack inside," Val said. "Didn't trust me alone with it, I guess."

"Did they have it when they came back out?" I asked.

"No," Val said. "The sack was gone. But the duffel was a huge one, so the jewels might've been in there."

"After Chinatown, where'd you go?" I asked.

"I drove them to a parking lot on Logan Street, off Sunset. They jumped out and took off. I wiped down the van, went to the parking lot across the street, and got in an SUV they'd left there. Then I drove around for an hour and picked them up at the corner of Logan and Sunset. They still had the duffel, but it was less full."

"Svetlana—Logan and Sunset," I said. "What's there?"

"I am already on it." She consulted a map on her phone. "It appears to be a combination of business and residential. They could have gone anywhere."

"Val," I said, "when they got out of the van, which direction did they go in?"

"I don't know directions, man."

"Well, did they go *toward* Sunset or away from it?"

He pinched his eyes shut. "Away."

"You're sure?" I said.

"Yeah. Away."

"Dakota," Coltrane said, "I know those parking lots. If they were going away from Sunset, the only place fairly close is Echo Park Lake."

"Coltrane is right," Svetlana said. "Logan feeds into Park Avenue and Echo Park Avenue."

"Good, that might prove useful," I said. "All right, Val…after you picked them up again, then what?"

"They made me drive a few blocks, then told me to stop and get out. I had to call a cab. Waited like an hour for one."

"Rough," I said. "Now go back for a second. Think about when you picked them up. Did they say anything else? Anything at all? Close your eyes and picture yourself behind the wheel."

"Yeah…okay, this might…as they were getting in, Davis said something about Hu and a ship. Something about smuggling. Then Bruce said, 'Shanghai,' and then they clammed up."

"Can you remember the name of the ship?" I asked.

"No, man."

"Svetlana, look into it, okay?"

"Yes."

"So, Bruce and Davis dumped you off," I said. "Where'd they go? Back to the Standard?"

Val shrugged. "All they told me was, they were going down the coast for a couple days before we do the split."

"When and where is the split?" I asked.

He shook his head. "They're supposed to call me."

"Here's the deal, Val," I said. "Right now you're an accessory to manslaughter, but the cops don't know where you are. Help me clear Hailey, and I won't tell them anything about you. But try to lose me, or give me bogus information, and I promise you, you'll go back inside for a long time."

"Okay," he said, "but what about my cut? Do I still get it?"

"*Oh, Val,*" I said. "What do you think?"

"No?"

"*Ding-ding-ding!*" I said.

"Here we are, Dakota," Coltrane said.

Through the rain streaked windshield, the neon lights of Chinatown blazed.

"All right, Val," I said, "you're on."

"I think it's the next block over," he said. "No, wait… that fabric store. Pull up across the street."

Coltrane pulled over.

"They went down that alley on the side," Val said. "Must be an entrance down there."

"Svetlana, Coltrane," I said, "if I'm still inside in fifteen minutes, something went wrong. Contact Barb and have her get the cops."

"A fabric store?" Svetlana leaned against me. I could smell her perfume.

"I'm betting it's a front," I said. "We'll see. Wish me luck?"

"What is luck to trained detective?" she said. "Go."

"Back in a flash."

I got out, hopped puddles in the street and strode down the alley. The rain was coming down hard. Two Asian women in lingerie stood by a door shivering beneath an umbrella. They were sharing a cigarette.

"Ladies," I said. "You must be freezing. Let's get you inside."

They giggled as I opened the door for them. I stepped inside and stood in a wide entrance hallway with plush carpet, tall plants, a coat check booth, and a bar. From speakers overhead, Sinatra sang his swinging rendition of "Luck Be a Lady."

Down the hallway I glimpsed a roulette wheel and a blackjack table (good thing Svetlana hadn't come in with me). The situation was clear: this was an illegal casino, and these two alluring young women with silky hair as black as crows' wings? More working girls. Lot of them in L.A., I gathered. I handed them each a $50 bill.

"It's Valentine's Day, ladies."

They giggled.

"I want a double date," I said. "Get me a drink would you? Macallan eighteen-year, neat. Make it a double."

"Double drink?" one of the women said.

"Yes."

"*And* double date?" the other said.

"Yes," I said.

At the end of the hallway, in the archway outside the casino, stood two thick-necked Asian men. Their suits strained against their muscles; they looked like the bigger, more psychotic brothers of Oddjob from *Goldfinger*. The Asian girls started toward the bar.

"Wait, ladies," I said. "I need to see Mr. Hu first. Where's his office?"

They pointed at a steep set of stairs. There was a door at the top.

"Thanks," I said.

Fortunately, Oddjob's brothers had to go into the casino to deal with something and didn't see me steal up the stairs. At the top, I opened the door and slipped inside. "Luck Be a Lady" was being piped in here, too; hopefully Lady Luck would stick with me a while longer. A trim middle-aged Asian man stood behind a desk with an unlit cigar in his mouth. He was flicking a lighter and banging it on the desktop. He glanced at me as I crossed the room toward the back of his desk.

"Mr. Hu?" I said.

"What you want?"

He was still fiddling with the lighter when a cell phone on his desk rang. The cell phone was closer to my side of the desk, next to a dish of dinner mints. As Mr. Hu reached for the phone, in one gorgeously smooth motion I pushed the phone away with my right hand and swiped him across the jaw with my left. He hit the desk on his way down to the floor. As I picked up the cell phone, I memorized the number and answered it on the second ring, mimicking Hu's accent the best I could.

"What you want?" I said.

"Mr. Hu? It's Jake. Bay City. Just wanted you to know, sir, we're keepin' a real close eye on those two you sent down our way, and—"

"Who?" I said. "What two you talk about?"

"Mr. Bruce and Mr. Davis, sir."

"Ah. Good. Goodnight then."

"Goodnight, Mr—"

I hung up and rifled through the desk drawers. In the bottom drawer was a crumpled brown grocery bag. I opened it. It was loaded with jewelry. I bunched up the bag and shoved it inside my trench coat. I ate a mint and walked out, snapping my fingers to "Luck Be a Lady." When I neared the bottom of the stairs, the two Oddjobs stepped in front of the doorway, blocking my exit. They were backlit and wearing tuxedos, which made them look ten times more menacing.

"You look for Mr. Hu?" said the one on the left.

"I just saw him." I touched my fedora brim. "Thanks."

I continued down the stairs, just another one of Mr. Hu's business associates dropping by for a three a.m. visit, and at the bottom brushed by them. The Asian girls were there, each holding a tray with one shot glass of liquor on it. Overhead, Sinatra belted out the final lyrics of the song. The girls smiled.

"Double drink!" they chirped.

Normally I didn't drink while on a case, but this case, and this day, had been anything but normal. I downed both shots, savoring the velvety warmth of single malt in my throat, and headed for the side door. With my luck, Mr. Hu was already coming to upstairs.

"You no want double date?" one of the Asian girls asked.

"Another time," I said, and left.

Halfway down the alley, I sprinted back to the car. I got in the front seat and Coltrane gunned it out of there. I didn't even have to say, "Hit it."

Svetlana spoke over my seat back: "I take it your foray was unsuccessful."

"You tell me." I reached inside my trench coat, pulled out the grocery bag and passed it back to her. She turned on a cabin light.

"Impressive," she said, "but surely the original score was larger than this."

"You bet it was," Val said. "We cleaned that place out. Must've been forty, fifty necklaces alone. Dozens of rings—lot of 'em diamonds—earrings, bracelets, not to mention—"

"We get it—you stole a bunch of jewelry," I said. "You also contributed to the death of your buddy Dan. Or did you forget about him? And there's something you haven't told us. The other girl—the hacker, Regina—when did you last see her?"

"When we ran out the door," Val said. "She was supposed to drive away with Hailey."

"Nope," I said. "Regina took off. Svetlana, we should check her out first thing tomorrow."

"Define *first thing*, Dakota. It is four o'clock in the morning."

"Let's shoot for ten o'clock. Coltrane?"

"Yeah?"

"To the hotel, please. Then dump Mr. Mullet at his place, wherever that is."

"You got it."

"Hey, man," Val said. "You don't have to keep picking on my haircut."

"Oh, yes he does." Coltrane tilted the rear-view mirror towards Val. "Dude, you ever want to get laid again, you got to cut that."

"Alright, I will," Val said. "Tomorrow."

It was quarter past four when I made it back to my room. I took a long, hot shower in the capacious marble bathroom, then wandered into the living room wearing a plush towel. I flopped onto a sofa. I lay like that for a minute in the dimmed lights listening to the reassuring white noise of the air conditioning. My eyes got heavy.

Sprightly knocks on the hotel room door—*shave and a hair-cut, two bits!*—brought me back to reality. I rubbed the exhaustion out of my eyes, slapped my cheeks and went to the door. I waved the "DO NOT DISTURB" sign in front of the peephole first, in case a bad guy was out there aiming a gun at the hole, waiting for me to put my eye to the lens. (In movies and TV, no one *ever* does this; I think I might have invented it.) When nothing happened, I peeked out. It was Barb, grinning hard without showing her teeth.

"It's me, Dakota," she said brightly. "Open up, please. I have something I think you're going to like."

What could she mean? A clue? The rest of the jewels?

Curious, I unbolted the door, and the second I got it open, she punched me in the face. It was a decent punch that turned my head. When she reared back to punch me again, I grabbed her by the dress bodice, hauled her into the room and slammed the door. My jaw smarted from the punch. I wanted to rub it, but I wasn't going to give her any satisfaction.

"You bastard!" she said. "You ditched me! Nobody ditches me!"

I leaned toward her and sniffed. "No offense, Barb, but your deodorant's slipping."

"My deodorant!?"

She slapped at me, and when I ducked her arm, my towel slipped off.

"Well, well…" She raked her eyes up my body. "Sorry. *Accident.*"

Her eyes met mine. She smirked. I stepped toward her.

"Yeah, accidents happen."

Hooking the cups of her bodice with my left hand, I reached under her arm with my right, yanked the zipper down, and tugged the entire dress to the floor. Under the black satin evening gown, the woman was stark naked. She gasped.

"Tsk-tsk, Miss Soames," I said. "My grandmother warned me to steer clear of fast women. And top on that list? Women who don't wear undies."

She stepped out of the dress in a pair of chunky high heels. Then she turned toward the door, giving me an epic view of her toned butt and her blonde hair down her bare back.

"Well, seems I'm not welcome here," she said. "Ta-ta, Dakota."

"Where do you think *you're* going?" I said.

I reached out and clutched her hair. Gently tugging her backwards, I turned her around and kissed her.

Over the next few hours, in a variety of locations around the suite, I witnessed Barb's bitch in heels persona disappear. By nine o'clock in the morning, with the hazy L.A. light seeping through the windows, and with the two of us having only dozed since dawn, we lay in bed and discussed the case.

"You punched out Mr. Hu?" she said. "Do you have any idea who he is?"

"No, but somehow I have a feeling you're going to tell me."

"The man runs Chinatown. He's got a ton of crooked cops and politicians on his payroll. He's Teflon, plain and simple."

"So who are Bruce and Davis?" I said. "And why the elaborate heist to knock over a jewelry store?"

"Maybe Hu's people found the score and hired the two producer clowns to do it."

"Wait a second…*clowns?*" I climbed on top of her and pinned her arms down. "That's my insult, doll. Patent-pending. Afraid you'll have to get another."

She squinted up at me defiantly. "It's mine. *You* get another."

"I thought I cured you of such insolence," I said.

"Apparently not."

She raised her head off the pillow and nipped at me with her teeth. When we came up for air again, we were twisted up in the sheets and perspiring.

"What time is it, doll?" I asked.

"Nine thirty. Why?"

"This case isn't going to solve itself," I said. "We have to get to work. Today I want Val to take us to the spot where he dropped off Bruce and Davis, and I want to talk to Regina. Let's move."

"Hey, New York, hold your horses. This *doll* ain't had her coffee yet." She rolled onto her side and grinned. "That's coffee like me, Dakota—light and sweet."

"*'Light and sweet'?*" I chuckled. "More like strong and scalding."

"Naughty boy." She slapped my bare chest. "That'll cost you."

"Uh-uh, no more of that," I said, "it's time for work. We'll shower, then I'll dress and go procure coffee." I nodded at the black heap on the carpet. "I'll also buy you a new outfit. There's a boutique down in the lobby."

She nibbled my earlobe.

"Let's go." I touched her cheek. "To the shower."

While in there with her, I developed a theory: Nothing in the world is as smooth and slippery as soap and hot water between two people's skin.

Afterwards I dressed quickly in a polo shirt, shorts and tennis shoes with no socks, grabbed Blaze's script and headed for the door. It wasn't until I was in the elevator that I realized I'd forgotten my phone and wallet. Oh, well—I could charge anything I needed to the room.

Stepping off the elevator, I spied a lavender sheath dress for Barb in the boutique window. I asked them to deliver one to my room and went to the continental breakfast across the lobby. I made coffees for the two of us, balanced a couple of croissants on top, and, with the script under my arm, was about to go back to the elevator when I felt the inimitable jab of a gun barrel against my spine.

"Put down the coffees, Mr. Stevens. *Real* slow," said a man's voice behind me.

Whoever he was, a miasma of bad cologne and cheap cigars hung in the air around him like dust does Pigpen in the Peanuts cartoons.

"Good," he said. "Now, you're going to take a little walk with us. Me and my colleagues have a car parked outside, so—"

"You mean, 'My colleagues and I have a car parked outside,'" I said. "You wouldn't say, 'Me have a car parked outside.' Or maybe you would."

"Shut up," he said. "What's that under your arm?"

"A script."

"Drop it."

"Nope," I said. "I'm being paid as a consultant, and the writer needs my notes, ASAP. I'm not dropping it, and if you try and take it from me, I'll make a scene."

"Fine, keep the script. Now, move!"

He drilled the gun barrel into my spine, and we shuffled toward the doors to the street.

"Fifty bucks says I can guess what you look like," I said. I glanced at the other men. "Any takers? No? Okay. Well, based on your voice, I'm guessing you're fat—at least a good two-fifty at about five feet seven. What a polite person might call 'portly' but on you is just plain *fat*. Blue five o'clock shadow, even though it isn't even ten a.m. yet. And a stain on your shirt from second breakfast this morning." I half-turned to speak over my shoulder. "Oh, 'second breakfast' is a reference to *The Hobbit* by the way."

"Shut up and keep walkin'."

Once outside, I squinted in the light. One of the men got behind the wheel of a blue sedan—a Chevy Caprice Classic, the quintessential unmarked cop car. A second got in the front passenger seat, and a third opened the rear passenger door at the curb and slid in. Spurred on by the gun in my back, I got in the middle beside him.

"Oh, come on, guys," I said, "not the *hump*."

"Shut 'ya yap!"

The guy with the gun, whom I hadn't seen yet, slid in next to me. As I looked him over, the car accelerated into traffic.

"Well, guys, pay up," I announced to the car. "Your buddy here is undeniably fat—try to park some of that surplus over there, by the way. He's a good five inches shorter than I, he has at least a day's growth on his face, and there's a big stain on his tie—which, by the looks of it, is from one of those free cherry Danishes at the Peninsula, which makes it second breakfast, which means—"

Fat man elbowed me in the ribs. Sadly none of that extra padding of his was on the point of his elbow. My scalp flashed hot and perspired the way it did whenever I ate heavily curried Singapore Rice Noodle. When I could breathe again, I continued my monologue.

"Call me crazy, but I have a hunch you're cops," I said. "Bay City. Am I right? One of you must be Jake. You'll recall we spoke briefly last night. Remember…'*What you want?* Come on, fess up. Who's Jake?"

Nobody said anything. We cruised through a few stoplights and got on the freeway heading south.

"'Forget it, Jake. It's Chinatown.'" I turned to Fat Man and grinned. "I've always wanted to say that."

Silence. Nothing but the purr of the engine. Up front, the driver cleared his throat. I sat quietly for a moment, until I became aware of that miasma again—now quadrupled—of bad cologne and cheap cigars.

"Could somebody please crack a window?" I asked. Nobody moved.

"At least tell me where we're going," I said. "No? All right, then, I'm not telling *you* anything about this fantastic script I'm reading." I opened to the page I'd dog-eared. "Anybody have a pen?"

III

I'd always thought that Bay City was a make-believe town on the Southern California coast invented by mystery writer Raymond Chandler and later used in the TV show *The Rockford Files*. I'd always thought it was a make-believe town populated by make-believe corrupt cops. But once they took me inside the cinder block Bay City Police station and down to the basement, and once the fat man shoved me in a chair, slugged me in the mouth, and I spat my own blood on the floor—I knew the place was real.

"Listen," I said, glancing at the four of them, "is this about my PBA contribution? How many times do I have to tell you? *Mail me the form.*"

"Boy, are you in for it, smart guy," one of them said.

He opened the door and Mr. Hu strolled in, followed by (the doorway cringing at their approach) Oddjob's two bigger, more psychotic brothers. I gulped so hard, I was surprised nobody else heard it. Mr. Hu slipped on a pair of what looked like Isotoner leather gloves. He held his fists up to the light and flexed his hands a couple times.

"Nice fit?" I said. "Remember those Isotoner TV commercials with quarterback Joe Montana? Or was it Dan Marino?"

Without a word, Hu removed his suit jacket, and laid it, lining side out, over a seat back. Then, with one last appreciative glance at how well his gloves fit, he composed himself with a deep breath and unleashed a flurry of punches on my face: *left, right, left, right, left, left, right, right, right* (you get the idea). They were the fastest punches I'd ever seen or felt, but they were hardly knockout blows by any means. The one swiping left hook I'd hit Hu with had more raw power behind it then all of these put together. Still, to be punched more times in a few seconds than you can count, and to have your head violently shifted left, then right, then up, then down is disconcerting to say the least. Like being on a nauseating amusement park ride, you can't help wondering when it will end. When Mr. Hu finally finished, I was dizzy and sweating, and I felt my face swelling up.

"Mistah Stevens," he said quietly, parking one of his barely existent butt cheeks on the corner of the table. "Why steal from me? You do not know me. Do you think it wise to invade a stranger's place of business and take items which do not belong to you?"

"No, it doesn't." I closed my eyes for a second to stave off a wave of dizziness that threatened to topple me to the floor. "But it also doesn't make sense to rob a jewelry store and frame desperate actors for the crime. It's especially stupid when one of the actors is the daughter of one of the most powerful men in Hollywood, Theodore Vance. Maybe you've heard of him? Vice President at Warner Brothers?"

Hu didn't reply.

"I'm curious about something myself," I said. "How'd you find me so fast? I don't recall leaving my business card."

The fat cop stepped out of the shadows.

"You're gonna find, buddy boy, that Mr. Hu's got eyes pretty much everywhere. There ain't much that happens in L.A. Mr. Hu don't know about."

"Your grammar sucks, Fat Man," I said, "but I get the gist."

Mr. Hu leaned toward me as his two Oddjobs breathed at my neck.

"Where are my jews?" he asked.

"*Jewels*, with an *L*," I said. "Enunciate, Mr. Hu."

The Oddjob at my left shuffled to the side, shouted and chopped off the corner of the interrogation table. The splintered wood clunked on the floor. I looked at Hu.

"I guess I'm next if I don't answer."

"Correct," Hu said.

"By now, the jewels are either with the cops or the store owner," I said.

"That is unfortunate."

He was perfectly still, staring at the Linoleum floor when he said it. Also unfortunate was Hu's pronunciation of "unfortunate," which sounded more like *"onfohchoo-nut,"* but I didn't say anything. Besides being rude, it probably would have led to my having an arm chopped off at the shoulder.

"Look," I said, "I work for Mr. Vance. All I care about is clearing his daughter of this thing. Why don't you shake down Bruce and Davis for a bigger cut, then give them up to the LAPD? The cops recover half of the jewels, the dealer collects the insurance on the rest, the DA gets a good conviction, and Vance's daughter gets cleared. Everybody's happy."

"Don't listen to him, Mr. Hu," Fat Man said.

Meanwhile, Hu was silent. What I needed here was a distraction, and I knew I could count on Fat Man to create it.

"Hey, Fat Man," I said. "Think of a bowl of Jell-O. You like Jell-O, right? Look who I'm asking—of course you do. Anyway, that jiggle a bowl of Jell-O makes…tell me…if I pounded you in the gut right now, is that what you'd feel?"

Fat Man rushed across the room at me, but I was ready, leaping out of my chair and hitting him in the gut with everything I had. He doubled over like a deflated accordion. I reached behind his hip, took his gun, chambered a round and dug the barrel into his spine. Groping over his shoulder, I found his tie and yanked it over his back to use as a choke collar. My back was to the wall and I had his enormity to shield me. The other cops pulled their guns, but they couldn't get an angle around Fat Man. Hu and the Oddjobs were motionless; clearly they didn't have guns.

"Everybody," I said, "guns on the floor! Now!"

The three cops dropped theirs.

"Kick them over here," I said.

They did.

"Now keys and cell phones," I said.

When there was a pile of guns, keys and phones at our feet, I looked around the room for something to carry all this stuff.

"Your suit jacket please, Mr. Hu," I said.

He tossed it at Fat Man's feet. I lowered my gun so it was aimed between Fat Man's legs.

"Put everything in the jacket, Fat Man. Note where the gun is aimed now."

"Guys, don't try nothin'," he said, stooping for the items.

"Come on, Fat Man, who taught you grammar?" I said. "It's, 'Don't try *anything*.'"

"Shut up."

"And get my script," I said.

One of the cops tossed it to him.

"Okay, got it," Fat Man said. "Now what?"

I reached to the side and opened the door.

"Now we back out together. Slowly."

I noticed that this interrogation room was sound-proofed and didn't have any cameras in it. Since we were in the basement, it could be hours before anyone discovered them down here. When we stepped backwards into the hallway, Fat Man shut the door.

"Give me that bundle," I said. "Good. Now get your keys, lock the door and snap the key off."

"But they'll be trapped," he said.

"That's their problem," I said.

He snapped off the key.

"Now," I said, "take me to your car—your *personal* car, not a department vehicle." I jabbed his spine with the gun. "Just keep moving. And don't have a heart attack on me."

He led us down a long corridor, up some stairs, and then we were outside, in the parking lot. I shoved the bundle in a trash can.

"Whatever you do, don't get cute," I said. "If you think I won't shoot you because you're a cop, you're wrong. I'm a distinguished former FBI Special Agent who stumbled on collusion between the Bay City police and the Chinese Mob. You, my friend, are a jumbo-sized corrupt cop whom the LAPD would love to nail for accessory to robbery and manslaughter. So play it straight and you'll live to eat another day."

"That's it." He pointed at a Cadillac SUV.

I whistled. "Boy, the corrupt cop business must be pretty good, Fat Man."

"Could you stop calling me 'Fat Man'?" he said. "I can't help it. It's a thyroid condition."

"Thyroid my ass, Butterball. Get in and drive."

My plan was to get to the pier and blend into the crowd, then call Coltrane and have him come pick me up. I kept the gun pointed at Fat Man, which had a conciliatory effect on him; he didn't say anything, nor did he try to drive recklessly or draw attention to us some other way. He drove the speed limit and even used his turn signals.

"I've got a Cadillac at home myself," I said. "Never ridden in the SUV before though. A surprisingly smooth ride. But I bet the mileage sucks. What do you get on this, ten, eleven per gallon?"

He frowned, which caused the fat folds in his neck to double up.

"*No*, like sixteen, seventeen," he said. "Twenty-*two* on the highway."

"Not bad, and that's carrying *you*," I said. "I'd probably get closer to thirty."

"Prick," he said.

I nodded. "Yeah, sometimes. But the ladies like it. It's part of my charm."

I had him roll down the windows, and after a series of turns down broad, clean streets, I began to smell the ocean. He turned us onto a road that ran along the beach. Ahead, a giant Ferris wheel loomed on the pier. Bikini-clad women rollerbladed by on the sidewalk beside the sea wall. I made him pull over and shut off the engine.

"The keys," I said. "And my script."

He tossed them on my lap.

"Now your wallet," I said.

"No way. I ain't giving you my wallet."

"Your wallet," I said, "or I tell Hu that you spilled everything you know."

Grumbling, he reached inside his suit jacket and took it out.

"Only the cash and credit cards," I said. "I know what a bitch it is to get your driver's license replaced."

He handed them to me.

"Oh, and your badge," I said, snapping my fingers.

"You *sonova*..."

He gave that to me as well. I shoved the keys, cash, credit cards and badge in my pockets.

"Last, and *definitely* least," I said, "strip."

"What?"

"*Strip*. Don't worry, I won't look. Believe me, I don't *want* to look."

"Boy," he said, unbuttoning his shirt, "I can't wait till Mr. Hu kills your stupid ass. I hope it's long and painful, too." He got the shirt off and started on the pants. "I heard that one time he put a guy in a tank with electric eels. Maybe he'll do something fun like that with you."

"Maybe," I said. "Or maybe he'll just do that to you."

Fat man shoved his clothes in my lap.

I got out of the car and walked toward the pier with the clothes and script bundled under one arm, and the gun hidden in the waistband of my shorts. A young woman jogged toward me.

"Excuse me, miss," I said. "Do you know how to get to Venice Beach from here?"

She smiled and pulled an ear bud out of her ear. "Venice Beach?"

"Yeah." I motioned at Fat Man in the SUV. "That guy was asking me, but I'm not from around here. Could you go help him?"

"Fer sure," she said.

As she jogged toward the SUV, I waved to Fat Man over her shoulder. The look of panic that came over his face was priceless. I savored it for a moment, then turned and continued up the sidewalk counting to myself—"one...two..."—and then the young woman screamed. I hopped the sea wall and dumped Fat Man's clothes, keys and badge in a rubbish bin.

I was about to continue toward the pier when I spotted something across the beach and was overcome by a sense of déjà vu. Floating in the water on this side of the pier was a series of docks, with a banner above them that read, "JET SKIS 4 RENT." I smiled to myself remembering the time I'd seen my friends' boys Jack and James escape from the cops on a videogame by doing this. I ran across the beach and strolled down the dock to the attendant. He was a tan and lanky young man, maybe 20 years old. I laid a $100 bill on the small table in front of him.

"I'd like to rent a jet ski, please."

"Money's no good, man," he said. "Need ID and a credit card."

"Lost my license," I said. "But I'll tell you what... rent it to me on the credit card, and you can keep the cash. Do I look like a Jet Ski thief to you?"

"No, but they never do," the kid said.

"Look, sonny, I just want to go out for an hour. There's no need to be a ball-buster here."

He snapped up the bills. "Okay, take that red one on the end. And wear the life vest."

I put on the vest, climbed aboard and started the motor.

"Hey," he said. "That a screenplay?"

"Yup. Listen, which way—"

"I've got a screenplay too." He reached into a messenger bag. "In fact—"

"Fascinating, kid," I said. "Which way is Malibu?"

He pointed north.

"And Venice Beach?" I asked. "South?"

He nodded.

"Thanks."

I floored the Jet Ski away from the dock and jumped some incoming breakers. At the end of the pier, I continued straight, the spray splashing up on my face. My lips tasted salty. I ran the Jet Ski at full-bore until I was out beyond the pier, then eased it back to three-quarters and turned left toward Venice Beach. My plan was to make the attendant and any witnesses think that I'd gone south. Once I'd gone a hundred yards or so, I made a wide, looping right turn out to sea and headed north farther from shore.

I kept the Jet Ski at half throttle and steered for a point to the north, several miles away, where the shore curved out to sea. There was a long stretch of beach with houses on it, and above the houses was a road. Every few minutes, sun glinted off the windows of passing cars. It had to be Malibu. Barb had a place in Malibu. Once I got to land, I'd ask to use a phone. I'd call Svetlana, find out where Barb's house was, and meet them there.

My face hurt. As far as I could tell, Hu's punches hadn't broken my skin or any bones, but I was certain I was badly bruised—probably black and blue—which reminded me of Val's blueberry-covered face last night, which reminded me of something significant Val had said. He said he dropped Bruce and Davis at a parking lot on Logan Street, off Sunset Boulevard, and that they were heading toward Echo Park Lake. Did they go there? What if they did? What if they buried the jewels somewhere in the park? Val *did* say he'd heard tools clanking together inside the duffel bag and that they were gone an hour. What if they buried the jewels, then hustled back to Sunset, where Val picked them up again? I had to get over to Echo Park as soon as possible to check things out. As soon as I got back on dry land that is.

When I was a mile from the point, the Jet Ski engine began to sputter. I was running out of gas, so I made an abrupt turn for the beach. Remembering I had Fat Man's gun, I dropped it in the ocean, and when the engine coughed and died, I was a few hundred yards from shore. I coasted in as far as I could, then jumped in—script and all—and swam for shore.

Even with the life vest, the swim was strenuous, and delightfully punctuated by a rogue wave that flattened me as I was climbing out of the water. It carried me in another fifty feet and beached me on the sand. Once I'd stopped coughing up seawater, I lay on my back for a moment, gazing westward at the sun, now low in the sky—five o'clock, I surmised. There was movement to my right. I turned and two nude and very good-looking people, a famous actor super-couple, were stooping over me. The man was holding my script.

"Hey, buddy, you okay?" he said.

"Yeah, I'm fine. My Jet Ski ran out of gas."

"We saw," the woman said.

Her face glowed. The rest of her was something to see as well.

The man waved the script. "This yours?"

"Yes," I said. "Thanks for rescuing it."

"Did you write it? Are you"—he glanced at the cover—"Blaze?"

"No." I sat up and gazed out to sea so I wouldn't be staring at their private parts. "My name is Dakota Stevens. I'm a PI from New York. I'm giving Blaze some notes on the script."

"'Gone Rogue,' huh?" he said. "What's it about? Give me the pitch."

I told him. I also gave him my alternate titles for the film: *Rogue*, *Rogue Agent*, and *Agent of Death*.

"I might be interested," he said. "Can I take the cover page to call this guy's agent?"

"Sure," I said.

He tore off the cover and handed me the script. "Who knows…maybe we can attach Gina here to direct."

"With my gorgeous husband as the lead?" she said. "Absolutely."

They embraced and stood on the sand kissing with the waves crashing behind them. I might as well have been a piece of seaweed. I got to my feet and tried to look elsewhere, but it was awkward. Finally, I cleared my throat.

"Sorry to interrupt, but I really need to use a phone."

"No prob," the husband said. "Come on up to the house."

"Where are you headed?" Gina asked.

"I need to get to Barbara Soames' house," I said.

"Oh, Barb lives just up the road," the husband said. "We'll give you a ride."

"You know Barb?"

"Everyone knows Barb," Gina said.

They started walking up the beach toward the house.

———❖———

When I got to Barb's place, the housekeeper, a Latina woman named Flora, let me in. Apparently there was nothing unusual about my showing up at Barb's door on a weekday afternoon soaked to the skin, fanning a water-logged script. Flora led me inside and even brought me a towel, which made me a little more comfortable. I still felt like a salt-encrusted sea otter, but at least now I wasn't *wet*.

From where I stood in the living room, I could see Hailey sunning herself on the deck overlooking the ocean. Knut sat in a chaise opposite hers reading to her from *Variety*. At least I *thought* he was reading to her; he might have been sounding out the words. Hailey lifted her head off the chaise and squinted into the house.

"That you, Dakota?"

"Yes."

"Come here," she said. "I need to talk to you."

"Not now," I said. "I'm off the clock for a while—at least until Svetlana and Barb get here."

Barb's place was predictably modern, cold and sterile: a lot of metal and glass surfaces, and no books or memen-tos of any kind—at least not out in the open. I strolled down a dim hallway and went up a set of stairs to the master suite. After a hot shower, I squeezed into a medium-sized terrycloth bathrobe with a Beverly Hills Hotel crest. The robe was hanging on a "His" hook beside an identical one under "Hers." Being a guy, I felt a pique of jealousy at the idea of some mystery man—a wealthy studio exec no doubt—shtupping Barb; but I put it out of my mind and went back downstairs.

I took my wet clothes to a utility room off the kitchen, where Flora offered to wash them for me right away. She placed my wet script atop the warm dryer and gave me a bag of peas to put on my bruised face. I settled into an Eames chair with my feet up, laid the peas on my cheek and took in the panoramic ocean view. So, this is what working in Hollywood can get you. Maybe I should give up the grind in New York and become a studio dick. I was relaxing into the chair and debating whether to break my no-alcohol rule again for a couple of beers, when the front door opened and banged shut.

The sound of high heels echoed down the tile hallway. The second Barb stepped into the living room, she slammed her Louis Vuitton handbag on the glass coffee table—so hard, I thought it would shatter.

"Where the *hell* have you been?" she said. "You leave to get me coffee and—"

I held a finger to my lips.

"Oh, get over yourself," Barb said. "Svetlana knows all about it. She's been worried sick about you."

"Hardly." Svetlana went to the kitchen island, sat on a barstool and crossed her legs. "I knew Dakota was on the scent of something and that he would eventually come back to us."

"Where's Coltrane?" I asked.

"Outside. He preferred to wait in the car."

Barb knocked my feet off the footstool and sat down on it facing me.

"All right, what was the hot lead you just *had* to follow?" She winced and extended a hand toward my cheek. "Oooh, and what happened to your *face?*"

"It wasn't a *lead*," I said. "I was abducted in the hotel lobby."

"Seriously, Dakota? The plot of *North by Northwest?* So you're Cary Grant, is that it?"

"I *was* abducted—by Bay City cops."

I told them about the abduction and the beating Hu gave me. I finished by sharing the highlights of my escape, including the Jet Ski ride and washing up on Barb's celebrity neighbors' beach.

"They were stark naked," I said.

"Yeah, they like to do that," Barb said. "Sounds like you've had a banner day. And it's only going to get better. By now, Hu's got every Chink in L.A. looking for you."

"*Chink?*" I winced. "Barb, that's—"

"You don't understand." She huffed. "Look, do you know what a triple threat is in movies?"

"Sure," I said. "Somebody who can act, sing and dance."

"Right. Well, in crime, Hu's a triple threat. He's smart, connected and ruthless. The man—"

"Might be a triple threat," Svetlana interrupted, "but in detective work Dakota is the *perfect* triple threat—deductive reasoning, forensic testing, and…" She turned to me and batted her eyelashes. "What is that third thing you do so well?"

"Oh, I don't know…there are so many," I said. "Questioning? Driving? Shooting? Fighting? Snooping?"

Svetlana snapped her fingers. "Yes, 'snooping,' or what he likes to call 'poking around.' As a detective, *Barb*, Dakota is the perfect triple threat. *Quod erat demonstrandum.*"

"Yeah, QED," I said, sitting up in my chair, "plus I have Svetlana, so I guess that makes me a *quadruple* threat. Screw Hu."

Hailey walked in from the patio, followed by Knut.

"Well, *quadruple threat*," Barb said, poking my leg, "we waited two hours for you this morning. Finally Svetlana said you'd want us to go see Val."

"And?" I asked.

Svetlana batted her eyelashes. "Gone…with the wind."

I smiled.

"Both Val and Regina," Svetlana said. "We tried her place next, and she too was gone. Then we went to the parking lot on Hogan—"

"Where I found the *van*," Barb said, glaring at Hailey.

"Good," I said. "What'd you do over there?"

"We did what you would do," Svetlana said. "We poked around the neighborhood. The most logical conclusion is that Bruce and Davis hid the jewels somewhere in the park around Echo Park Lake."

"Great minds think alike," I said. "I came to that conclusion on the Jet Ski earlier."

I glanced at Knut. He looked like he'd just been audited by the IRS. Flora walked in with a small pile of folded clothes.

"Mr. Dakota, your clothes, they ready now. I put in bedroom for you, *señor*?"

"*Muchas gracias*, Flora."

"Your script dry, too."

She walked down the hall.

"I have a theory," Svetlana said.

"Let's hear it, Champ."

"Why do you call her 'Champ'?" Barb said. "It's annoying."

"Because she's a U.S. chess champion," I said.

"Sure, *former*," Barb said.

"No," I said, winking at Svetlana, "once a champ, always a champ. Let's hear it, Svetlana."

She stood, walked to the window and gazed out. The sun was low over the water and backlit her dramatically. She wore a cream shift with a long side slit, which boosted the effect.

"What if," she said, "Hu, Bruce and Davis have been working together? They concocted the fake reality TV show and to distance themselves from the crime, they used *Hailey*"—she glanced at her—"as the ultimate scapegoat, because her celebrity—as Mr. Vance's daughter—would distract the police from the real perpetrators."

Svetlana turned away from the window and sat down on the chair next to mine. I nodded at her.

"I think that's exactly how this went down." I moved the bag of peas to my other cheek. "But…Hu's involvement doesn't matter. All I'm concerned about is clearing Hailey, which means the priority is finding the jewels." I nudged Barb with my toe. "Barb—Bruce and Davis are probably waiting for the heat to die down before retrieving the jewels, right?"

"Sure," Barb said.

"Svetlana," I said, "remember when Val said he'd heard Bruce and Davis talking about Hu, smuggling and Shanghai?"

"Yes," she said. "And I discovered that Hu owns a ship departing for Shanghai at one o'clock tomorrow morning."

"Bruce and Davis might be trying to make a run for it," I said. "That could be why they gave Hu some of the jewels after the score—to buy passage on the ship for Shanghai."

Knut shook his head. "I will be in guest room, Barb."

As he walked out of the room, I gave Barb a look. She shrugged.

"I don't hire my assistants for their brains, Dakota."

"You don't?"

She pouted and kicked me gently in the shin.

"Moving on," I said. "We need to find the jewels, then get word to Bruce and Davis that we found them so we can flush those two out. Barb, can your L.A. grapevine get the word out?"

"Of course."

Barb went to the kitchen island, uncorked a bottle of red wine, and poured herself a glass. She sat down on my footstool again and sipped her wine.

"I hate to be a bringdown, Dakota," she said, "but... let's say you and Svetlana are right about the jewels being somewhere in the park. That park is *huge.*"

"No, Barb...Central Park—you know, in *New York?*—that's huge."

"Whatever," she said. "It's still a needle in a haystack. Val said they were gone for an hour, right? In that amount of time, they could have hidden the jewels anywhere. For all we know, they put them in a safe house nearby. Or a dumpster. Or a culvert, for crissake."

"I know, Barb," I said, "but Val also said he heard tools 'clanking together.' You know what 'clank together'? Shovels. And shovels mean *dirt*, and in a city, dirt means a park."

"Okay," she said, swirling her wine, "maybe you've got the location of the jewels down, but how can we guarantee that Bruce and Davis hear that we found them? I mean, I can put the word out on the grapevine, but—"

"What if I called them?" Hailey said.

"What?!" I said. "You have their number?"

"Dammit, Hailey!" Barb said. "Are you a *complete* idiot? We needed to know about this yesterday."

"Screw you, Barb," Hailey said. "I flaked, okay? I've been under a lot of pressure. When they cast me, they gave me a burner with one number on it. If anything went wrong during any of the shoots, I was supposed to call them on it."

"Where's the phone now?" I asked.

"Beverly Hills. My dad's place."

"What if someone called it?" Svetlana said. "Would your father answer it?"

"Relax," Hailey said. "It's in the pool house—that's where I crash—and I've kept it shut off."

"All right, everyone, be ready to go in ten minutes." I laid the bag of peas on the floor and stood up. "It's Beverly Hills, then some kind of hardware store—for shovels, flashlights and such—and then the corner of Park Drive and Echo Park Drive. Let's move. I'm going to get dressed."

I started down the hall. Barb followed me and cut me off at the stairs leading to the master suite.

"Need any *help*, New York?" She wagged her eyebrows.

"Not *your* kind of help," I said.

———◆———

From Malibu, the six of us split up temporarily. While Barb, Knut and Hailey went to Beverly Hills for the phone, Coltrane, Svetlana and I stopped at a Home Depot and bought spade shovels, headlamp flashlights, and six pairs of work gloves. When we were back in the car, I asked Coltrane to drive to the corner of Park Avenue and Echo Park Avenue, then I settled in to read my now-foxed copy of the script. Svetlana pushed the script down.

"What?" I said.

"*Barb*, Dakota?" she said. "And during our case no less?"

"I know, I know. It just happened. I can't explain it."

"*That* does not 'just happen.'"

"No, sometimes it does," I said. "She came to my room at four thirty this morning and punched me in the face. Things got out of hand. It couldn't be helped."

She sighed.

"*Yakshcho dyyavol bezsylyy, poslaty yomu zhinku,*" she muttered, then opened her book on classic Hollywood.

"I didn't catch that," I said.

"Ukrainian proverb," she said. "'If the devil is power-less, send him a woman.'"

"You and those damn proverbs. I don't understand. Are you calling me the devil?"

"You are the great detective," she said. "Figure it out."

We spent the next half hour in silence—she reading about Clark Gable and Vivien Leigh; I, about rogue and implausible FBI Special Agent Brock Tangier. When I finished up to page 80, I called Blaze's number, gave him my notes and told him to send two copies of the script over to Gina and her husband first thing in the morning.

"That's me, Blaze," I said into the phone, "Dakota Stevens—Hollywood dealmaker. *You're welcome.*"

I hung up.

"Park and Echo Park, Dakota," Coltrane said.

"Great," I said. "Find a spot to pull over, and then could you give us a hand?"

"You bet," he said. "Remember—"

"—you like the action."

"That's right." He grinned in the rear-view.

"I, however, do *not* like the action," Svetlana said, flipping a page in her book. "I do *not* dig holes, Dakota."

"Really?" I chuckled. "You think I don't know that? Relax, kid, you're with me. We're going to put those predatory eyes of yours to work as my spotter. That, and I need you to wear one of the headlamps." I nudged her. "It'll look great with that sexy shift you're wearing."

"*Zadnitza,*" she said.

Outside, Barb, Hailey and Knut met us at the trunk of Coltrane's car. I handed out the equipment.

"It's a needle in a haystack, I know," I said, "but we have to try." I pointed a shovel at the park. "The jewels are somewhere in there."

"You're sure about this?" Hailey said.

"No, I'd say I'm about seventy-five percent sure."

"You sound like a friggen weatherman," Hailey said.

"Well, Hailey, now that you mention it," I said, "there *is* an eighty percent chance of showers tonight.

And there's a one *hundred* percent chance of a certain young lady going to *prison* if we don't find the jewels and clear her bratty little ass."

I thrust a shovel and a pair of gloves at her.

"Sorry," Hailey said.

"Forget it," I said. "We fan out around the park, starting at this end. Each person alone, except for Svetlana, who's with me."

"What are we lookin' for, Dakota?" Coltrane asked.

"Good question, Coltrane. I like where your head's at. Look for places where the ground is disturbed or there's a rock or some other object that might be acting as a marker. Check under trees, near benches and trash cans. Anyone finds something—the jewels, I mean—you call the others and we meet back here at the car. Questions? No? All right, let's head out."

I led the way into the park, pointed where I wanted the others to start, and continued with Svetlana. As we swept our headlamp beams across the ground, I became vaguely aware of light shimmering on the surface of the lake to our right. I stopped to dig at a small mound of dirt beneath a tree, but found nothing but rocks. Faintly in the distance I heard the clanks of other shovels on the hard ground.

After half an hour of searching and digging, Svetlana and I found ourselves standing in front of Echo Park Pedal Boats. We looked at each other.

"What if they did not bury the jewels?" Svetlana said.

"Exactly," I said. "Digging takes too much time. Too easy to get caught. But if they hid them in the lake—"

"—and were able to retrieve them again easily."

I snapped my fingers. "Val...the duffel bag. He said he heard a *chain* rattling in there."

"To the water then," she said.

The pedal boats concession was in a tan stucco building with a brown tile roof. A miniature lighthouse stood behind the main building. A canopy of trees blocked out most of the light from street lamps, but a floating dock on the side of the building was well-lit. Chained to the dock was a flotilla of pedal boats, bumping against each other in the water. I pointed at the scene and patted Svetlana on the shoulder.

"Our chariot awaits, madam."

"No, no," she said. "*Your* chariot awaits."

"Whatever. Follow me."

We hustled down to the dock. I found the chain that secured all the boats and pulled it out of the water. I aimed my headlamp beam at the chain as I ran it through my hands.

"What are you looking at?" Svetlana asked.

"This chain is brand-new," I said. "No rust, no algae, nothing. If I'm right, Bruce and Davis cut the original chain, took out one of the boats and sunk the jewels."

"Perhaps." Svetlana stood in the shadows at the end of the dock, so I could barely see her. "But where? In case you have not noticed, this lake is sizable."

"I realize that," I said. "Let me think."

I gazed out at the water and tried to put myself in Bruce and Davis' shoes. They'd just committed robbery, and one of their people had been shot at the scene. They didn't have a lot of time, so burying the jewels—especially in a remote spot in the park far from the road—was out.

The best option was to sink them in the lake someplace, but again it couldn't take too much time. The hiding spot would need to be close to the dock, and they needed some kind of marker in the water to retrieve the jewels later.

I scanned the water. The cove surrounding the dock was brightly lit by streetlamps, but directly across the cove, about fifty yards away, the water was cloaked in shadow. Something was floating out there. It looked like water lilies. I started taking off my clothes.

"You're going to swim?" she said.

"Yeah," I said, "unless you happen to have a pair of bolt cutters in your magic bag."

"I do not."

"You might want to turn away," I said.

Svetlana smirked. "And miss a chance to watch you swim across a lake wearing a flashlight on your head? Certainly not."

"'Yet this be madness,'" I said, "'there is method in it.' That's *Hamlet*, my dear."

"Wait," she said.

A second later a bright light flashed. She'd snapped a photo of me.

"For posterity," she said.

I crouched on the edge of the dock and lowered myself into the water. Svetlana picked up my clothes and looked down at me with a thin smile.

"How is it?"

"Cold." I switched off my headlamp. "I thought this was California."

"It is," she said. "In February."

"Stay in the shadows," I said, pushing off the dock. "If anybody comes, whistle."

I used a breast stroke so I could keep the headlamp above the water, and headed straight across the cove humming "Luck Be A Lady" to myself. Of course that's when it began to rain—fat drops that made rippling circles on the still water. Unlike the palpably clean, chlorinated water of swimming pools, the lake water was slimy and smelled like a neglected aquarium. I ignored the sensations the best I could and focused on the lily pads drifting in the darkness ahead.

When I reached them, I switched on my headlamp and angled the beam so I could see the water beneath the lily pads. The rain intensified. I swam through a submerged mass of algae that enveloped my fingers, my toes, my legs, my arms. I thought of the black racer water snakes that lurked in the ponds on my Millbrook estate. Ugh, the sacrifices I made for this job.

Once I got the algae off myself, I slalomed through the water lilies, studying each one under the beam of the headlamp, and extending my arms and legs as far as I could through the water to feel for anything that shouldn't be there, like a rope or a chain.

I was halfway through the field of lily pads when I saw one ahead glint a harsh bright green in the light. As I got closer, it was clear to me the lily pad was plastic, and when I turned it over, the underside was styrofoam. The falling rain made it difficult to see beneath the surface of the water. I swept my hand through the water a few times and hit a line. I pulled it to the surface. It was a thick length of monofilament—the type used for deep-sea fishing. Looping it around my hands, I pulled on the line until I came to a chain, then hauled up on the chain. There was something heavy at the end of it.

When I got it to the surface, I took hold of it by the handle. It was a steel box. Holding the handle in one hand, I swam a quick sidestroke with the other, cutting through the rain-dappled water, dragging the lily pad float behind me. At the dock, Svetlana squatted by the edge, holding an umbrella over herself, making me very aware of the long slit on that shift of hers. I averted my eyes and held the box out of the water. When she grabbed the handle, I gave it a slight tug.

"I'm tempted to yank you in here with me," I said. "Where'd you get the umbrella?"

She patted her Gucci bag.

"Ah," I said.

I let go of the handle, and she pulled the entire apparatus—box, chain, line and lily pad float—onto the dock. I climbed out of the water.

"Refreshing?" she said with vivacity.

"Only if you find slime and muck refreshing."

"I do not," she said.

"I hated swimming in the lake at Scout camp," I said. "Hey, any chance you have a flathead screwdriver in the magic bag?"

"I might," she said.

"Check while I get dressed. Where are my clothes?"

"End of the dock."

I found them, stripped out of my shorts, threw them in the trash can, and put on my dry clothes. Although they wouldn't be dry for long; the rain had become a downpour. When I went back to Svetlana, she held a screwdriver up to the light.

"*Voilà!*" she said.

"Thanks."

With Svetlana holding the umbrella over us, I kneeled beside the box and, with one quick push, pried it open. I shone my headlamp inside. The box was filled with Ziploc bags. I grabbed a couple and examined them under the light. They were filled with jewelry. Rain pattered on the umbrella.

"Excellent, Dakota." In a rare warm gesture, Svetlana rubbed my shoulder. "Even if you do smell like a swamp."

"Let's get everybody over here," I said. "It's time to set the trap."

There were footsteps down the dock. Out of the shadows came Knut. He was holding a ridiculously large gun—a .454 Casull, I saw when he stepped into the light. A favorite sidearm of big-game hunters, this revolver was capable of bringing down a water buffalo. To say it was overkill for the streets of L.A. was an understatement.

"I will take jewels now," he said.

Instinctively, I put myself between the gun and Svetlana. A lot of good it would do; a bullet from this gun would go straight through the two of us, downtown L.A., and half of an East L.A. cement factory before stopping.

"Knut, put the gun down and *think*," I said. "If you fire that thing, you're going to set off every car alarm within half a mile. But if you put it down right now, I'll forget this even happened."

Rain streamed down his face. He looked at the gun, then the box of jewels, and appeared to be calculating something—albeit laboriously—when there was a clang against his head. He toppled to the dock like a sequoia hitting the forest floor. Barb stepped out of the shadows holding her shovel. She dropped it on the dock and dusted her hands.

"That's the last dumb assistant *I'm* hiring," she said.

I took the gun out of Knut's hand, removed the shells and put them in my pocket.

"Thank you, Barb," I said.

I moved toward her to give her a hug. She backed away.

"Whoa!" she said. "What are you doing?"

"I was going to hug you."

"Uh-uh," she said. "No PDA."

"PDA?" I said.

"Public Display of Affection," Svetlana said.

"Right," Barb said. "Especially in the rain."

"Fine," I said. "Make the call. Time to catch us a couple of jewel thieves."

Barb called her contacts in the LAPD, and within half an hour the park was surrounded by unmarked cop cars. When everyone was in place, Hailey called Bruce and Davis on the burner phone and told them she was at the park right now retrieving the jewels. She hung up.

"All right," I said to Hailey, "let's join the others."

Hailey and I, along with Svetlana, Barb, and three detectives, sat inside the pedal boats concession building in the dark. Outside, the rain had stopped and night noises rose up around the lake. Whenever a car crept past the park, we all craned our necks toward the windows, but every time it was a false alarm.

An hour after Hailey made the call, there were footsteps out on the dock. The detectives pulled their guns. Quietly, we filed outside and caught Bruce and Davis trying to cut the chain on the boats with a bolt cutter.

"Don't, guys…you're surrounded," I said. "And do you really want people knowing you tried to get away on a *pedal boat*? Come on."

They raised their hands, and the detectives cuffed them. Barb walked over with Hailey.

"We're going to follow Bruce and Davis down to the station so she can make a statement," Barb said.

"Okay," I said. "See you in the morning. You can join me and Svetlana when we go talk to the store owner."

Svetlana and I started back for the car. When we got there, Coltrane opened the door for Svetlana.

"Coltrane," she said, "would you join us for coffee and pie?"

"Golden State? Love to."

We got in. Coltrane shut the door behind us.

"Case closed, Svetlana," I said. "Time to get paid."

"And"—she brushed her neck with her fingertips—"time to get my reward."

<hr />

For our last two days in L.A., as if the gods were smiling down on Svetlana and me for solving the case, the haze and rain lifted, and we were greeted by brilliant sunshine, blue skies and a cool ocean breeze.

For the brief foreseeable future, L.A. was clean and beautiful again.

Mr. Vance showed his gratitude by inviting us to stay at his Beverly Hills mansion, where for two days we swam, played tennis, and discussed Blaze's script—now titled *Agent of Death*. Barb gave me a tour of locations in Raymond Chandler's mysteries, as well as where Jim

Rockford's mobile home used to be. On the final afternoon, Mr. Vance personally accompanied Svetlana and me to his jet. Barb and Hailey stood beside him on the tarmac.

"Don't you have something to say to them, Hailey?" Barb said.

"Thanks, Dakota. Thanks, Svetlana."

"Stay out of trouble, okay?" I said. "No more TV shows with strange producers."

"Not a chance of that," Vance said, putting an arm around his daughter. "When Barb told me how she just *took* all that equipment off the studio lot—the van, cameras, lights—and how she sold everybody with her pitch, I said to myself, 'My little girl's a *producer*.'"

"Daddy's right," Hailey said. "Besides, that's where the real money is anyway. Screw being a star. I want points on the back end."

"That's my girl." Vance kissed her on the cheek. He reached in his jacket pocket, pulled out a check and handed it to Svetlana. "A little bonus for you two."

I gestured at Svetlana's neck. "You mean *besides* the diamond necklace the jeweler gave Svetlana?"

Vance chuckled. "Yes, I suppose so."

Svetlana glanced at the front of the check and put it in her purse.

"It is very generous, Mr. Vance," she said. "Thank you."

"Consider it a capital investment," he said to me. "You're still getting your agency off the ground." He shook Svetlana's hand, then mine, firmly. "I can't tell you how much I appreciate your clearing this up so fast. If you ever need a favor someday, give me a call. A lot of people out here say that, but I mean it."

"Thank you, sir," I said.

As he and Hailey went back to the car, Coltrane got out and opened the door for them. I gave Coltrane a friendly salute; he saluted me back. Then Svetlana, with a polite nod to Barb, climbed the jet stairs and disappeared inside.

"Well," I said to Barb, "looks like it's just you and me, kid."

Her hair fluttered in the breeze. Her eyes, a deep chestnut brown, were misty.

"Hey," I said, "we'll always have the Peninsula."

She grinned. Behind me, the jet whined to life. I glanced over my shoulder, and when I turned around again, Barb grabbed me by the jacket and kissed me. It was a long kiss. Finally she let me go.

"I thought you didn't like PDA," I said.

"A woman can change her mind, can't she?"

"Maybe we'll meet again someday," I said, brushing her bangs out of her eyes. "On a case in New York next time."

"No way, honey. I'm an L.A. gal. I can't function anywhere else."

"L.A. it is then."

I hugged her. She felt and smelled great.

"Take care of yourself," I said.

She sniffed. "You too, New York."

"Such insolence." Still hugging her, I reached down with one arm and slapped her hard on the ass. She squealed. I whispered in her ear, "Don't *make* me come back out here."

I pushed us apart so I could look at her face one more time. She smiled.

"Goodbye, Dakota."

She gave me a final peck on the cheek and turned for the car. I had to get on board before I did something pathetically sentimental like wave at the car's tinted windows. I ran up the jet stairs without looking back, sat in the seat across the aisle from Svetlana and tightened the belt across my lap.

"New York, here we come," I said. "If we can make it there, we'll make it anywhere."

Svetlana lowered her magazine—*New York* magazine—and smiled.

"First thing tomorrow," she said, "we deposit these checks."

"And second thing?"

"A field trip to Fifth Avenue of course."

"Of course," I said.

The door shut. The plane began to move.

I closed my eyes.

Acknowledgements

If a writer is good, he doesn't allow the seams in his work to show. Besides elements of craft, these seams include any turmoil in his life while writing the work, and any doubts he might harbor about how the finished work will be received.

If a writer is good, the reader sees only the alchemy of his personal life, interests and imagination into art. This means that the reader also never sees the unlikely sources of inspiration and encouragement that cross the writer's path.

For this writer, the past three years have been full of trials and mistakes, but certain people—family, friends, fans and colleagues—have inspired me and helped me to heal. These people are presented below, with my wife Alexas Martine first as always.

Thank you, Alexas—my devoted wife, my Muse, my angel—for doing for me what John Steinbeck's wife Elaine did for him: "…taking care of all the outside details to allow me the amount of free untroubled time every day to do my work." As Steinbeck further put it, "I can't think of anything else necessary to a writer except a story to tell and the ability to tell it." Alexas, your endless moral, financial and creative support has kept me writing and living all these years; were it not for you, I would likely have self-destructed by now, and I certainly would not have begun to write in earnest the way I did 20 years ago, when I came home from my teaching job and you had organized my many crates of writing. You gazed at me in wonder with your lovely pale blue eyes and said, "You're a writer, Chris. You *have to* do this." Although I had been writing since I was 13, it was on that October afternoon in 1996, at age twenty-six, that I made the decision to pursue mastery as a writer, even knowing Hemingway's maxim that, "We are all apprentices in a craft where no one ever becomes a master." I didn't care; I was going for it anyway.

Thank you to my friends Brian and Maia Maloney, and to their wonderful boys Jack and James, for providing me with inspiration, and, on a more practical level, for giving me the use of their beautiful vacation houses over the years—on Cape Cod and in the Green Mountains of Vermont. Nowadays, besides "a story to tell and the ability to tell it," a writer needs solitude and quiet; the din of modern society is antithetical to the creation of literature. Brian and Maia's beautiful, tranquil places have enabled me to hear myself think again, to reconnect with Nature, and to rekindle the joy I feel when working the sentences.

Thank you, Brian Maloney, for being such an ardent cheerleader of my work since our college days together; for buying copies of my books and foisting them on your friends and relatives; for sharing your home and your family with Alexas and me; for pulling me from the pit of despair about the state of my career; for giving me subtle financial assistance in the form of meals, day trips, golf outings, and occasional loans; for seeing me through personal crises and helping me to remember my priorities; and for reminding me that the painful wallowing in emotion and personal memories, a necessity of my work that I so often complain about, is, as you wisely put it, Brian, "exactly why you became a novelist in the first place."

Thank you, Jason Scott Sadofsky, for being my friend for nearly 40 years; for always being the first person to read and review my published work; for imparting to me your wisdom about how to navigate this maddeningly mercurial, modern world of technology, even if you sometimes impart such wisdom using circumlocution and oblique analogies; for sharing with Alexas and me the many benefits accrued to you through your professional, financial and personal successes; for being my guardian angel when I've been poised to jump off the bridge of self-destruction (yet again); and for tolerating my sometimes delightful, but often annoying, sudden shifts in mood and behavior.

Thank you, Tony Scotto, for reminding me regularly that I need to do what I do for the *ages*, not for day-to-day sales or moment-to-moment *trending* popularity; for being the one person on Earth who can consistently make me laugh (there's a guy on Uranus who's also pretty funny); for reading the early "final" drafts of all of my work and offering me your creative and encouraging ideas; for coming up with Svetlana's one-liners about how *rare* she likes her beef cooked (e.g., "Simply coax the cow through a warm room"); for sharing with me as a technical advisor your knowledge and many talents; for pushing me to go further with my writing, to invent my own genres, to write books that are "the pure nectar of Chris"; and for being a brilliant, loyal friend and a most honorable human being in the tradition of Benvenuto Cellini.

To Palomino, the California pencil company, thank you for bringing back the Blackwing and the Blackwing 602. Your pencils are a godsend, enabling me to write my first drafts in longhand. Special thanks and kudos go to my younger sister Mandy Mahoney for typing up my first drafts by deciphering my cryptic, all-over-the-page handwriting. For their respective technical expertise in the areas of golf and motorcycle clubs, special thanks go to PGA Professional Rhett Myers and AMA motorcycle club member Bob Hanaburgh.

Thank you to all of the following people for being oases of encouragement and support in the vast desert that is the serious writer's daily existence. In some cases, your support has been as little as an encouraging word, a positive review or a piece of sage advice, but it has always been exactly what I needed most, when I needed it, and for that I am forever grateful: Lou Abraham; Dave, Ren, Alfie and Goliath Adams; Dave Antonucci; Fenway Bark; Cynthia Barnes; John W. Barry; Karl Reid Beck; Wally and Elaine Bixby; Michelle Bolser; Lindsey Bourassa; Dana Buffin; Mark and Laurin Sydney Burk; Ruth Buteau; Stephen R. Campbell; Kari Stroup Capkowski; Jill Cassidy; Tom Chavonelle; Eric Chen; Alexis Coleman; Virginia Crawford; Howard Crothers; Callie Davisson; William DeAngelis; Cindy Santora DeCelles; Danielle Decelles; Maria Deefay; Dana DeNunzio; Lisa DeSpain; Laura Phaneuf-Devine; Lori Dritz; David

Duncan; Lucie Fleury Dunn; Tori Eldridge; Cindy Ellis; Genevieve Fiedler; John Filiberti and Diane Santiago-Filiberti; Barekah Fisher; Mary Busque Fowle; Theresa Frangos; Megan Gallant; Chrys Chavonelle Glascock; Alberto Valdez Godoy; Kate Goldsmith; Mohammad Golpayegani; Penelope Hall; Todd Hall; Zach Hampton; Clare Havens; Shayna Rothenay Kapple; Ed Kerbs; Dave King; Elisabeth Konokolova; Carole Csillag Kosakowski; Kristine Zanno Kratky; Joseph Kubancik; Bill and Jody Lape; Hillary Leftwich; Nicole Lichwick; Angelo Limardo; Rachel Lovinger; Tom Lyons; Christine Sozio Magliaro; Dennis and Mandy Mahoney; Ann Matkins; Blanca Quintana McBrien; Steven and Leanne McDowell; Donna DeNunzio McFarlin; David Menon; Marcie Moline; Al Musumeci; Rebecca Huggins Nanna; Mark Neumann; Jen Eastman Nolan; Tracey Francis Olmoz; Al and Susan Orcutt; Shelley Owen; John and Tara Pantalone; Michael Papetti; Dakota Perez; Elisabeth Pinio; Albertina Marisella Pistis; Donje Putnam; John Quinn; Paul Raines; Orgel Jones Redhaven; Kirie Reveron; Raymond Robinson; Ron and Dianne Rodrigues; Kenny Roemer; Melissa Orcutt Routson; Andy Saemann; Barbara Scotto; Chris Shave; Robb Sherwin; Stu Shinske; Meghan Simonds; Michele Simonetty; Navjot Singh; Alma Sparks; Nicole Sparks; Pam Stack; Rebecca Stanley; Dakota Stevens; Vera Struchkouskaya; Danielle Swartz; Frank Tartaglione; Michael William Teamer; Thanasi "Tom" Theodoropoulos; David Tutein; Anna Vallinakis; Mary Ward; Randy Weir; Anya Wilhelmi; Peter Willhoite; Kathleen Wisbauer; Jessica Anna Zellars; Ivar Zirnis; Dominique Zuzelo; and Jeff and Thelma Zwirn.

Finally, I would like to thank the following institutions and businesses for either giving me a "clean, well-lighted place" (as Hemingway called them) in which to write, or for promoting me and my work over the past decade: Half Moon Theatre; The Millbrook Diner; The Millbrook Free Library; Momiji Restaurant; The Northern Dutchess News; Panera Bread, Poughkeepsie, NY; Penobscot Theatre Company; The Poughkeepsie Journal; Poughkeepsie Junior League; and Vassar College Library.

With gratitude,
Chris Orcutt
Millbrook, New York
October 30, 2016

ABOUT THE AUTHOR

Chris Orcutt has written professionally for 25 years as a fiction writer, journalist, scriptwriter, playwright, technical writer and speechwriter. He has also taught high school U.S. history and college writing.

He is the creator of the critically acclaimed Dakota Stevens Mystery Series, including *A Real Piece of Work* (#1), *The Rich Are Different* (#2), *A Truth Stranger Than Fiction* (#3), and *The Perfect Triple Threat* (#4). For information on future installments and his other writing, visit his website (below). His short fiction has been published in *Potomac Review* and other literary journals. It has also won a few modest awards, most notably 55 Fiction's World's Shortest Stories. As a newspaper reporter he received a New York Press Association award. Orcutt's short story collection, *The Man, The Myth, The Legend*, was voted by IndieReader as one of the best books of 2013. And his modern pastoral novel *One Hundred Miles from Manhattan* (an IndieReader Best Book for 2014) prompted *Kirkus Reviews* to favorably compare Orcutt to Pulitzer Prize-winning author John Cheever.

If you would like to contact Chris, you can email him at corcutt007@yahoo.com. For more information about Chris and his writing, or to follow his blog, visit his website: www.orcutt.net.

EXCERPT FROM
A TRUTH STRANGER THAN FICTION

Book 3 in Chris Orcutt's Dakota Stevens Mystery Series is also available. *A Truth Stranger Than Fiction*, the 3rd novel in the series, delves into the bizarre, interconnected world of foreign spies and fangirls, mobsters and murderers, government bureaucrats and corporate profiteers. Following is the opening of *A Truth Stranger Than Fiction*.

At nine o'clock in the morning I stood at the windows of my new office overlooking Madison Square Park. I was sipping Jamaican Blue Mountain coffee, admiring the early October foliage, and exchanging naughty text messages with a 30-year-old divorcée on the Upper East Side.

Texting was a new skill for me, but apparently I was a natural. My latest message caused its recipient, Clarissa, to message back, *"OMG Dakota! I almost fell off the damn treadmill!"*

I fired another salvo, a steamy text guaranteed to knock her on her berry-ripe backside for good this time, then turned my attention to the moving boxes. Svetlana had agreed to handle most of the unpacking, but she was in Connecticut at a speed-chess tournament and book signing. In all, since our last case a couple of months ago, Svetlana had managed to win four tournaments and write a second chess book. Meanwhile, I hadn't even dropped off my dry-cleaning yet.

Standing there in the stillness, three floors above rush-hour traffic, for perhaps a minute I was at peace with the world and my place in it. Then my cell phone rang. With its new ringtone—the theme from the 1970s TV show *The Rockford Files*—I usually reveled in the theme, letting it play for a while. But today the music was ominous. Today it shattered the silence in the room and foretold trouble on the other end of the line.

And if I'd known how *much* trouble, I might not have answered it.

The ringtone played insistently. Soon the phone would go to voicemail. I didn't want any trouble today, but too bad. Like the title of the Raymond Chandler story goes, *trouble is my business.*

I put down my coffee, took a seat and answered the call.

"Dakota speaking."

"Mr. Stevens?" It was a woman's voice. "Where are you? Your office is closed."

I leaned back in my chair and looked down Fifth Avenue, as if I could see all the way down and across town to East 10ᵗʰ Street. *Dumbass.*

"I'm at my new office. The directions should be on the door."

"There they are," she said. "You really need to update your website, Mr. Stevens."

"I'll get my I-T department right on that."

"Madison Square Park?" she said.

"Yes. My building is the ancient one with the bay windows. Third floor."

"I'll be up in fifteen minutes. Please be there. I think someone is following me."

"Do you want me to—"

She hung up. I stared at my phone. Most likely, no one was following her. New clients, enamored with the novelty of hiring a PI, often imagined they were being followed. I got up and freshened my coffee at the credenza.

The new office lacked a break room, not to mention the old one's slick glass walls and hi-tech conference room. One could say the new office was retro. *Very* retro. It had been occupied for decades by an ancient pair of accountants, then had lain empty for years after the second partner died. They left behind two elephantine oak desks, frosted glass doors and about an inch of dust. The walls, probably eggshell white 40 years ago, were now the color of a paper bag. And the dozens of moving boxes strewn everywhere only underscored the shabby feel of the place.

Svetlana had decorating plans though, and what the office temporarily lacked in creature comforts was made up for by its address—an address I wasn't sure we could afford: Fifth Avenue.

I went to the window and looked down at the street. Traffic was at a standstill. The sidewalks teemed with jostling people late for work. I sipped some coffee and thought about the woman on the phone. The woman had sounded attractive. Attractive and confident. I wondered what color her hair was and decided she sounded blonde. Blonde and tall. I scanned the heads of tall blonde women walking past the park, and waited for one of them to cross the street to my office. None did.

After a couple of minutes I realized I couldn't put off unpacking any longer. Surveying the sea of boxes, I saw one labeled "Dakota Desk," and, with a leaden sigh, started to unpack it.

Out in the hallway the elevator grate banged, followed by a knock at the door. The glass rattled.

"Enter," I said.

The door swung open and a bobbed head of hair—cotton candy pink and blue hair with Cleopatra bangs—entered the room. She was a petite woman—early 20s, I surmised—dressed in a short black leather jacket, white tank top, denim shorts, and Doc Martens boots with black knee-high socks. A canvas messenger bag dangled from her shoulder.

"Mr. Stevens?"

"Are you the one who just called?"

"Yes."

So much for my deductions based on the woman's voice. She shut the door…

CPSIA information can be obtained
at www.ICGtesting.com
Printed in the USA
LVHW032213031019
633101LV00013B/936